Praise for
Nebuchadnezzar

"In *Nebuchadnezzar: The Head of Gold,* author Joseph Chambers provides dramatic insight into the life of the ruler who controlled the most powerful world kingdom history has ever seen. Nebuchadnezzar's encounter with the prophet Daniel laid the foundation for the future governments of the earth, and more than twenty-five hundred years later, we are still seeing these prophecies unfold before our eyes. As students of biblical prophecy know, the importance of Nebuchadnezzar's Babylonian kingdom cannot be dismissed, for it will soon rise up again in the last days prior to the return of our Lord Jesus Christ."

    —Dr. Tim LaHaye, co-author of the Left Behind and Babylon
       Rising series

"A captivating novel!"

    —Thomas Horn, noted novelist

NEBUCHADNEZZAR

Nebuchadnezzer: The Head of Gold
The Battle of the Gods, Book One

And, forthcoming,

Darius: The Wings of Silver
The Battle of the Gods, Book Two

NEBUCHADNEZZAR
THE HEAD OF GOLD

JOSEPH CHAMBERS

HighWay
A division of Anomalos Publishing House
Crane

HighWay

A division of Anomalos Publishing House, Crane 65633

© 2009 by Joseph Chambers

All rights reserved. Published 2009

Printed in the United States of America

09   1

ISBN-10: 0982211937 (paper)

EAN-13: 9780982211939 (paper)

A CIP catalog record for this book is available from the Library of Congress.

Cover illustration and design by Steve Warner

Dedication

The most important person in my life has been and still is my wife, Juanita Laverne Huffines Chambers. I call her the "Queen of Joseph." She is not a pushover—that goes for me or anyone else. She is a fully capable lady in all needed skills and personality. A pastor's wife is a pastor's best helper. She has excelled in sharing our burden as shepherds in the Lord's church. If you do not like me, leave her alone because she totally stands beside me. She has given up my attention for many, many of hours when my heart aches to be alone with God.

I love her with all of my physical capacity!

Summary

A series of novels on the "battle of the gods" could not be more representative of both history and the present. All wars result from clashes of religion and the ego of rulers. Man is inarguably a religious entity and will almost always fight for what he believes. Every culture that loses the will to battle soon lands in the ash heap of history.

Nebuchadnezzar: The Head of Gold is the first in The Battle of the Gods series. While this novel illuminates history, it is far more than a historical novel. The romance of Nebuchadnezzar with Amytis his queen is exquisite and engaging. His relationship to the representatives of the gods is just as intriguing and breathtaking. There is great history in the story, but it is full of the present in its many movements.

This empire of Babylon is unforgettable and to read of it in a passionate novel is absolutely thrilling. The connection to many different religions makes this novel broad in its scope. As much as the present world tries to reject the idea of kings and queens, the mystique of a palace and the glory of kingly settings never fail to grip the heart.

This novel takes us from the Garden of Eden, where Nebuchadnezzar was born, to the greatest palace ever built. It passes through a love affair with the princess of Mede until he builds for her the "Hanging Garden of Amytis." The glory that comes to Nebuchadnezzar drives him to a height of pride that leaves him insane. Then, he spends seven years in the wilderness of southern Mesopotamia (modern Iraq) in the marshes now famous to the world. His Queen Amytis is a highlight of this novel when she secretly escapes the Palace of Gold to search for her king and her love.

The people of the book transplanted from Zion are Nebuchadnezzar's powerful rulers and faithful helpers. At the end he rewards them with an international university on the outskirts of his capital.

The gods never cease to battle and the story will move on into other empires, great capitals, and intriguing personalities. The Battle of the Gods is the ultimate picture of life on this planet.

Forthcoming,

Darius: The Wings of Silver
The Battle of the Gods, Book Two

Contents

foreword

I can think of no one better prepared to write the story of King Nebuchadnezzar in novel format than Joseph Chambers. When Dr. Chambers asked me about writing this foreword, I did not hesitate for one simple reason. God has blessed him with the highest regard for the absolute authority and trustworthiness of the Bible. Therefore, one can expect that faithfulness to God's inerrant Word throughout this story.

Biblical "fiction" sounds like an oxymoron. The Bible, of couse, is not fiction. But biblical truth is communicated with complete faithfulness to Scripture in the parables of Jesus, in the report of Nathan to David (2 Samuel 12:1–7), and in other instances. That is what Dr. Chambers so ably does with this beautiful story of Nebuchadnezzar and the Jews who were held captive in his kingdom of Babylon. He essentially takes the biblical account of those days and—with the heart and understanding of a Bible-believing pastor, a careful Bible teacher, and a meticulous Bible scholar for over fifty years—walks a mile in the shoes of those biblical characters, all of whom were real people in real and momentous times.

And few are equipped to understand better what those days were like and who those people actually were. Dr. Chambers has visited Iraq, and ancient Babylon, several times. His scholarly and scripturally faithful work on the rebuilding of Babylon predicted in Bible prophecy, called *A Palace for the Antichrist*, has become a much sought after reference work. His lectures on the Bible's placement of Babylon as the epochal city of evil and age-long adversary of God's Holy city, Jerusalem, are powerful.

But still, for me, it is Dr. Chambers' love and devotion to the-God of Abraham, Isaac, and Jacob and to the Name of His only begotten Son Jesus, his discernment of all truth through Scriptural lenses, and his belief in the presence and work of the Holy Spirit in the saints of Jesus Christ that makes this book. And what makes it a compelling and powerful read is Dr. Chambers' ability to put flesh and bones and heart into the facts, transforming them into a story. Be sure and read this book with open Bible, for it will shed light on those great passages that deal with the days of Nebuchadnezzar, King of Babylon, and upon those prophecies that saturate the pages of the Bible about rebuilt Babylon's coming role as a signal of the soon return of our Lord and Savior, Jesus Christ.

Phillip Goodman
Prophecy Watch Television & Thy Kingdom Come Ministries
www.prophecywatch.com

Introduction

A breathtaking love story that is right out of the ancient land of Sumer. Visiting the "Garden of Eden" where nature and plenty was all created splendor. Joining such a story is King Nebuchadnezzar, the one most noted King of the Chaldeans. Then, a beautiful and vivacious princess enters the scene, and she will become his queen.

Royalty is always beautiful unless someone makes it ugly. In either case, royalty offers an undying mystique. It is loved, hated, pursued, and denied; but never forgotten. The tales that are told and the rumors that are spread about royal persons never die. They are intriguing and only grow more so as they are repeated.

Add to all of this the religious component and especially the prophesies of holy men called Seers and the battles begin. Nebuchadnezzar's story was written in the Scrolls of these holy men and their God had called him, "The Head of Gold."

This love story includes the constant battling of these gods. Every culture in the Middle East, where Nebuchadnezzar ruled, worshipped a different god. Every war and conflict was attributed to the will of the gods, whether it was Inanna at Ur of the Chaldeans, Marduk of Babylon, Ashur of the Assyrians, or Jehovah of the Scroll people. In most of these cultures, the kings were themselves considered demigods or at least the physical representations of these gods. Young maidens were often called goddesses and declared to have come down from the gods as tokens of success.

Nebuchadnezzar, the Head of Gold, was the ultimate king. Amytis, his princess, then his queen, added tenderness to his strength and stature. The first world government became a reality through this stunning marriage of Nebuchadnezzar and Amytis with their two empires uniting as one.

Fifty-six miles of walls that stood three hundred feet tall circled the golden capital. A second inner wall formed a moat, which was flooded with the waters of the famed Euphrates. Multiple golden gates guarded the capital and entering through each gate was a royal experience. At night the walls were lighted with giant torches, which were visible for miles across the flat plains of the Fertile Crescent.

To approach Babylon, it was necessary to cross many bridges. The canals they spanned watered the abundant estates filled with delicacies and flowering vines. Date farms and banana groves flourished. Oranges, grapefruits, pineapples, and every garden delight were in abundance. It was a paradise all around while viewing the splendor when approaching the capital city.

The king built his mountain princess a "Hanging Garden" that reached upward like steps reaching into the sky, reminiscent of Nimrod's ancient tower. This Garden was a wonder of their day and soon became known as one of the "Seven Wonders of the World" and was visited by multitudes. Within the inner walls of this garden, there was a home to many beautiful creatures. Every animal known in the empire was represented. Part of the garden was netted in order to protect and care for every exotic bird from the empire. The sounds of birds and other animals created music for the entire city. Walkways carried visitors to heights and sights that brought the world into this living garden.

Massive pulleys, operated by the captives of defeated kingdoms, carried an ample supply of water to the peak. The entire garden flourished by this carefully planned system. It was a tropical landscape right on the Euphrates River inside the golden city.

The palace beside the garden was the most beautiful one in the history of the world. No one would dare, nor could afford, to match this mansion. Its grand size and the great pillars wrapped in gold surrounding three sides and standing forty feet tall left the viewers dazzled. It was called both, "The Golden Palace" and, "The Palace of the Gods."

This celebrated empire and all of its greatness did not arise until the demise of the Assyrian Empire that had ruled at Nineveh for hundreds of years. The Babylonians and other nations were ready for the end of the brutality that had characterized Assyrian rule. The world of the Middle East was changing.

A former Assyrian king brought a beautiful princess out of Samaria and married her. She was the mother of the next king and her granddaughter, Zakutu, became the princess of Assyria. Her death marked the beginning of the end of the Assyrian Empire. While Zakutu was dying, the princess of Medea was born. Zakutu's death left the Assyrians with a sense of doom, while hope and excitement was rising to the south and east. Zion, the principle city of Judea, was under judgment. In the Royal College, behind the city walls near the Temple of Solomon, young men were studying the Scrolls. They were being prepared to help govern the Golden Empire for King Nebuchadnezzar. This Golden Empire could not rise to its glory without the acumen of these servants of their God. Their seers spoke and the divided nation of Zion was in turmoil.

From the story of the Golden Empire, this futuristic novel of human history continues toward a final day when the kingdom of God will rule the earth. There was ordained in the prophetic scheme five kingdoms after the Golden Kingdom and before the last kingdom that would never end.

There will be no lasting peace during the six kingdoms of human design. The future kingdom will be perfect. It is all a battle of the gods. The true and living God will win and will rule the world forever. The end is too beautiful to forget. The princess of this last kingdom will become a queen and live in a palace far exceeding the golden palace in Babylon.

A King Born in the Marshes

630 BC

nebopolasser is a chieftain among the many ethnic groups that presently live in the southern part of Chaldea. He is also the general over the Assyrian Army of the south. Many of the inhabitants call their homeland by its ancient name Sumer, whereas others say, "Akkad," "Akkadian," "Babylonia" or "Mesopotamia." The Assyrians have united these city-states by force and often employ vicious tactics to maintain their dominance. Keenly aware of the developing political events, Nebopolasser is determined to be part of the Chaldean effort for independence. Encouraged to declare himself king, he has many supporters. He has served Assyria well and honorably and has been a powerful leader for peace. He is not of a rebellious nature, but neither is he an Assyrian by birth. He came from a famous family of Chaldeans. It is clear to Nebopolasser that the end of peace is near. In the not too distant future, events will soon get out of hand without a strong leader.

Nebopolasser viewed his large herd of water buffalo from the impressive deck standing over the waterway. His thoughts again return to Hanna, the love of his heart. His lovely wife is expecting their first child at any time, and he is staying close to home until all is well. Their home has been painstakingly built and richly adorned. It is beautiful as well as comfortable. He lives in the midst of an area commonly known as the "Garden of Eden." He plies the marshes as the sea-people do: fishing, farming rice, raising water buffalo, building reed houses for others, and has become rich in the ways of these strong people. The last thing he desires is to leave it all for the intrigue of state and government all intertwined with the temples and priests. However, he responds when either opportunity or duty calls. To be part of a New Babylonian Empire would complete his life's dreams of future greatness for his people. He ponders these matters as he sits on his large deck among the teeming world of nature and plenty.

A maidservant hurries from his beloved wife's quarters with good news, announcing, "General Nebopolasser, you are a father! Your wife has borne you a son!"

"Is my wife alright? How quickly can I be with her and the baby?" he asks with anticipation.

"It won't be long," she replies. "Your wife is a strong lady, and you have a strong son."

"Sir," she continues, "Do you know what you will name him?"

"Yes," he answers, "but we will tell everybody together."

Slipping quietly into their bedroom, Nebopolasser quickly kneels beside her bed. They are very religious and have declared their worship to Marduk and the gods of his large pantheon. The first thing they do is offer up thanks to him for his answers to their prayers.

"You have given me a strong son," he says proudly to his wife. "We will dedicate him to all of Chaldea and the many peoples of the earth for their good. We have discussed a name, and I believe it is the right name."

His wife Hanna simply responds with the same beautiful smile that first drew him to her.

"Our people of Chaldea have suffered much and many nations have ruled over us and brought us horrible destruction. We need a son that will help to reset the boundaries and protect them. Nebuchadnezzar is the name of a past great king of Old Babylon and means exactly what we want for our people—someone to keep the old boundaries and protect our way of life!"

Smiling softly, Hanna gently reaches over, laying her hand over her husband's, and replies, "He will be our king."

Thanking him for giving her such a handsome son, Hanna agrees to name him Nebuchadnezzar.

She whispers, "Let's call him 'Young Nabu' until he reaches manhood. He will love that name, it sounds so much like his honorable father's, and it will be easy to repeat as often as we will need to do so."

"Agreed," he says as he squeezes her hand and tenderly kisses her forehead. "Now, get some rest. You deserve it."

Nebopolasser knows he must hurry back to the soldiers at Erech and tend to the duties of security for the entire south. The soldiers are officers of the law and are responsible for peace as well as war. He has already decided that he will resign from his Assyrian post as soon as possible, but wants to do so honorably after finishing his job well. His relationship with King Ashurbanipal of the Assyrians has always been excellent and must never be allowed to deteriorate unless the king himself chooses to end their friendship.

After staying with Hanna and young Nabu for a few days, he sets out to visit his father and mother and their entire clan. Traveling by his superb high prow reed boat, he delivers the good news of his firstborn son.

"My father, my father," he declares, as the canoe is tied to the deck, "we have a son and he looks like his father!"

There is an exchange of kisses on both cheeks amidst exciting chatter.

"Son," his father says, "I have heard talk of your declaring yourself 'King of Babylon.' I am ready to share in the extensive task."

His father continues, "Do remember, your father is a warrior. I would love to put my life on the line to share in the struggles that will certainly follow."

"Yes," replies Nebo, as his father affectionately calls him, "I will depend much on your superior skills. I believe you would be the right general to lead the defense of our small city-states and to drive back the Assyrians if they choose to resist—and I certainly believe that they will."

"Nebo," he says, "we must do more than drive back the Assyrians—we must end their torturous methods of war forever."

"My father, you must not say those things out loud until the time is right. The hour is not yet come, and we must wait until all of Southern Chaldea is ready to join us. Listen, and be careful."

After a splendid celebration with the entire clan and a dinner of young, roasted lamb and wild pheasant, Nebo returns to his Hanna and young Nabu.

After some days he is back in Erech, where the talk of tributes and the heavy hand of King Ashurbanipal have unsettled his men. General Nebo, as they all call him, is greatly loved and has a tender way of maintaining total authority. He is preparing for a trip throughout the very marshes that everyone refers to as the "Garden of Eden." Along with a contingent of his best warriors, he will travel to the seacoast and put to rest some troubled spots of disorder. Before leaving, he addresses everyone under his command.

"Our salaries are paid by the Assyrian Empire and our duty is to defend the same. We must always remember that a warrior's strength is in his submission to authority. Talk of rebellion is not acceptable to a champion warrior," he said passionately.

"On a lighter note," he continued, "we have the greatest appointment in all of the empire—to work and live in the garden spot of the world. All of you know that from the earliest time, our fathers have told us that this southern landscape is the ancient Garden of Eden. We have many Sumerian tablets and writings that speak of our past. Defense of this renowned place should be the joy of us all. My family has lived in the middle of this wonderful world filled with splendid creatures and birds and I am proud to be a keeper of it all.

"Remember," he added, "this city of Erech where we are stationed is the oldest city of ancient Sumer, who were the first people to live in this paradise. Also the celebrated Gilgamesh, the most famous of all Sumerians, actually lived right here in Erech. It is believed that he built our ziggurat as his tower of worship. He is sometimes called Nimrod, and our city is sometimes called Uruk. The history of this wonderful city is rich and great, and we are its protectors."

The towering trees and other beautiful forms of nature are visible everywhere as they travel cautiously toward the sea. General Nebopolasser and his top commanders ride chariots pulled by four *onagers*, a type of wild donkey. The general is enthralled with the animals that dart from their many hiding places as the voice of this large contingent of warriors makes its way south. At times the men must load their chariots on large prows and travel by water. A tiger hurriedly climbs an exceeding large oak. Water Buffalo graze under the watchful eyes of their keepers. The crystal clear waters are dotted with fishermen drawing their nets and seeking out the wealth of their world of plenty. "This is truly a garden of life everywhere and no one can doubt its abundance," exclaims General Nebopolasser.

The general and his men talk of their families and their homes. General Nebo speaks, "I have told you of my firstborn son and my Hanna. I have named him Nebuchadnezzar. We will call him Young Nabu. Some have suggested that his name is prophetic as names should be. I simply want my son to protect our ancient boundaries and our way of life, just like we are doing night and day."

He then continues, "Our king is getting older and he has reigned for 39 years. All of us ponder what the future may hold when he is dead, and we must be careful to keep ourselves ready to defend what is right. We must not speak of rebellion, but of protection. Rebellious men miss the way, but protectors find the way. Let's be careful to be protectors."

629 BC

Young Nabu is now one year old and his father, General Nebopolasser, spends as much time as possible in the marshes. Young Nabu is being trained in every skill needed for the future.

"Son," he says to the babbling little Nabu, "you are a joy to me. I would do anything for you. You can trust your father." Smiling, he looks down proudly at his son, who is happily playing on the floor in front of him, knowing that his words have brought little response. Suddenly looking up at his father and catching his adoring eye, Nabu jumps up and rushes into his father's outstretched arms. The sight of the two of them romping throughout their house and wrestling on the floor evokes giggles and much laughter from Hanna.

The rumors only grow louder that General Nebo would soon be King Nebopolasser. He tries to dispel rumors so that the matter does not surface until the proper hour. He knows all too well the fierce treatment a man who is labeled a traitor will receive from the arrogant commanders of the Assyrian army. He still conducts himself as their willing servant. Conscious of being watched, General Nebo assigned faithful men as guards to watch over him, his beloved Hanna, and Nabu.

The Princess of the Assyrian Empire

628 BC

The princess of the royal palace at Nimrud is a beautiful young lady characterized by vigor and laughter. Zakutu is only in her teens, but already extremely mature and captivating. All who see her quickly consider her the loveliest and most vivacious young lady in all of the Assyrian Empire. She actually appears as a goddess to their mythological minds and is said by many to have come down from their god Ashur. Her presence with King Ashurbanipal at royal functions is proof of Ashur's blessings and favor on the Assyrian Empire.

Her father, the king of the Assyrians, is viewed by his enemies as brutal and overbearing. To Zakutu, his favorite, he is the joy of her heart. She was named after her great-grandmother, Sennacherib's queen, whom he brought back from Samaria.

The queen's beauty has been rivaled by none in Nineveh save that of the new princess, and in her life provoked grave jealousy throughout the king's court as well as among family rivals. She was known as the "queen from the land of the Scrolls."

In an act of wicked jealousy, Princess Zakutu's two great-uncles murdered their father, King Sennacherib, because they saw the strong influence that Queen Zakutu held over him. They greatly feared that the inheritance of the throne would be given to her son, their younger sibling and half-brother. Her grandmother's influence was indeed so overwhelming that these two sons had been forced to flee after their father was viciously murdered. Her grandfather, who was Queen Zakutu's son King Esarhaddon, inherited the throne.

Princess Zakutu is so proud of her father. Possessing superior wisdom, her father is far gentler than the Assyrian kings of their history. His mother had instilled a degree of compassion in him that marked a change from the past. Also, his learning was acquired at her feet.

When Zakutu hears her father's voice, she rushes through the palace corridors, the sound of her sandals echoing rapidly on the cool tile floor and off the walls. "Father, father, is it really you?" she cries.

Gently, he embraces her as only a father can do. He even weeps because he has been gone so long. They immediately retire to the family quarters where the famed royal family lives. Amidst such splendor, their normal pattern of family life often escapes them.

"Father, please tell me of your extensive trip into our kingdom!" she pleads as she throws herself down on a huge, overstuffed Persian cushion. "And tell me about our wonderful friends that you saw. Tell me, Father, if everything is well."

She knows that her father is often overwhelmed by the affairs of the Assyrian Empire, and that he tries earnestly to protect her from all bad news. However, she still wants to know everything. "Father, I want you to share the good and the bad with me because I love you," she pleadingly whispers.

"Zakutu," he says, "you are exactly like your great-grandmother. We should never have named you after her!" he teasingly says. "You would be ready to take on the throne with all the affairs of the kingdom if you had but the privilege. My grandmother certainly did and made a lot of enemies for everyone. Please, just be my princess for now, and someday I will give you to be the bride of the most handsome man in the whole kingdom. Everywhere I go, I'm already searching for him."

"O, Father!" she exclaims. "I do not ever want to leave you!"

Ashurbanipal suddenly has a desire to tell his daughter all that is in his heart. As he settles himself down on a cushion beside her, he realizes just how good it feels to be home and with the joy of his life. He is also excited about spending time with her mother, his very special queen. The king and queen are extremely captivated with their daughter.

"In the mountains of Medea," he begins, "Our king, King Cyaxares, and I had a thrilling lion hunt. I must tell you that he killed three to my two, but it was unforgettable fun. My wonderful horse was at his peak, and we raced after those lions until we were exhausted. You know that your father loves to hunt, and hunting the lion is my most challenging joy," he says with a smile on his face.

"King Cyaxares and his father before him have been wonderful, submitted constituents of our famous kingdom. As was the tradition of his father, King Cyaxares pays large tribute to Nineveh."

"Father, will he ever become your enemy as so many of our distant citizens have often become?" she asks with an obvious show of concern on her young face.

"Zakutu," he sighs, "let's talk about the enjoyable things I did and saw. The mountains of Medea," he suddenly recalls, "are breathtakingly beautiful and this trip was taken during their prime time of spring. Every hill was filled with flowers and the fruit of Medea, some of the best in our kingdom, was ripe and abundant." He tells her of the pelican birds and majestic tigers that he saw almost everywhere.

"The hills," he says, as he tries hard to relax and give Zakutu his deepest attention, "are filled with life and the beautiful wild beasts that are so special to all who live in the Medean Mountains."

Excitedly he says, "The skies there are full of beautiful winged creatures created by Ashur and his son, Belit. Of course, King Cyaxares believes it was Ahura and Mazda, his holy spirit."

"We constantly watched for the good omens of the birds during our time together, but I cannot say there was even one. Yet, the hunting was terrific and honed our skills as warriors."

Trying hard to satisfy the curiosity of his princess, he continues, "King Cyaxares spoke of his son and you, but I was not interested. His son showed me little kindness. There were only the forced gestures and formal honors required of all my subjects."

"My princess," he continues, "you are the fairest in the entire kingdom. Everywhere I go they speak of you as the most beautiful symbol of the Assyrian Empire. I must secure the most honorable husband for you someday soon."

The king finishes his time with his favorite princess by saying, "The Medes have fought us in the past and I know too well the pain of their treatments. The next peaceful trip I go on to one of our extensive regions I shall take you with me to show all the people my beautiful princess. Your beauty has already been heralded throughout the empire, and many speak of you as the heart of all Assyria. You are more than my princess—you are the Assyrian princess! My Zakutu, you are a goddess to all of us. I believe Ashur gave you to the queen and me."

Later that evening after Zakutu has slipped off to bed, King Ashurbanipal and his royal court meet to talk of the troubles brewing and the forces they need to handle them. Not one of them doubts that the young King Cyaxares of the Medes has something planned. A well-placed Assyrian in his court tells them of visits by Babylonians, Scythians, and other small nations that would profit by their freedom from the honorable kingdom of Assyria. The king is the first to speak.

"My honorable lords," he says, "Our kingdom is strong, but most of our subjects have learned of our military tactics and more and more are training to resist or implement the same. We must devise new schemes and train our feared warriors with even greater skills."

A more conservative lord from the northern section of the empire speaks of reducing tribute to inspire the subject cities and small kingdoms to value their protection. Riches of gold, silver, and other valuables constantly flood the storehouses of Nineveh from every direction, and, for this reason, no one else speaks kindly of such thoughts.

"We must warn all of our subjects that to rebel will only serve to provoke the most brutal results such that only we Assyrians are schooled at effecting," says one of the old Assyrian lords. "We must show them that rebellion will never be tolerated!"

The Assyrians are known to impale their victims with sharpened poles driven up their backs and then leave them hanging to suffer a most painful death. They also often flay their victims alive and display their mutilated bodies in public to be mocked. Their methods are so utterly brutal and feared that the Assyrian lords are sure that making an example of all rebels will quickly quench any uprising.

They go on to discuss the extensive library that King Ashurbanipal has poured his heart into creating. With nearly one hundred thousand tablets and cuneiform writings, it has become one of the world's respected marvels.

Again the king speaks, "While in the capital of Medea, I met with the lord of the highest school of learning and have returned with several valuable tablets from its rich treasure of learning to be copied. These will help us to quickly transform our library into the largest in the world, if it is not already," he says with much enthusiasm. "We must train our subjects from every part of our vast kingdom to understand their need of the wisdom that comes from Nineveh, their capital."

They discuss the recent repairs made to the many aqueducts that bring in the large supplies of water—making their capital the world's premier city. One of the lords of the empire, whose duty it is to supervise the actual city of Nineveh, speaks of the care of physical matters. They applaud him for his role in bringing in the supply of water that now flows in rivers to the city through fourteen aqueducts, one of many improvements he brought to the capital.

The minister of the armed warriors speaks of one of their leading generals among the southernmost part of Chaldea saying, "There is some talk from our faithful Assyrian post that this general, one of the toughest and best, may himself be beginning to think of rebelling. There is no proof, but his temperament has changed. Also, his positive talk of our Assyrian Kingdom does not sound strong as it once did. His loyalty seems rather questionable."

He goes on to say, "This trusted man of our faithful Assyrians warned me that if this general should rebel, it would mean enormous trouble for us with all of the city-states from Babylon, south, to the sea. He even suggested that if he shows definite signs of defiance, we should swiftly eliminate him with a dreadful demonstration of painful treatment. He believes that such action on our part will serve as a strong warning to all and will secure that part of our empire."

There is a murmur of agreement throughout the room that if rebellion arises, quick action will have to be taken. Extremely exhausted, the king dismisses everyone for he knows this will be a sleepless night.

Zakutu wakes up her father the next morning as she alone has the privilege of doing. While his queen is loved, she does not have the right to call on him unless he sends for her.

"Father, can we talk about your God Ashur today?" Zakutu asks with a sober curiosity. She appears to be embarrassed by her own question.

The king is taken by surprise at her words because she has never called Ashur "his god." He has always been their god.

"Yes, but why did you say 'my god'?"

Zakutu suddenly realizes that for the first time she has spoken to her father in a way that casts doubt on her faith in Ashur, the Assyrian namesake god.

"Father, my great-grandmother for whom I was named was from Samaria and her God was different from Ashur. She guaranteed your father the kingdom by her prayers to her God. My maid, that you have given me, is also from great-grandmother's country, Judea, and she talks much about her God and her love for Him. Father, I fear for our world empire, and I wonder if we should pray to your grandmother's God. He could save us from the sorrows that I often fear," she explains.

For the first time ever, King Ashurbanipal is angry with his princess. The king replies, "We have served Ashur and his gods for many, many years and they have made us awesome! We have won many victories as we marched under his name. My princess, I have no interest in this God of Judea."

Zakutu reminds her father of the holy man named Jonah that had come to their city, how the entire city had fasted and repented of their sins, and how wrath had been averted. The king has heard all of this before, and knows of the memorial that had been erected to this seer, which gives him credit for saving Nineveh.

"I know the story, but I do not believe anything would have happened if no one had responded to that old seer," he says with grave disinterest.

To her astonishment, he briefly taunts her and dismisses her from his presence.

The princess does not see her father for days. She knows that he is bothered by the very thought that she might doubt his god. When he returns from Nineveh to the royal palace, the king tries hard to treat Zakutu with his usual love and affection. He has missed her attention greatly.

"I have planned a memorial trip for us to beautiful Southern Chaldea all the way to the sea," he says.

"We will ride our Arabian horses and take along the royal carriage for comfort when you need to rest. You have never visited Babylon or Erech and other beautiful cities in our kingdom or the ancient area of utter abundance known as the Garden of Eden. We will visit with the strong general who leads our garrison of the south. I will be involved with matters of state at times, and the greatest of all of our cavalry and soldiers will be with us to insure that we are perfectly safe."

Then he adds, "I want you to enjoy some special time in horsemanship and the study of royal decorum over the next few weeks to prepare you to ride at your father's side. The crown prince, your brother, will go with us and be with you constantly when I am busy. You will see the son of our general, Nebopolasser, who is only about two years old. His name is the ancient name of a past Babylonian king, Nebuchadnezzar. This trip will be a treat, my princess."

He tries hard not to show that he is concerned about this general and his son. The name, Nebuchadnezzar, has a ring of impending trouble to all of the Assyrian lords.

Zakutu is extremely busy with her royal teachers of the special skills that her father wants her to develop, while King Ashurbanipal is busy with state affairs. Completely unknown to Zakutu, her father is planning a strong offensive to secure some rebellious matters and ideas being reported daily by his Assyrian posts throughout the southern kingdom. His general, Nebopolasser, who is the father of the baby, Nebuchadnezzar, is apparently being discussed in a manner that the king considers rebellious.

King Ashurbanipal plans to shield his princess from the real purpose of the trip and use her personality and beauty to show his subjects the fatherly side of their king. He believes that they will be inspired by her goddess-like appearance and even be tempted to think like Assyrians. He also plans several stops to secure tablets of learning and business to enhance the Library of Tablets that has already become a wonder of the known world. He has not yet found the original copy of the "Epic of Gilgamesh," but has learned of its possible presence in the temple at Erech, which is now called Uruk.

The personal horse of the king is the most beautiful in all of the empire. It is a well-bred Arabian stallion of a glistening golden hue whose very gait has an air of royalty. He is the envy of all who see him.

The horse that Zakutu, as the king's princess, has been presented is unquestionably the next in beauty and strength, but gentle and steady. Even the crown prince Ashuretililani is envious of the princess' horse. It is a silvery stallion, only a bit smaller than her father's horse. The crown prince's horse is clearly third in beauty, yet nonetheless a fabulous beast. As they leave Nineveh, the tens of thousands of people are there to see their king, the crowned prince, and the beautiful princess off with the highly trained garrison of the cavalry and marching warriors ever to leave Nineveh. It is a royal scene to behold. The king's carriage follows immediately behind that of his princess. When the princess is exhausted, the king wants to provide her with a comfortable means for part of her travel.

Zakutu says, "Father, this must be the crowning day of my life. To be with you on this state visit to many parts of our empire is a young daughter's dream come true."

As they leave the city, they notice that the city is sparkling clean and towering palm trees line every boulevard. Elaborate statues that represent the Assyrian Empire are ubiquitous. The fruitful orchards of this fertile stronghold are neatly trimmed and hang with fruits. The fields are full of vegetables and the flow of water from the aqueducts steadily traces its way through the multiple channels that guarantee their perfection.

"Father," Zakutu continues, "our country is beautiful and our people are truly blessed. Do you think they really understand how necessary the Assyrian Empire is and what an exceptional king you are? Father, you are different from many kings of our past, and I am happy about the changes you have made against many odds."

"Yes, my princess, I do feel loved and honored, even as my father, grandfather, and many other past kings before my time must have felt. I have been their king for thirty-nine years, most of which have been peaceful years," he replied softly.

They begin to discuss the "Great Tablet Library" and how the implementation of that tremendous idea could lift the empire to another renowned height of glory that would be awe-inspiring to the whole world. The king discusses the languages that he can speak such as Chaldean, Akkadian, and Scythian, and the value of learning that he brings into the empire.

The king adds, "I dream of our Tablet Library being copied and made available to every major city and the educated teachers that will instruct our next generations, instilling in them the values of learning." The crown prince noticeably lacks interest.

Turning to the crown prince and Zakutu, he says, "I have told you that I am the first king of the Assyrians that can read and write, and we must guarantee that all future leaders are taught the superior wisdom of the world. I dream of kings that can speak every language in the empire."

Views of Nineveh fade as the royal company proceeds south toward Chaldea and Babylon. It is a tremendous show of Assyrian powers to the king, his crown prince, and the princess. The gentle breeze that sets every field waving in the sunlight is calming to every nerve in the body. The abundance of natural beauty on the fertile crescent of plenty, paired with the great royal presence of the king and his great entourage, is spectacular to behold.

The king is at the height of his glory, but all of his leaders and family members are unaware that the forces of destruction are too far along to turn around. The success of this trip will be short lived, and the individuals they will visit are indeed the new future for the land of Mesopotamia. The magnificent and most powerful army in the world marches to its last triumph.

With Babylon now in sight, Zakutu can hardly contain her excitement. As she looks toward the city, she says, "Father, you have told me often of the beautiful walls and towering city, but it is far greater than I have ever imagined!" She is clearly overjoyed.

The advance cavalry and soldiers have secured everything and all of the enemies are silent. "It all seems so peaceful," the king says. He thinks, *Maybe our Assyrian posts have overstated the dangers.*

The vassal-king King Kandalanu is fully prepared to honor King Ashurbanipal in the royal fashion. As they enter the gates of Babylon and continue down the processional way, it is to the shouts of an excited crowd. They continue on to the palace for a royal banquet. The priests from every temple are dressed in the robes of their religious attire, and the honorable King Ashurbanipal is careful to honor one and all.

King Ashurbanipal stands for their loud ovation and then speaks to one and all, "To you, King Kandalanu, I bring the honor of the Assyrian Empire. To you, wise and honorable lords, I applaud this great city and your careful authority. To you, esteemed priests, I honor Marduk, your namesake, and I equally honor all your faiths. To you, faithful citizens, I give respect and good will." Then he offered, "Let me present to you the crowned prince of the Assyrian Empire."

As Crown Prince Ashuretililani stands, there is roaring applause that seems to never end.

Finally, Ashurbanipal says, "Now, let me introduce the most beautiful lady in the empire, my daughter, my princess, the namesake of the renowned queen of Sennacherib, Princess Zakutu."

Her beauty has already stolen every heart, and as she stands the crowd goes completely wild. It is a great while before she is able to reclaim her seat, as royal protocol requires that she stand until the honor is finished. She has won the day for her father.

Three days later, the king and his great army are off to the city-state of the southernmost part of Chaldea. There is to be a great celebration in Erech, where the general of the Chaldean garrison is stationed. General Nebopolasser, with his newborn son, will be there to meet the king.

The famous *ziggurat* of Erech, where the Chaldean goddess, Inanna was first worshipped, is visible from a day's journey away. Inanna was the first worldwide goddess, and all future goddesses will be named after her. This ziggurat is more than a place of worship as it also serves as an observation tower from which to study the heavens. The king is the first to spot it.

"Zakutu!" he shouts, "Look! That is the oldest worship ziggurat in the world, and your father is the one who orchestrated the reconstruction of it. This city is certainly the oldest in our empire, and the ancient story called the 'Epic of Gilgamesh' that describes the worldwide flood was written here. Our tablet library has several different versions of that great catastrophe, and our scriptorium has made copies to be used throughout our empire. I am expecting to find the original copy while we are here for our visit. We believe that our god Ashur and his gods, along with Ninurta, the god of war, whose temple is behind our palace, sent this flood to correct and judge the evil in man."

His princess Zakutu greatly desires to tell her father about the creation story that her great-grandmother and her maid have shared with her. It is a story so different and so believable that she has indeed embraced this God of the Scrolls. She knows however that her father is not ready to handle this kind of talk from his favorite. She silently prays.

As they journey on towards the great tower in the distance, she is amazed at the beautiful oak, beech, and basswood trees. Occasionally, she sees porcupines and even ostriches. The great Chaldean crescent of plenty is a stunning sight to Princess Zakutu. The country is replete with the beauty of living and vibrant nature.

Groves of palms are everywhere, each palm standing stately and bowing slightly in the breeze.

Her father comments, "Zakutu, the beautiful landscape expands and the vast array of animals increase as we journey toward the marshes and the Persian Sea. You will love this beautiful part of our empire and the marshes where our General Nebopolasser, was raised and still lives when duty allows. His mansion is wonderful to behold. He has accumulated his extensive wealth from the bounty of this rich land and waters and we too, enjoy so much of this abundance."

The time in Erech is wonderful, and the celebration is rich in royal grandeur and pomp. Zakutu loves being the king's daughter and carries herself as a royal princess should. Time is spent with the family of Nebopolasser, and all appears well on the surface. Nevertheless, her young mind knows something is not right. She loves the marshes. Leaving behind the horses and chariots for a time in the exquisite pirogues (canoes), they ply the waters of abundance. Seagulls, ducks, herons, partridges, and storks are abundant. Hyenas, wildcats, water buffalo, gazelles, and even panthers roam freely.

Zakutu comments, "Father, this is a real living zoo, and it's beautiful to see these wild animals in their own natural world." Her laughter is a pleasure to all.

Soon, they are on their way back to Nineveh, and Zakutu feels like she has grown into a young lady—and is better prepared to face her world. She and her father have grown closer and the crown prince, her brother, appears to have accepted his sister. Knowing that the princess is part of the royal family, he has learned to appreciate her strong personality and absolute beauty.

Zakutu is unaware of many of the activities performed by the greater part of the Assyrian cavalry and foot warriors. They have indeed put down several rebellions, made examples of the unruly in the vicious way of the Assyrians, and are hoping that they have paved the way for lasting peace. The Assyrian leaders traveling with the king have collected a considerable tribute and much booty as is the custom of this empire. The princess cannot help but notice the extensive amount of gold, silver, and other goods that they are bringing back to the capital. She knows that this is their way of life, but much of it makes her uncomfortable.

King Ashurbanipal is careful to see that the princess rides proudly at his side. She says to her father and brother, "Our country is indeed extravagantly rich, and we have a wealthy life. I want to spend my life helping the many poor people we have witnessed on this trip—those that live so meagerly in the midst of so much abundance."

The crown prince is annoyed at her statement, but the king seems to understand her tendency toward a more compassionate view of the Assyrian Empire.

The Seers Have Spoken

627 BC

The Assyrian Empire has removed thousands of people from Samaria, her cities, and her countryside and planted them throughout the cities of Mesopotamia, Medea and Persia, wherever they rule. Many within the Assyrian world have become aware of the voice of destruction that is making pronouncements against their empire. No one doubts the hatred that Assyria's strong arm and vicious treatment of her enemies have instilled in the minds of those who have heard of or witnessed their fury. They have brought with them their own Scrolls, and know the latest words being spoken by the seers: Nahum, Jeremiah, Habakkuk, and Zephaniah. These pronouncements are constantly being secretly passed among them. They are also keenly aware that they are in Assyrian cities because of their flagrant disregard for the "words of their Scrolls."

A greatly respected seer by the name of Nahum is speaking. The people that love the Scrolls or at least respect the people of the Scrolls believe that his words come straight from the living God.

Nahum says, "Nineveh, there is no healing of thy bruise; thy wound is grievous; all that hear the fruit of thee shall clap the hand over thee: for upon who hath not thy wickedness passed continually?"

Amirta, Zakutu's maidservant, upon hearing these words, trembles for her own safety. She is determined that as soon as Zakutu

has rested from her magnificent trip with her father, she will tell
her about these recent proclamations from the God that she has
known from her childhood. She knows that the princess will be
deeply troubled for her father, whom she adores so very much, and
for her brother, the crown prince, whom she does not trust.

Nahum declares, "Woe to the bloody city! It is all full of lies
and robbery; the prey departeth not."

"I will discover thy skirts upon thy face," he shouts. "Thou
hast multiplied thy merchants above the stars of heaven. O, King
of Assyria: thy nobles shall dwell in the dust: thy people is scattered
upon the mountains, and no man gathered them."

These words from God are too much for Amirta, a slave in
King Ashurbanipal's palace and totally separated from her family.
She must talk to someone.

At the palace of Nimrud, it is a beautiful day and the princess is
rested and exuberant.

"Amirta," she says to her trusted maidservant, "I trust your
God, but I fear for my father and our land. I see so much that is
beautiful, but I also see so much that I fear."

She asks with deep concern, "Can we pray today for the Assyrian Empire?" Amirta has not yet had the opportunity to share the
words of Nahum.

Since she has come to know about this awesome God whom
Amirta serves, Zakutu has grown especially close to her maid-
servant. Through the many hours she has spent learning about
Amirta's faith and listening to the stories of how God delivered
His people, they have developed a strong bond of kinship that she
cannot explain.

"Zakutu," she replies, "I'm also fearful, for the words of God
that I trust are dark and foreboding and I dread telling you all of

them. If our seers are right, and I believe they are, then there is no hope for Nineveh or even this beautiful palace. The wrongdoings of Assyria are far too great to be forgotten!"

With tears in her eyes, Zakutu responds, "But God heard us when the seer named Jonah spoke to us; will He not hear us again?"

"I'm just a lowly maid," says Amirta with compassion. "I cannot know what will happen, but I will join you in prayer to seek God for an answer."

Together the young women pray earnestly that it is not too late for Assyria.

All is not well in the land of the Scrolls. The evil of the people there is just as dark as it is in the capital of Assyria. The light they have from their seers makes their darkness even more foreboding. Josiah, a good king that does pleasing things in the sight of his God, is only successful on the surface. A seer named Jeremiah is stirring up the people with his constant pronouncement of the coming judgment. For him, the nights are filled with bitterness and weeping as his mind races with the thoughts of the coming sorrows. He loses hope for his nation and its capital. His heart is profoundly heavy as he proclaims the evil of Judah and the destruction of Zion to a people that refuse to hear. There is still hope, he says, but only if the people act quickly and repent for all their wicked sins. He speaks words straight from his God, "Consider you and call for the mourning women. And let them take haste, and take up a wailing for us, that our eyes may run down with tears and our eyelids gush out with waters. For death is come up into our windows, and is entered into our palaces."

Jeremiah meets with King Josiah and they open their hearts to each other. Josiah knows that this seer is speaking for the God of the Scrolls. With great respect, Jeremiah says, "King Josiah, I am grateful for your tremendous efforts to change the direction of our nation, but the change is insufficient. The voice of God is awesome and I tremble with fear. The priesthood in our temple is still a false priesthood, and you must act to return the temple authority to the true appointed ones of the Book."

Jeremiah continues, "Also the breaking of our Sabbath, a day commanded by God, has polluted our land and only the pure among us still keep this holy day before our God."

"Man of God," King Josiah says to Jeremiah, "that is impossible because my lords will not allow it. We have torn down the groves to other gods and have destroyed their idols. We have forbidden the sacrifice of children unto Molech and have returned to the faithful offerings of the proper sacrifices on our altars, but the removal of the present high priest and his appointed priesthood cannot happen."

"I tremble for you, my king, but our only hope is a complete cleansing of that entire act in the office of priest. Then our sacrifices will be received by our God and His favor will return."

King Josiah is in tears as he hears the words of his seer, but the cost to act is beyond what he is willing to pay.

"O, Jeremiah," pleads the king, "please intercede for me—that I be given the wisdom to do all that you have commanded me."

He begs Jeremiah to stay near him and Jerusalem, as though the seer has magical powers of protection rather than a voice of truth speaking for his mighty God. The superstition of the king is greater than his love for the truth, and his failure to fully obey is witnessed by all. He is a good king, but too weak to withstand the strong princes that advise him.

Two other seers, Habakkuk and Zephaniah, from the Land of the Scrolls, add their voices. Habakkuk speaks, "Therefore the law is slacked, and judgment doth never go forth: for the wicked doth compass about the righteous; therefore wrong judgment proceedeth!"

He speaks again regarding the people of the Book, every citizen of Judea, and of all the land, "Because thou hast spoiled many nations, all the remnant of the people shall spoil thee; because of men's blood, and for the violence of the land, of the city, and of all that dwell therein."

The seer Habakkuk is quick to pronounce that from the beginning his people were ordained to bless others, but they have grievously failed. Soon, they will have to answer for their sins and failures.

By the Spirit of his God, he promises, "Shall they not rise up suddenly that shall bite thee, and awake that shall vex thee, and thou shalt be for booties unto them?"

Yet, in the midst of such ominous words, Habakkuk sees far into the future and speaks of hope, "For the earth shall be filled with the knowledge of the glory of the LORD, as the waters cover the sea."

Zephaniah, another seer, hears similar words, which leaves his heart in anguish for his people. The voice of the Lord echoes in his mind and fills him with a sense of urgency for the hour of darkness, which is to come upon his nation.

"I will utterly consume all things from off the land," Zephaniah pronounces.

He further declares as he has heard from the God of the Scrolls, "I will also stretch out mine hand upon Judah, and upon all the inhabitants of Zion; and I will cut off the remnant of Baal from this place, and the name of the Chemarims with the priests."

Zephaniah also promises that Assyria will suffer the same judgment as Judah and Zion, concluding, "…and he will stretch out his hand against the north, and destroy Assyria; and will make Nineveh desolation, and dry like a wilderness."

As these words are repeated in Zion and secretly spread by every Scroll lover that has been carried away captive into every corner of the Assyrian Empire, almost everyone is listening. Throughout the empire of Assyria, there is much fear and trembling. Many of its inhabitants know nothing of a voice from a seer, but they know the emotions of their slaves from Judea and those of their own souls. The entire land is troubled, and there are movements toward a new king as they witness what appears to be the last year of King Ashurbanipal. The citizens, with the exception of a pious remnant, have no voices to give them hope. The whole land of the Assyrian Empire is greatly troubled. The future looks bleak.

The Assyrian Princess Is Dead

627 BC

Before the birth of Nebuchadnezzar's Head of Gold Empire, the Assyrian Empire must be finished. The stage is set. The famous names that must pass off the stage are legendary and invoke intense emotion, but pass they must. From one of the greatest kings of the Assyrian Empire, King Ashurbanipal, to one of the most pious kings of Judea, King Josiah, their time to make history is in its closing moments. Other exceptional names must have their time in the sun.

Zakutu is always a living example of beauty and royalty. Not once has she ever appeared in the courts of her father, King Ashurbanipal, the city of Nineveh, or elsewhere in the empire without the air of a goddess. She is the symbol of the grand scheme of mortal man that has come to be known as the Assyrian Empire. She is the king's most captivating asset and the people would worship her if she would allow them. She has embraced the faith of her namesake, her great-grandmother Queen Zakutu, and her humble maidservant, Amirta.

But to the Assyrians, who know nothing of her new faith, she is still the assurance of their future. Assyria can be nothing but great as long as she lives.

As she sits in the splendor of her private room, she reads the Scrolls brought to her in secret by her maidservant. Her eyes begin to swell with hot tears as she pours over the words they contain. She knows the future of her world in Nineveh is coming to an end. A cold numbness fills her body as she lifts herself up from her bed. Walking to the window, she stares out, unable to move, as if she is beholding this view for the very last time. Filled with sorrow to the innermost part of her soul and gripped with fear for her beloved father, her will to live ends. There is not one ray of hope for her life as an Assyrian. She knows that the Assyrian dream is ending in despair.

Her last visit with her father is almost immortal. She speaks freely.

"Father," she says, "you will be remembered as the wisest of all the kings in this empire. Your heart is no longer set in the cruelty that we, as Assyrians, are known and feared for. You are a champion to me. Your change from a cruel king to one of wisdom, learning, and benevolence has made me love you beyond words."

King Ashurbanipal is moved to tears (unheard of amongst the Assyrian monarchs) as they converse. He is thankful that she has laid her head on his shoulder as she curls up beside him because he does not want her to see his tears.

"Zakutu, your beauty and faith have wooed my heart to respect your happiness in believing. I know that you are ill within, but altogether vibrant without." He says sadly, "The Assyrian Empire cannot survive without you."

Over the past months he has noticed the deep sorrow that seems to have taken hold of his princess. The vibrant life that so effortlessly flowed from her has vanished. Although she tries to hide it, he sees through her brave facade.

Trying to lift her spirits, he says, "We must plan another trip together! I want to take you to Judea, Tyre, and Egypt to see our world to the west."

"Father," she says, "there is not time for me, but maybe for you. You must learn about the faith of your grandmother. She, too, knew that prayer to her God was real and longed to pass her heritage on to others. She passed it on to me, and for that I am grateful."

Knowing his princess is exhausted, the king kindly dismisses himself. He leans over and tenderly kisses her on the top of the head. He will never see her alive again. That night she quietly passes to another world.

Princess Zakutu's body, clothed in the most costly of garments, was laid in state for all of Nineveh to mourn. Her funeral was nothing less than a royal event, filled with all the majesty and splendor befitting a princess. She is now laid to rest under the floor of the exquisite palace in Nimrud, beside her a chest filled with precious gems and stones from the farthest corners of the earth. The empire is in the throes of death, even as the princess is placed in her cold tomb beneath Assyrian splendor.

Young Nabu is now three years old. The son of Nebopolasser is a striking young child. The magnificent army under the command of the general has taken to the lad and he romps among them as the center of attention. By exposing young Nabu to his army, the general hopes to instill in him a sense of duty, leadership, and the bravery of a mighty warrior. The talk of a new Babylonian Kingdom has grown into a whirlwind. As much as possible, all discussions are kept within the tight circle of dedicated supporters, the elite of the southern region of Mesopotamia. The general and his father meet often to discuss the proper time and place to carry out their plans.

"Father," the general says with boldness, "my choice for declaring independence for all of Babylon from the Assyrians is next year at the ending of the harvest. If the harvest is good, we will have some months to solidify our declaration and place the soldiers in the planned strategic locations."

His father listens intently as he continues, "We are exercising our mighty warriors and expanding the numbers of men. Our strength is now at its peak. We are managing, with extreme caution, to perform these exercises under Assyrian guidelines and to show no sign of the planned defection."

His father agrees. "My son, I believe that you are right. I have labored much to get all matters of our business and farming in order. I have hired the best help available, and I am ready to be at your side.

"Son, your mother is proud of you, but she also fears for you. She knows that anger and brutality will come to you from Nineveh if all does not go as we plan."

"I believe the right time has come. Faith, plus our beliefs in Marduk, must sustain us."

In the fall of AD 627, the King Ashurbanipal of Assyria died. The king, father of Assyria's most beloved princess of all the empires in history, never recovers from her early death. Adored and loved by all, Zakutu literally gave life to a dying system. The king has buried her with a trove of riches, jewelry of gold, silver, and precious stones. In the months that pass, he spends most of his time at the site of her entombment beneath his favorite palace in Nimrud. It is impossible for Ashurbanipal to conceive of his princess in the cold stone tomb beneath his own splendor. The palace walls of delicately carved alabaster stone had been transported to this location. The Assyrians rerouted the Tigris River to bring these exquisite carvings to Nimrud. The story of King Ashurbanipal's many triumph and victory are written into the rich slabs in a continuous circle around the walls. Even the beautiful stone in the floor is filled with stories of this king. The palace is a history of his superior kingship.

The crown prince is ready to see his father pass from the scene and is appointed the co-regent with his father in the last months of his reign. The king is concerned for the kingdom because Prince Ashuretililani does not seem to possess the gentle sense of diplomacy that comes naturally as it had to the late princess. His character is rough and not noble like Zakutu's. He does not appear to have the same love for the Assyrian Empire that was so dear to her heart nor has his father's love of learning that produced one of the most astounding libraries of learning ever assembled.

"Son," the king says, "your temperament is very different from mine. I hope that you will balance the old Assyrian style of brute force with a more diplomatic form of control. Our world is changing, and quality learning can become our emerging personality."

He continues, "You know that our tablet museum has over one hundred thousand pieces of literature that your father searched our empire to compile. Already, educated leaders are traveling to the kingdom to study and learn. I long to know that you will protect it and make it even greater."

Ashuretililani replies, "Father, I applaud you for your learning and your love of the ancient and modern cuneiforms. You have helped lead all of Nineveh to know the riches of our past and the grand empires that we have inherited. You have proved that we are, indeed, the completion of their efforts.

"Assyria will never die!" he haughtily exclaims.

King Ashurbanipal seeks to warn his son of his overconfidence and to inspire him to put more trust in the gods, but his words seem to fall on deaf ears. His son, he fears, will not rule as he has.

Worn out, the king retires early. The next morning, as is their usual duty, the king's servants come to his quarters to attend to him. The king is lying awake in bed too weak to lift his head. He is ghostly pale. Although he is cool, there are beads of sweat about his forehead. He seems barely conscious of their presence. Deep concern washes over their faces, as they quickly exchange worried glances. The servants know their king is gravely ill and time is of the essence. Immediately, they summon the empire's best wise men to the palace. The high priest of Ashur is asked to petition the gods. Soon, the king's room is filled with priests, wise men, and servants.

The queen is also summoned to be at his side. She sits there, quietly staring, knowing that this great man of strength and valor does not have long to live. A tear slowly runs down her cheek as sadness fills her heart and uncertainty fills her mind. Their relationship has always been distant, yet she has a strong love and respect for her husband, the king. She had long ago accepted her position and the conditions of their marriage. Rarely has she been in the presence of the king, especially since the death of his beloved Zakutu.

As the sun is setting in the western sky, the king draws one last breath as his life slips away. The death of Princess Zakutu was more than this grieving king could survive.

A New Princess for a New King

624 BC

The mountains of Medea are lofty and even breathtaking, giving the appearance that they touch the sky. To be born in the midst of the grandeur of these peaks is to be addicted to them for life. It is as if the very life of these mountains runs through the veins of their inhabitants. They are more than high hills of emptiness; they teem with life and nature. They remain filled with what appears to be the original abundance from the ancient power of the God that created them.

A new princess has been born to the new King Cyaxares and his queen Akkadiya, who now rule Medea. She is considered by all of the Medes to be a gift from the gods. Her overwhelming beauty is captivating beyond description. Written in her face is an appearance known to the ancients as a "proper child" or as one predestined for future greatness. Both the king and his queen know that mystery. It is written all over their princess and they believe that she is certain to be part of a future that will touch the world.

King Cyaxares says to Akkadiya, his queen, "Our princess is a gift from the gods to replace the beautiful Princess Zakutu. Our Amytis is even more beautiful."

He continues, "The heart of the Assyrian Empire was devastated by Zakutu's death, but our Amytis will be at the heart of a new empire."

"O, Cy," Queen Akkadiya replies, "Our daughter is so very

beautiful, but I want her for us and not for another empire that so ruthlessly destroys others. The Assyrian Empire has destroyed so many great lives of even our own people."

They talk for many long hours of how they want freedom from the Assyrians and to see the Medean riches going to all Medes instead of as tribute to Nineveh. The queen, aware that he seldom speaks to her of state affairs, is careful to listen attentively and comment only when necessary. She loves the fact that he is now sharing his feelings and struggles with her. As he speaks about his concerns, he paces the floor. Her eyes, filled with admiration, follow him as he moves about the room.

He truly is an exceptional man! she thinks to herself.

He is considered by many Medes to be the most capable king that has ever ruled their empire. His natural ability to understand military and state concerns far exceeds that of many of his peers and is unusual for his young age. His strong stature and incredible personal bearing seem to be exploding since he has become the father of this young and charming daughter. The beautiful princess brings King Cyaxares great joy and inspires him to act more like a husband and father than he ever has in the past.

"Cy, is it safe for you, the princess, and me to go for a carriage ride up through the mountains of Elburz all the way to the Caspian Sea? The mountains and the lands of our country are so inviting and beautiful, and we must allow our princess to be the joy of all Medea," his wife says.

"There is nothing that she loves more than to sit on the balcony and gaze at the mountains. She always asks question after question about the beautiful trees and the animals that live among them."

The king loves this idea and immediately begins to ponder how he can use this trip as his first visit to large areas of his kingdom. The king of Medea wants to remove any fears of his ability to succeed his father. They will ride among the people of their country, and he will show them that he is a genuine family man. The king, riding with his family, will be an enduring symbol of strength to the people of a strong and growing Medea.

The mountains are at the peak of spring and will be a treat for his personal security guards and intimate lords, as well as for his queen and princess. The day is planned, and the people that live along the chosen route are informed. It is to be a trip long remembered by the entire nation. King Cyaxares speaks to his lords at their next council, "My wise lords and counselors, I want to demonstrate my love for you and my gratitude for your faithfulness. I want to show the people of our land my love for them as well.

"We are going on a trip through the mountains, and among some of the poorest of our people. I want to take the princess on her first experience out of the palace and away from the capital. She is nearly five years of age, and her beauty and love for everyone will show them a picture of our future." The lords of Medea are excited about such a grand show of themselves to the Medes.

"No one in the entire world can manifest love and show the face of their palace and the home of their king like a beautiful princess. Our people will love the thought of watching her grow up into the lady she is sure to be," the king continues.

Each of Medean's lords shares in the planning and executing of this exciting event. The king's carriage is carefully prepared and the entire city is invited to share the departure.

A feast is arranged for the celebration that will begin as their king, queen, and princess leave to visit the mountains and other parts of the nation. Every possible plan to make the entire capital and travel route a well-planned scene of excitement is carefully created. The princess will be the showpiece.

Amytis is dressed as only the king's daughter can be attired. Her long, naturally jet-black locks are more than beautiful. Her features are charming, and she knows that she is the star of the occasion. To see and adore the princess is to be under the sway of her father, the king.

She clearly revels in every expression of the celebration. The king and queen gladly conduct themselves as proud parents, knowing that the Medes' love of the princess is really a love of them.

"Father," she says, "I love you and mother for taking me to see the mountains. I can hardly wait to view the wonderful scenery you have described to me. Papa, I'm so glad you were grandfather's joy, even as you have told me that I am yours."

As the celebration is erupting all around her, she snuggles up to her father and kisses him on the cheek, to the absolute explosion of cheers from the crowd.

Along the route, the princess is sitting, standing, waving, and acting just like a five-year-old. Her exuberance is evident to everyone, and the crowd strains just to get a glimpse of the star of the passing court of their king. The lords are perfectly happy to ride their royal appearing stallions and just to be seen as the voices of wisdom preserving their Medean lifestyle. The queen has never viewed herself so clearly as the special one in the king's life. The princess is truly beautiful, but it is evident that her beauty came from the queen. She is outstanding in her own appearance and loveliness.

"Papa, look at those pretty flowers!" Amytis exclaims.

The king tries to explain the names of the different flowers, such as the Catnip and the beautiful Gold Dust. The walnut, oak, ash, and pistachio trees literally line the roadways. There are also beautiful poplar and hackberry varieties, and the princess marvels at their towering height and great size. Many of these trees are hundreds of years old and mammoth in size. She has been taught that the gods made all of this beauty for the Medean Empire.

Nothing thrills the princess more than the wild animals that constantly dart across the road. The lions are her favorite, and her father dares not tell her of the lion hunts of which he is so fond. The tigers are beautiful, and she even sees one chase a small deer for his evening meal.

The pheasants, suddenly flying from the roadside, never fail to excite her to let out a childish yell. Ducks and geese are always near the waterways and lakes that dot the landscape.

Amytis constantly asks the names of the animals, and tries hard to repeat them.

Of the lions she asks, "Are they dangerous, Father?"

"Yes, unless you are with other people that clearly outnumber the lions," he responds.

He describes the forest and trees as he tries hard to help her understand the value of these natural treasures. The king wants the princess to know about the value of her own part of the natural world. He wants her happiness to be in pure things that are the gifts of the gods.

They spend the night in a mountain estate belonging to one of the king's lords. It is set in the side of the mountain and is surrounded by breathtaking gardens and a natural zoo. This lord is a transplant to Medea that King Sennacherib had displaced from Megiddo of Samaria. He has become rich and powerful and has been elevated to new respect by the Medean elite. His wealth had given him a powerful position with King Cyaxares' father, and with King Cyaxares himself. Secretly, he is a man of the Book and prays often with a host of friends for the end of the great brutality from the Assyrian Empire that troubles his world.

The princess thinks she has never seen anything so beautiful. All of the varieties of animals and birds they have seen as they journeyed to the mountains are represented in the lord's mountain estate.

Amytis asks questions incessantly, "What is this flower? How big is that tree? Do these beautiful animals hurt one another?" The king's lord, who owns this outstanding estate, takes delight in showing the princess everything.

"Amytis," he says, "you bring life and joy to our mountain home, and you must come and spend a few days every season."

They feast on lamb and wild turkey until everyone is full and sleepy. The mountain air makes the night of rest perfect.

Many of the Medes are having their first personal visit from their young king in their own cities and villages. The king always addresses the people with brief remarks. The princess wants to dash among them but she is not allowed for her own safety. The crowd is ecstatic. At a breathtaking celebration near the Caspian Sea of which almost everyone in traveling distance has come to be a part, the king says, "My honorable subjects, I bring you greetings from the capital. All of our wise counselors could not come, but they send their gratitude to you. The queen, your princess, and I promise to seek the best for all of Medea. Our dream is for all of you to have greater freedom, greater wealth from your labor, and greater happiness. We will protect our nation with our lives."

The crowd roars their approval by shouting, "Long live our king!" On the spur of the moment, the king holds the princess high in the air and cries, "Here is our princess, a spiritual symbol of a great future for all Medea!"

Princess Amytis throws up her little arms and blows a kiss to the crowd. It is electrifying. The crowd almost goes insane.

While the king is enjoying this great presentation of royalty he knows that when he arrives back at the palace and capital, the time will come to throw off the yoke of the Assyrians. This trip has convinced him that the wonderful people of this nation are ready to follow him into a new freedom and hope. He begins to share his heart about this dream with the lords who are traveling with him.

"My lords, let us meet apart from families and guards."

When only the leaders of Medea are near, he says, "I am ready to declare our freedom from the Assyrians."

The awesome adventurers of this time of celebration have warmed their hearts to his kingship, and they respond in complete agreement." We are ready to declare ourselves the 'Medean Empire' and to break all alliance to Nineveh. You have shown us your leadership and wisdom, and we are ready to follow."

They talk at length during this happy experience with the king and his family. They speak of dreams long held in silence because of the powers of brutality known in the Assyrian Empire. The time has come for change and the king and his lords know it.

Finally the king and his entourage journey home after many days of celebration in every city and every village possible. Amytis says to her father, "Father, I love these beautiful mountains, but I love you and mother most."

Her quick laughter and ability to learn and act almost royal, even at her young age, thrills King Cyaxares. Forgetting all the protocol of being a king, he takes her in his arms and simply gives her the kind of affection a daughter needs from her father. "I love you, my princess," he triumphantly says.

The Assyrian Yoke Is Broken

624 BC

General Nebopolasser goes swiftly to his father's home in the marshes. His father meets him on the deck of his beautiful home built of reeds.

"Father," Nebopolasser says, "The time has come. Tomorrow, I will proclaim myself king of Babylon and all Southern Chaldea."

"It's about time," his father says. "Your delay has been wise, but further delay will only open the door for someone less qualified. There will be much danger for the next month, and I am ready to lead the palace guards. For months I have been enlisting the best men in the whole of Chaldea, and we will protect you with our own lives.

"Son, be prepared," he continues. "You will have to make tough decisions and good men, many of them our friends, will die. But, we are ready to be free of the Assyrians at any cost."

Nebopolasser speaks with great concern and passion, "I know the location of every cavalry band and group of foot warriors of the Assyrians throughout the southern region of Chaldea. Our best guards in each location will be waiting for the news to reach them, for my decision, or for any reaction from Nineveh. The king of the Assyrians, the son of Ashurbanipal, is not a strong leader. The whole empire is in disarray, and I believe he will withdraw his men to save lives and prepare for a frontal attack. They are very aware of the news forthcoming from King Cyaxares of Medea and will be most concerned to protect their capital, Nineveh.

"Father, we are in the best possible condition, and the time is favorable to us. We have planned well, and the time is now."

"I believe you are right, my son," says his wise old father.

"My father," speaks the general, "my overwhelming concern is for my Hanna and Young Nabu. We must have the best guards to protect them and our families. When they learn of our decision, they might have someone that is pro-Assyrian among us, unknown to you and me that may try to hurt us at the source of our strength and love. Remember that Nabu is only six years old. He is a handful young child, quick to learn, and roams these marshes with pleasure and freedom. As of tomorrow, he will be my crown prince. He is also our future leader of the army, and we must carefully protect him for the New Babylonian Empire."

"Son," says his wise father, "I have three brothers who have taken charge of our own local borders. They are already organized with at least three hundred men from this part of the garden we call Eden, and they will die before anyone touches our families. They have been on guard for weeks and will now intensify their actions."

"My father," says Nebo, "that's why I felt watched as I slipped down from Erech to make this visit. I now feel complete peace for my family."

The next day as General Nebopolasser, his father, and a very large contingent of the best of his fighting men approach Babylon; they find it locked down like a siege has already occurred. A Babylonian guard speaks through the imposing gate and asks of their affair. He knows that this is the general of the Assyrian Empire of the South, but he also knows that the news from Nineveh is to be obeyed.

The guard says, "We have been instructed that no one is to enter Babylon until further notice."

Nebopolasser speaks without hesitation. "Today I will proclaim myself the new king of Babylon. We are fully capable of taking down this gate, but we want to spare bloodshed. No one will be hurt, and King Kandalanu and all who desire will be given safe passage to the new lines of Assyrian territory."

The guard runs swiftly to the palace and delivers the news. The king does not doubt that the general, well known and absolutely respected, is fully capable of taking Babylon. To turn his few guards loose would be suicide for everyone.

The king says, "Open the gates. I will wait for Nebopolasser at the entrance of the palace."

Nebopolasser goes first to show respect to the king at the appointed place. King Kandalanu is informed of the declaration to be made in his throne room of Babylon.

Everyone of the city makes quick choices and, immediately, either declares loyalty to General Nebopolasser or begins preparations to depart for Nineveh.

After his short meeting with King Kandalanu, Nebopolasser quickly goes to the temple of Marduk while the inhabitants of the city prepare for the news to reach everyone. The high priest, having already received the news, knows that this new king is a great worshipper of their god, Marduk, and he is excited for their future.

The priest says, "I welcome you, King Nebopolasser, to this famed and ancient city, and I welcome you to represent our chief god to the new kingdom of Babylon." The priests of the Temple to Marduk are the first to call the general "King Nebopolasser" even before he calls himself the same.

Without hesitation the general speaks, "This Temple of Marduk will be the 'First Temple' of our empire, and we will bestow on this place our greatest of all riches. This temple will be the most beautiful in all the earth and it shall be enlarged and magnified beyond measure."

The priests of the temple begin a lively ceremony to worship and praise both the new king and their silent god. Immediately, Nebopolasser is given godlike status.

From the temple, General Nebopolasser goes directly to the capitol building and throne room. It is already filled to capacity with his own lords and guards, residents of Babylon, and, especially, business leaders who have assembled to hear the proclamation of his kingship.

The general speaks, "To the priests of Marduk and to all the priests of the temples of Babylon, to my lords and counselors that have assembled to help me serve you as your king, to the brave warriors who are ready to lead or fight, to the business leaders of this city, and to all my subjects of a New Babylon; I declare myself your king. Today, I am the King of Babylon and of all the Mesopotamia Valley. Today begins the end of the Assyrian Empire.

"It will be a new day," he declares. "We will seek to lead you in the defense of our borders, to unite you for greatness, to lead you in worship of our gods, and to bless all the people of the ancient land of Babylon. I am your king for good and not for bad. We shall free all peoples of the terrors of the brutal mastery of that which we call Assyrian."

The crowd is now alive, ever electric with enthusiasm, and there is no possible ability to speak further. The city is filled with their cries, "Great is our king! Great is our king! Great are our gods; great is Marduk! Great is King Nebopolasser!" It is a day of unfettered joy in this ancient city of many sorrows.

A new feeling floods the city of Babylon, and only the thought of the Assyrians marching down to battle keeps everyone from the perfect joy of a new day. No one doubts that the battles will be deadly, and the task ahead only to be won by the brave.

Across all of Chaldea, the dedicated warriors of the many ethnic groups immediately unite behind King Nebopolasser. After many years of Assyrian brutality and the high tribute demanded of them, the peoples of this rich fertile land are delighted to be their own.

Their riches and abundance have been carried off to Nineveh for too long, and they are quick to accept a New Babylonian Empire.

In the capital of Medea, the exceptional King Cyaxares is preparing to address thousands of the Medean population. Announcements have gone throughout the land to invite every possible fellow citizen to hear the king make a long to be remembered speech and proclamation. The city is primed for a celebration. The streets are gleaming clean. His trip with the queen, the princess, and his lords has opened the nation for greatness. Excitement is everywhere!

The respected vice chairman of the governing council stands to speak. Everyone present quickly becomes quiet and reverent. "My People of Medea, citizens of our great nation, fellow neighbors, and lovers of our beautiful land, I present to you our loved King Cyaxares," he says.

As the king stands, the crowd shouts, "Great is our king! Great is our land! Great is all Medea!"

They shout over and over again until the king holds up his hands for silence. He proclaims, "My fellow Medeans, this is a new day in the history of all Medea. Even as I speak, our well-trained cavalry and foot soldiers are stationed on our borders with Assyria. I have spent valuable time with General Nebopolasser of all the southern Assyrian warriors of the Assyrian Nation. Today, in the city of Babylon he declared himself king of all Babylon.

"I have been your king only a short time, but my father was your king for many years while I was your crown prince. We have been a vassal state of Assyria and paid our wealth into their treasury as tribute money. Today, our lords, all the council, and your king declare our nation free from the Assyrian Empire."

Immediately, the excited host of Medean people is exuberant and shouts their approval. It is a long while before the king can speak again.

"Many of your own families were mercilessly killed in battles with the Assyrian warriors. I believe the gods of Medea will avenge these deaths."

The king continues, "I believe the days of the brutal Assyrian soldiers and cavalry are over. Their new king is not Ashurbanipal, but a weak son. Their present development appears to be the defense of Nineveh, not aggression towards Babylon or ourselves."

"King Nebopolasser is, without doubt, the greatest general that has ever commanded the Assyrian army. Our general, myself and the king of Babylon, and his general, his own father, will be in constant unity to guarantee the safety of our great land and borders.

"Hear my last words to you," he continues. "We are a strong nation with great riches. Now, they will be reserved for our nation and not carried away to enrich the lives of others. Every able man will be needed, and some shall die in the struggle; so, be prepared to defend that which is yours. Our brave warriors are ready."

After a magnanimous time of shouting and declaring their love of the king, the princess, and their nation, the celebration of the happy feast began. The best food of the nation, from the Caspian Sea on the north to the borders of Babylon and Assyria, is spread all over the city. Games are announced at the theater, where all the enjoyable celebration events are occurring. There is joy throughout the land as the king's speech is repeated over and over by one and all.

The Assyrian offices in the capital are quickly vacated and all Assyrian representatives are granted safe passage to Nineveh. Every precaution is taken not to stir anger with the Assyrian post that has lived among the Medeans for years. Many are friends of the people of Medea. Some even ask permission to become fellow citizens of the nation of Medea.

For the next period of years, King Nebopolasser of Babylon

and King Cyaxares of Medea are busy building their armed forces
into powerful machines of warfare. They grow and consolidate their
two nations into small empires. They experience close cooperation
between themselves and their people as they build elaborate buildings, repair buildings destroyed by the Assyrians, and learn to trust
each other for future defense against invading armies.

The Assyrian yoke over these two nations is over, but skirmishes
occur. Within less than two decades, Assyria, as an empire, no longer
exists. Nineveh is soon to be in ruins, just as the seers have written
by the God of the Scrolls.

The Rise of New Babylon

623 BC

King Nebopolasser in his royal palace of Babylon speaks to his lords, "You are my wise company of Chaldea's finest and I welcome you to our first council of wisdom. From the coast of Southern Chaldea to the lavish crescent of our northern tip and both east and west of our capital, the greatest, most successful men of New Babylon that I have chosen are present. Your proven wisdom for which I honor you must be applied to the future of our empire if we are to be worthy of our name. To everyone gathered in this new council, I ask you to put the future of all Chaldea above your own."

The king continues, "I am presently assembling from among those that know the gods and deal in divining and sorceries, wise men that read the signs and know the good and bad omens. Their wisdom will be constantly available to all of you so that this council can have the latest words of the gods in every decision we make."

As he speaks, the king is seated in his royal chair in the preeminent court of his lords. Already, there is a kingly air that surrounds King Nebopolasser and his lords tremble before him. They believe that the gods of Babylon rest on him and have put the powers of life and death in his hands. After his opening address to them, the court chambers echo with chants and worship to the king.

"The gods have come!" they proclaim. "Long live King Nebopolasser! Long live the king of Babylon!"

As they shout these acclamations, oblations are made before the king. The chants continue until the gigantic chamber becomes a pulsating temple-like scene and all business must be put on hold. The overwhelming acclamations and excitement continue until the guards protecting the council join in and it spills out into the city streets. Soon all of Babylon becomes a roaring place of worship to the gods and the king. The revelry continues for hours.

The chefs from the king's estate and his palace servants prepare a delicious feast for his lords, and the celebration moves to the palace banquet hall. It continues as they feast on the best cuisine of Chaldea. The main fare is water buffalo from the estate of the king himself. The menu for this occasion is modeled after the great recipes of these great marsh dwellers. All the banquet delicacies are prepared in the ancient styles of Sumer.

By the time the evening is finished, the lords from all across Babylon have given their hearts and soul to their new king. The governor of Ur is chosen as the final voice for this first noble council of wisdom. He is the honorable lord of the grand city of Ur.

Lord Tehra steps quickly to the podium and speaks, "King Nebopolasser, I honor you as the king from the gods. To all of my fellow lords, I honor you as the best of Babylonia. To all of our great people of the kingdom, I honor one and all as the finest and most honorable of all mankind. We are the Chaldeans, the first dwellers in this ancient land of Sumer. We represent the people that the gods have sent down to dwell in this rich land. We are the creators of the first language and are the favorites of the gods. Our land is a garden, with the wealth of the world arising from our treasures.

"Today we have conducted our first council of wisdom and have declared before all that New Babylon will be the kingdom that honors the gods. It will be a kingdom for the people of all Chaldea. Never again will we be subject to the nations around us. We are free," he explains.

"The challenge that lies before us must begin with several

important tasks. We must secure our borders against all possibility of foolish attacks and we must plan and assure our worthy people of a prosperous lifestyle. Next, we must prepare our warriors and cavalry to stretch our borders to secure the trade routes that of necessity pass through Mesopotamia. We must control the wealth of those routes both in revenue and the needs of the empire."

He continues, "The king has honored me with the position of Lord of Agriculture. We must redesign and improve the canals to water all our fertile fields and strengthen the sciences of successful farming. We should devote ourselves to vineyard development and the needed task of harvesting the riches from the land. I have assembled a special council and the king has promised to provide this task with sufficient revenue. New Babylon must become a bread basket for the entire kingdom to enjoy."

The lords are wealthy men and their estates receive their wealth by the prosperity of the land. The news is like a final crescendo to finish the excitement of the first council of the king's lords. One after the other speaks excitedly of the prosperous results that are sure to follow. The day ends in exceeding triumph.

Before the king had announced his kingship, news channels had been thoroughly planned and a complete system developed so that all news carriers moved by relay to every corner of the kingdom. News of the first "Council of Wisdom" and the words of Lord Tehra, the new Lord of Agriculture, reach all in the New Babylonian Kingdom before the next two days have passed. The news is a double joy, coming quickly after the announcement of separation from Nineveh and the Assyrians. For years, their wealth has been carried off for others to enjoy, while little has been done to improve their own lot in life.

The support for King Nebopolasser soars. Thousands of young men quickly begin to join the growing number of warriors ready to defend the new borders and expand the kingdom. Chaldea overwhelmingly accepts the promise of a "New Babylonian Empire."

The most powerful man of Erech is Lord Sarhaddan. He is a man that has such charm he is easy to follow, but enough firmness that he is impossible to ignore. He is a natural leader, a skilled warrior, and a devoted lover of Inanna and her ancient temple ziggurat. This ziggurat has long been the religious mecca of all Chaldea. It is at the heart of great religious celebrations and no one dares to speak evil of it.

The huge wealth of Sarhadden's personal empire is lavished on this goddess and his influence is powerful. The king appoints him as the new general of all his warriors and the cavalry of horses and chariots. His duties are to train the king's cavalry and to extend the number of chariots and warriors into a fighting force that cannot be defeated. He is also responsible for directing the large fleet of ships that sail the seas. Lord Sarhaddan has complete command of Babylon's military. He is fully able to perform the task.

His first commander is an excellent merchant that has traveled the world and become exceedingly rich in the selling of purple and other finery in ladies apparel. His grandfather had been brought from a quaint town south of Samaria by King Sargon II and transplanted in Erech. His grandfather had told him of seeing friends and many of the Samarian lords impaled outside the gates of their capital city, Samaria.

His grandfather was led in chains from his wealthy home and brought across the desert, where many died from the savagery of the Assyrians. This first commander has never forgotten the imagery, fastened in his memory, of the sorrow he was told. He is a lover of the Scrolls that his father had received from his father and always prays toward the east for the end of the vicious Assyrian Empire. All of this has prepared him to help train the warriors for the end of Nineveh.

The portion of the Scrolls his grandfather had secretly stowed in his meager belongings is from a shepherd turned king, who was himself a tremendous warrior. The commander's inspiration lives out of that fragment from his homeland and he worships the God of the Scrolls. He always finds business to give his attention to when these devotees of other gods are worshipping and is careful to worship only the God of his grandfather.

A news item is sent throughout the kingdom challenging the best of all the Chaldeans to become warriors for New Babylon.

The news release from Lord Sarhaddan states, "I accept the appointment from our honorable king as the general of all our military. The success of a kingdom depends on the security of its borders. Every city, every small town, and every Babylonian must be safe. The king has committed the riches already flowing into our treasury to the building of our forces of warriors and cavalrymen. Large chariots are being constructed, our unique armory is being prepared, and every instrument of the best of warfare is quickly being readied for the trained and brave men among us."

He continues, "Our new kingdom will be challenged and we must be ready. Our training will be tough, and only the best of men will be able to endure the rigor. But, when your training is over, you will be a man your family can be proud of.

"I challenge you," he adds, "to become the men that will make New Babylon greater than it ever was in the past. Babylon is rising again and we will train to see that it never falls."

The challenge is accepted and thousands of Chaldea's best respond as expected. The trusted general wastes no time. Soon the cavalry and the warriors will be ready to defend and expand every border and to control every trade route of the Mesopotamia Valley.

King Nebopolasser arrives unexpectedly at the training camp of Erech. Hundreds of the best cavalrymen from his old garrison, which he had commanded for the Assyrians, are his guards. These warriors protect him day and night. The king rides in his special chariot, which is pulled by four fabulous horses, into the camp. When the recruits realize their king is present, the place turns into an enjoyable celebration. General Sarhaddan immediately assembles the entire camp for the king's visit.

King Nebopolasser chooses to approach the crowd in his own chariot to display his awesome warrior mystique. With his royal chariot gleaming in the desert sunlight, a gleaming sword buckled on his side, and a dazzling spear in his hand, he rides right into the camp like a warrior out of a storybook. General Sarhaddan is by his side and the camp is set where they can ride through the midst of the great training area. All the recruits can see the king and his kingly chariot. The results are electric. Once the opening display is finished, the king and his general, Sarhadden, approach the speaker's stand.

The king addresses all of his warriors and trainees, "The strongest and best of all Chaldeans are standing before me."

Turning to his respected general, he says, "General Sarhaddan is a champion. He and I have fought together often and I have trusted my life to him in many battles. He is your general and he will train you until the warrior of Babylon can make our kingdom prosperous, safe, and respected. Every kingdom must know that you are the bravest and strongest.

"I am here because there are many challenges that must be faced. Soon we shall end forever the Assyrian Empire. We cannot wait for them to recover from their present weakness. The kingdom of Assyria is vicious. They know no mercy and many will suffer unless Assyria is no more! You are the men that will end a thousand years of suffering and savagery from the north."

The king quiets the crowd because they are continually crying, "The gods have come! The gods have come! Great is King Nebopolasser! Great is the kingdom of Babylon!"

The king continues, "The trade routes that pass through the Mesopotamia Valley reflect the riches of the world. The people who control those routes eventually control the world. They have made the Assyrian Empire rich and strong. Those riches and the strengths of them will eventually make them strong again. That cannot be allowed to happen. We must prepare to extend our kingdom to control every route that passes through our valley and through the Persian Gulf. The goods for building the great temples to our gods, protective walls around our cities, and securing your wealth as we build the New Babylonian Kingdom are carried along these routes. These routes must be under our control.

"The abundance of this fertile land can be traded for the growing wealth of peoples in distant lands. Our splendid warriors that stand before me today and those that follow can secure these routes for Babylon. I'm here to challenge General Sarhaddan and his commanders and all of you for our excellent future."

His eloquent speech is godlike and mesmerizing. "Will you accept my challenge and my instruction?" he cries.

The response is wonderful. His words of bravery create such joy that every soldier is ready to pour himself out for his king and the kingdom. He has set the course for greatness. They are ready to train with an enthusiasm that thrills the king and all the warrior brass. The king in his warrior's attire and the general in his official uniform, with the tokens of many past victories on his chest, stand side by side. The skilled warriors of past victories stand with all the trainees in rigid attention. Babylon's bravest are prepared to build and protect the kingdom of Chaldea.

As the king breaks from his professional response, he declares, "And, now, a special announcement. Unknown to General Sarhaddan, I have planned a special treat for all of you today."

Suddenly a grand chariot appears from the side carrying a young man dressed in the attire of a warrior. This chariot comes to a stop beside the king's chariot and the young man steps out of the driver's side and stands quickly beside the king. It is his son Nebuchadnezzar. The silence of the crowd is spellbinding. This young man has not been to Erech for over two years and has grown greatly in size.

Already he is well over five feet tall and weighs one hundred and fifty pounds. With his broad shoulders, he is masculine to look upon. He is almost an idol to his father, King Nebopolasser.

The king speaks proudly, "Today, I am presenting to you the crown prince of Babylon. General Sarhaddan, I bring my son to you to begin intensive training in your camp. He must be an exceptional warrior if he is going to be a great king."

Quickly, the king adds, "He will be an exalted king of Babylon, and the world will never forget his name.

"General Sarhaddan," the king declares, "Strong warriors standing before me, I present to you my son, Nebuchadnezzar, the next king of Babylon."

It is almost more than the crowd can endure. Explosions of excitement fill the crowd of warriors, cavalrymen, and charioteers.

Again the king speaks, "His grandfather and I have been training him for all of the seven years of his life, but now I put him in your hands for the rigorous improvements my general and his commanders are fully capable of accomplishing."

The king then instructs Nabu to make a drive of his chariot to show the warriors and recruits his youthful skills. The crown prince steps into his chariot and off he goes, spear in hand, with a skill that leaves even his father speechless. It is the end of a day that no man present will ever forget.

Every lord in the king's court is given a place of responsibility. No one can serve King Nebopolasser and just give him wisdom they have acquired. Every man is asked to be among the lords so he can do for the kingdom what his experiences of life have prepared him to give. With such talent, the New Babylon almost leaps out of the Mesopotamia Valley. When the crown prince becomes king, his father wants to make sure the kingdom is already secure. The beginning of New Babylon is not an ordinary beginning. Every event and action appears to be the action of humans and gods joined together.

Wedding Time for Nabu and Amy

614 BC

Sixteen years old, the crown prince of Babylon is a giant of a man and still growing. The covenant with the king of Medea for his princess Amytis to wed Nebuchadnezzar was made many years earlier. For these two kings Nebopolasser and Cyaxares, it was a union joined by the gods.

The Medean and Chaldean palaces have been the scenes of several banquets of the two families as they have built their two empires as partners. From the beginning, this alliance has enabled their survival from the onslaught and challenge of the Assyrians.

The expanded empire of the Medes requires that the Medean capital be moved. The new palace of the Medean king is magnificent to the extreme. It is situated in the crest of the mountains under the towering pistachio and poplar trees. Every walkway and roadway is paved with granite, while ancient statues and memorials of Medean successes fill the center spaces of lush gardens and flowers.

In the springtime, when the air is filled with the newness of life, Nebuchadnezzar and Amytis take a walk in the midst of climbing clematis vines and blooming roses. They walk in silence, holding hands since the two kings told them only minutes earlier that it is time for a wedding.

Nabu and Amy, as they call each other, have always been in love as far back as they can remember. He is the most handsome young man in the Babylonian Empire, and she is even more beautiful. She is a princess of rare beauty and charm, with jet-black hair that flows like silk, fabulous eyes, and a golden complexion. Nabu is a man of strength and character that will arrest attention. They look as a royal couple even in their youthfulness. Nabu longs for her to become his wife.

"Amytis," he says with such emotion that she almost shudders with joy, "I am the proudest man alive. I am a warrior, and I have trained to be the best.

"Remember," he says, "I am also a man. I intend to be your husband and friend and for us to never forget our love for each other. Other kings may have harems of women, but when I become the king, I will still be for you alone. And you will be for me alone."

Amytis buries herself in his arms. Beholding his tender expression, she simply says, "Nabu, I love you and you alone. I will be yours, and you will be mine.

"I promise my all forever," she says.

The joy between them can only be described as a lover's dream.

This wedding will be more than a private happiness for a loving couple. It is the marriage of two empires, and not just of only two families or two persons. The Babylonians and the Medes have often battled with each other. The wars between them made them susceptible to other warring nations, especially the Assyrians. King Nebopolasser and King Cyaxares are natural friends, but also wise kings. Both kings are success stories, and they want greatness for their families after their time on the throne.

The wedding will be a twin affair, celebrated in each capital of their two empires. It is planned for the end of the harvest in the fall, a beautiful time of the year. Nebuchadnezzar and Amytis have both asked their fathers for the wedding to be performed as quickly as possible. As the wedding is planned, both empires find themselves facing threats that must be settled.

The Assyrian city of Ashur is not far from the borders of the Medean Empire. King Cyaxares has been warned of an Assyrian attack developing from Nineveh with the garrisons of Ashur, and he is ready to respond preemptively. His noted general, Kumrama, has gathered this information and is already convinced that they must act swiftly.

"General Kumrama," the king speaks, "we are fully capable with the trained cavalry warriors of the Scythians that we have incorporated to take Nineveh and Ashur. How quickly can we act?"

The general is a brave man and a genius at tactical warfare. He is a lord in the king's wise Council of State and owner of the beautiful mountain estate where the princess spent her first night away from the palace. He is also secretly a man of the Scrolls, whose family had been transplanted from Megiddo.

"We are ready, King Cyaxares. If you will ride with me, this will be our victory together. All of the world will call us champions as they celebrate the end of Assyrian savagery. I have told you of the sorrows my family suffered decades ago, when we were chained together and led by force from our homeland. This is the moment of my dreams," says the general.

King Cyaxares replies, "Yes, I will fight in this battle. My father, King Phraortes, trained me to be a warrior, and I knew the day would come when I would repay Nineveh for the brutal suffering of all Medeans. We will ride tomorrow."

The skilled warriors of the Medean Empire and over one hundred thousand Scythian warriors that have been incorporated into the Medean Empire are ready. The Scythian king that ruled the Medes was slain by Cyaxares, and the Scythians are now under tribute to the Medeans and King Cyaxares. It is a formidable force ready to march against an equally impressive force of Assyrians.

As the king marches beside his general Lord Kumrama, they

devise the tactics they will follow. The general says, "We should march straight to Nineveh, but send a sufficient force toward Ashur to block the garrison committed to its defense from strengthening the warriors in Nineveh."

"Agreed," says the king.

The battle in Nineveh rages for days and a tremendous amount of damage is done. The Scythians are cavalry fighters, fierce and unafraid. A Scythian commander, a brilliant man, is killed on the seventh day, which greatly demoralizes the Scythian warriors.

King Cyaxares speaks, "We have effectively reduced their fighting force here in Nineveh. We have already lost over one thousand of our brave warriors and two strong commanders. Lest we lose many more of our own, we must march as in retreat, but quickly divert to Ashur and take that city. That's the city of their god, and to gain it will be favorable for us."

The general loves the idea and sees it as the right step toward the end of the Assyrian Empire. He declares, "We can easily take Ashur, especially with the warriors in Nineveh weakened and in much disarray from the damage we have inflicted. They will not have time to come to Ashur's defense."

While the city of Ashur is under attack, the flag of surrender appears from the center tower of the city. The governor appears on the wall and asks for an opportunity to surrender. Already he has lost a large number of warriors and knows the city is about to be sacked, even possibly torched. Diplomatically he states, "We are your neighbors and are ready to serve the Medean Empire."

When the general meets him outside the main gate, he is surprised to find an acquaintance and trading partner. He is also part of a family that was approximately one hundred years earlier brought as captives from a small town north of Samaria. "We are ready," says the governor, "to declare our freedom from the Assyrians and to become a family part of the Medean Empire." Only recently appointed, the governor is a secret lover of the Scrolls.

King Cyaxares states, "Governor Gallo, I will appoint you as the Medean governor of Ashur. I am requiring a tribute of one thousand talents of gold and three thousand talents of silver. We will leave a garrison of our warriors to protect the city. You are to dismiss every Assyrian and grant them safe passage to Nineveh. But they have only twenty-four hours to leave as we wait outside the city walls."

When the city is secured, and all proper stations of the warriors are established, the victorious army of the Medean Empire return to Ecbatana with much bounty from Ashur and Nineveh, plus the large tribute from Ashur. The capital city of Medea erupts into joyful celebrations as the king and his general lead the warriors down the broad street from the main gate of the city to the palace of the king.

Not one Medean in the city has ever before celebrated a victory over the Assyrians. It is a new day in their loved mountains!

Meanwhile, in the capital of Babylon, King Nebopolasser is debating the answer to a very different circumstance. The City of Nippur has raised a small and yet formidable band of warriors and is threatening the empire with revolt.

The king speaks to General Sarhaddan, "My General," he languishes, "these are our own Chaldeans, and some of them are from my family clan. It pains me to attack them, but to do otherwise is unthinkable. I will march with you and take the city."

"We will take the city with the least casualties possible," speaks the honorable general.

The next morning the imposing army marches out of Babylon and the armed camps of the new empire. It is the third time it has been necessary to go to battle. Once, they had marched north to drive back a force of warriors from Nineveh. Another time, they had put down an earlier uprising in Nippur.

This time the king is sympathetic, yet determined to end the revolt. "General," he says, "We will need to end this revolt and eliminate some very strong and good Chaldeans. They are putting the entire empire in danger when they follow their petty interests. One of the key leaders is an uncle of mine, the elder brother of my father. He defended me before but has become a strong enemy. I must personally slay him with the king's sword. Another is my Hanna's brother, and he, too, must be sacrificed for the empire."

King Nebopolasser fights side by side with his general. During the battle, the general fights himself into a dangerous corner. King Nebopolasser spurs his horse and swiftly rides, sword in hand, to defeat the general's assailant. It is a narrow victory for both, but the king's courage and willingness to risk his own life, inspires the entire band of warriors to participate.

Nippur falls on the second day, and the warriors take the city. It was ransacked and burned, and the bounty was hauled back to Babylon. To be near the Persian Sea, the trade route from many lands makes Nippur rich beyond measure. All of this wealth will help to make Babylon stronger than ever. The two leaders, Nebopolasser's uncle and his brother-in-law, are slain before the entire army by the king himself. The king speaks to his army as they are gathered before the burning city. "Today is a sad day. We have killed our own, but if this empire is going to protect us from the Assyrians and even the Egyptians and other powers of nations, we must be strong and united," he says powerfully.

With sorrow, he adds, "I have slain some of my own family members today, and I pray to Marduk that I will never need to do so again. I ask that we march to Babylon with tears, not with shouts."

Their wedding takes place in a time of peace. Nabu is sixteen years old and Amy is fifteen. Their excitement for their wedding day knows no bounds. Most weddings of royalty are arrangements, but their love for each other is deep and real. The two kings want nothing but the best for their families.

The wedding date has been set for 6 October 614 BC. There will be seven days of feasts: the first two in Ecbatana, the new Medean capital; followed by three days of travel in a caravan from Ecbatana to Babylon; and two days of feasts in Babylon. They will celebrate the wedding with large crowds at every possible location between the two palaces.

"Amytis," says Nebuchadnezzar, while spending a few days in Ecbatana with his father, King Nebopolasser, planning this exciting occasion. "I have prepared and replenished the second palace of Babylon for our first years together. It is beside the rushing Euphrates River, and our private quarters tower above this large and roaring lifeline of our city. At night the waters send a relaxing echo throughout the palace. Our servants are some of Babylon's best, and our chef is a cuisine champion that will bring the delicious recipes of our two worlds together."

With tender words, she says to Nebuchadnezzar, "My father has given me the three servants that have cared for me since I was born. With your household servants and my personal and faithful friends, our home life will be a happy place."

Then, even more tenderly, she says, "Nabu, you are my love. I remember the first time I saw you and fell completely in love with you. You are strong, a giant of a young man, who is also handsome and brave. But, most important to me, you are mine. Tell me you will still be 'Nabu' when you become the king."

"Amytis, we must save this love talk until the final wedding day. My heart is racing like a lovesick groom, and you are not to be defiled. On our wedding day you will know that this crown prince has no passion except for his chosen princess. Your beauty is the fairest of all maidens. Only the gods could make someone so beautiful. You are mine," he says passionately.

As the capital at Ecbatana finishes preparations, the entire city is turned into a wedding chamber. The palace sits at the highest point on the north side, almost hidden in the pistachio and poplar trees, along with many others. Exotic flowers are awash in blooms. Roses, clematis vines, orchids, and blooming bushes are everywhere. Because of its location on the very edge of the mountains, animals and birds are constantly seen in the city parks and even on the streets. It is a capital that blends nature with city life.

On the last day of September, the celebration begins. Nebuchadnezzar and Amytis start the day as they walk from the palace down the processional way to the center of the city. A throng of Medeans has filled the city. One glimpse of the couple is worth the day to all observers. Warriors are everywhere, and the couple's protection is top priority. There are constant exchanges of words with the crowd.

Amytis often says, "I love you," to her admirers. "You are our princess," she hears over and over.

There is a constant flow of words, even to Crown Prince Nebuchadnezzar. "Our princess has found herself a great king," he hears them say. He remarks often, "I love your princess, and I love you." Over and over words of happiness are spoken. The crowd borders on euphoria.

The wedding dress is of rare value and beauty. The king's general Sarhadden, who is a trader and the owner of an extensive date plantation, purchased the material from his friend, a dealer in many other materials of extreme worth. He traveled from Erech in Chaldea, his home, to help plan her attire for the seven days of celebration. She and her exquisite beauty will be remembered long after the wedding.

Godlike in splendor, the attire of the crown prince always borders on the kingly. The crown prince cannot compete with the king, but the king requires that he never dress in an uncultured or common fashion. Nebuchadnezzar appears regal and manly beside his queenly princess.

On each of the seven days they will woo the crowd as much by the uniqueness of attire as by the grandeur of their glowing personalities. They are clearly the symbol of both grand empires, Medeans and Babylonians. A marriage is occurring, not just between a young man and his princess, but also between two empires that will last nearly one hundred years.

On day two in Mede, there is the grand ceremony by the Medean high priest, followed by the banquet for the nobles. Again, the princess and the crown prince walk—to the sheer joy of all the cities' inhabitants and visitors—from the palace to the city temple. The high priest performs an elaborate ceremony that was especially written for these two. It must be destroyed immediately after the ceremony. No one else is ever to be married by this same rite. His final words are, "To the princess of Mede, to the gift of our god, to the beauty of this shining symbol of this empire, and to her seed—I dedicate this marriage.

"To the crown prince of Babylon, to his strength as a warrior, to his future as a king, and to the empire he shall rule, I dedicate this union.

"May the god of Mede and the god of Babylon unite these two grand persons to be one in marriage. May kings come from their union, and may peace keep them always."

The banquet is set, and the royal families and their court move quickly to the banquet hall. Provisions have been prepared for the overwhelming crowds in the capital of Ecbatana. Tents are set at many locations, and unique Medean dishes of the kingdom's best have been prepared. Thousands of lambs have been butchered and dressed with all the trimmings. Desserts with figs, dates, raisins, and other local sweets are ready for all to enjoy. The city is set for celebration.

As hosts, King Cyaxares and his queen stand to begin the feast. The king says, "Our princess has been our heart throb for fifteen years, and the crown prince is both her choice and ours. The only sorrow we have is in sending her on a three-day journey from the palace. She has made us happy thousands of times, and we love her above what words can express."

Raising their glasses in a toast, he adds, "To our princess we offer this banquet of plenty, and to her prince we transfer her future." To the people gathered, the king exclaims, "Eat, my great friends, to your delight!"

The tremendous caravans of royalty, counselors, lords, and families leave Ecbatana the next morning to celebrate all the way to Babylon. Tents are already set up in two locations for the necessary stops on the three-day journey.

The king of Babylon, King Nebopolasser, and Queen Hanna ride in the rich Babylonian carriage at the head of royalty. Fifty yards behind follows the crown prince and his princess in his royal carriage, fifty yards behind is King Cyaxares and his beautiful queen.

On one side of this wedding company ride one hundred of Medean's best charioteers with full armor, and on the opposite side are one hundred of Babylonia's best charioteers, also with full armor.

At every possible location en route to Babylon, there will be a brief stop and a time of celebration allowed for the people. There will be a feast at each of the night stops, both for the caravans and the people. These three days of travel have been planned so as to carry the wedding events to as many in the empires as possible. The only common laborers among the Medeans and the Babylonians during these seven days of celebration are those preparing and serving the great feast and those caring for the royalty, along with the two trained armies guarding every border to guarantee the absolute safety of all.

The caravan stops the first night in a quaint town of Medea. Citizens from many miles have traveled to view the royal scene and celebrate. The local chieftains have planned a banquet for their royalty. One of King Cyaxares' lords is a local merchant, and the tents are spread out on his grand estate. The princess and her crown prince appear at many gatherings to both show their love and to be loved. The same great expressions are everywhere from, "We love our princess," to "You will always belong to us," and "We share you with the prince."

She responds, "I will always be your princess. You will always be in my heart. These are my mountains, too," she declares.

The prince never fails to win their hearts with his towering strength and tender love toward their princess.

The second stop is in the fertile farmland called Chaldea. The crown prince now steps ahead of his princess. He has been careful to keep her at the front, but, now, it is his duty to be the Babylonian crown prince.

A respected lord of King Nebopolasser's court is the host at his grand estate of date palms and orange groves. Large canals that direct waters from the Tigris River dot the entire estate, and it is a picture of the emerging riches of the New Babylonian Empire. The Tigris River flows right through the middle, and the tents for the night are situated in a valley of flowers and luxury right beside the river.

Nebuchadnezzar takes his princess and shares her with every possible crowd. She is attired as the goddess the Medeans have made her. Her beauty is so captivating that the people are ecstatic. As the crown prince stops to speak, they listen with total attention.

"Your love is strength to me," he says. "I have been trained by my father, your king, to protect our land and our borders. I dedicate myself to you." These words were repeated often.

Then he would share his princess, saying, "The gods have given me a queen. Our neighbors, the Medeans, have given her to me. I love her as the greatest gift this life can give a man."

Then he asks, "Will you love her?" The response makes Amytis feel like a Babylonian. She actually weeps with love for her new admirers.

"I love you," she repeats many times.

Babylon is in sight and the roar of welcome can be heard for a great distance. This is the end of day five and the exciting finale will occur on 6 October 614 BC.

It is the sixth morning of this celebration, and the wedding begins as the crown prince and his princess walk ceremonially down the processional way that has been totally rebuilt just in time for this day. They leave the palace of King Nebopolasser and gracefully walk the entire length facing the temple of Marduk. They speak often to the ecstatic crowds along the way.

"I am dedicated to be your protector," Nabu, as they affectionately call him, declares. Amid their loud expressions of love, he speaks again. "I have brought to you my princess. Someday she will be your queen. I love you, and she will love you," he finished.

Amytis is truly a royal soul. She speaks carefully—always with her attention focused on the crown prince. "I love your prince!" she exclaims. "And I love you."

The high priest of Marduk conducts a lengthy rite of cleansing and worship. Their silent god must be given great attention, and a good omen is patiently awaited and expected. A priest secretly allows a white pigeon out of its cage, and it flies throughout the grand temple and out the window. It is the omen of this ceremony, and the crowd gives homage and emotional worship to their chief god.

The day is given to dances, theatrical performers, and entertainment. Each event ends with the appearance and presentation of Nebuchadnezzar and Amytis. The entire city and many visitors from the empire, as well as guests from friendly countries, enjoy a banquet for all. The menu is the best of the New Babylonian Empire and exceptional recipes from the past. Every culture that has touched Babylon is represented on the menu. It is a feast of exceptional taste.

The wedding day has finally arrived, but none too soon for Nabu and Amy. She is dressed in the most elaborate attire of the seven days. Pink is her chosen color. With her jet-black hair and beautiful Medean complexion, Amy looks gorgeous. She is ready to be the bride of the crown prince.

His attire is a blend of the kingly and the warrior. His entire person, both attitude and appearance, must inspire both fear and awe. He is someday to be worshipped, and the foundation of that day must undergird all that he is and represents.

After a morning of rest and enjoyment of the refreshing preparations made by their personal attendants, they are ready to make their final march before the ceremony by the high priest begins. They leave the palace and, with lots of love between them and the crowd, slowly make their way to the temple. "I love you! This is my princess! We are yours!" says the crown prince over and over.

Amytis joins in with many sweet remarks as she walks beside her prince.

After many sacrifices, oblations, and music, the high priest begins, "Nebuchadnezzar and Amytis, your fathers have presented you to me. The kingdoms of Mede and Babylon have joined you together in their hearts. Today, I will take their commitments of the two of you, and, by the power of Marduk, make you as one.

"Nebuchadnezzar, a wife is a grand gift of your god, Marduk, and he has chosen for you the most beautiful one possible. The god of Mede has nourished her, and, now, your god will magnify her above all the women of the empire. Her beauty will only flower as she worships in this temple. Magnify her in your heart, and your god will magnify her in the hearts of all. You have done a rare thing for a king—you have vowed yourself to her alone. All the people that you serve will love you for it.

"Amytis, you have been chosen by a striking young prince to be his wife. Make yourself his lasting pleasure, and the gods will shine light upon you and you will have a family to love. The god of Marduk will give you an heir to the throne. May the light of all the Babylonian Empire shine from this hour on your union. You are indeed a man and his wife. Amen!"

Nebuchadnezzar and Amytis are married! The king of Babylon and his queen, together with the king of Mede and his queen, lead the way from the temple to the courtyard. A carriage is waiting to carry the newlyweds to their nuptial hideaway in a very special private location.

Two additional carriages are present. When Nebuchadnezzar and Amytis are seated and the curtains pulled, the three carriages move together. They swap leads, maneuvering in different positions until no one knows which carriage is bearing the crown prince and his princess.

Then, they are off, each seemingly going to a secret location in the great empire of Babylon. Each carriage has guards carefully barring all that may seek to follow. When all three carriages have lost any followers, two of them return to the city.

The afternoon sun sets as the newlywed couple is swiftly carried to the location of their honeymoon. It is an estate of a wealthy Chaldean clan; the head of household is one of the king's lords. The lord's mansion is hidden in a quiet orange grove on the Tigris River.

Great Nineveh in Ruins

612 BC

The name of Nebuchadnezzar has become famous throughout the world. Still in his teens and happily married to his princess, his warrior abilities are unparalleled. King Nebopolasser wants to protect him from possible harm in battle, but recognizes the need for his potency and skills in the volatile clashes of different empires as each one seeks ascendancy.

Babylon and Medea have eliminated all warring between themselves in the wedding of Nebuchadnezzar and Amytis. Medea would be as happy to claim Nebuchadnezzar as their future king as the Babylonians have. The two kings, Nebopolasser and Cyaxares, meet with all of the primary leadership of their two armies of warriors.

"It is time to eliminate forever the threat of Assyria," speaks Cyaxares. "Our recent capture of Ashur has proved successful and of great value to our empire. That is the city of their god, Ashur, and their loss of that city is a crush to their sense of safety. It is clear that their god has failed.

"None of us can win," he adds, "without the help of the gods." He continues, "Together, we are fully capable of taking Nineveh. The strategy for our assault that my son-in-law, Nebuchadnezzar, has been sharing with me is brilliant, and we are ready to march in lockstep. The Scythians that are subject to me are also ready, and they are formidable in battle."

Nebopolasser, visibly proud of the attention Cyaxares is giving to his crown prince, agrees. "My general, Sarhadden, has proven his own skills and has been successful in our struggles. Your general is also brilliant. We have a winning coalition."

He adds, "I suggest we march immediately. We will recover the riches and wealth that has been extracted from us for many seasons. We must leave nothing but ruins in the location of Nineveh."

Nebuchadnezzar joins the discussion. "I agree. Nineveh must be totally destroyed. They have recovered from many defeats. We should leave no possibility of a future recovery. I am in favor of scorching the earth beneath the city." No one disagrees!

A day and place to meet is arranged and each empire sets about the business of total mobilization. Only enough warriors to keep peace and protect the kings' households are to be left. Every warrior is needed. This will be the "mother of all battles."

The formidable army of the vassal king of the Scythians is to attack from the north. This army and king are subject to King Cyaxares and the leaders readily agree on the strategy described to them. The Medes will attack from the east and southeast, and Babylon, the largest army of all three, will attack from the west and southwest. The city walls are a three-day journey and a strong barrier that must be breached. The fourteen aqueducts flowing with rivers of water into the city provide possible entrances and can hopefully be easily destroyed.

The three armies represent several hundred thousand. Almost every man knows the fear of the Assyrians. It is a day for vengeance, and no one thinks of mercy. To these armies, every woman is a potential mother and every child a potential warrior that must be eliminated.

Slowly, after the city is completely surrounded and all avenues of escape are sealed, the armies begin a methodical killing of every warrior that appears on the walls. The aqueducts are destroyed while fierce fighting rages and many lives are lost until all water into the city is halted. Thousands of Assyria's best are destroyed while trying bravely to protect the water supply and the years of tedious labor spent building these rivers of life.

Nebuchadnezzar suggests that several hundred separate bands of their most skilled warriors be organized. He speaks to the council directing the war, "Tomorrow, let's set fire to every gate simultaneously. These fires must be arranged by night with a mountain of flammable debris piled against them. At the moment the sun arises a flaming arrow can be shot into the piles before the gates. Let them burn all day while we allow no one to escape. From our safe bulwarks we can eliminate every effort they make that appears to try to save the gates.

"Remember," he says, "the city has no water to douse the fires."

"When the trumpets sound on the second day, our bands of soldiers will enter the city and sweep the entire boundaries free and drive the inhabitants into the center of the city.

"When they have secured several hundred yards of its entire perimeter, our armies will then march inside. The warriors will be helpless after they have been driven into the middle of the city dwellers and more easily destroyed one by one.

"Because we will not need to rush and lose many of our warriors, we will then slowly sack the city. No one is to escape, and no one is to be left alive."

The slaughter continues for days and appeals for surrender are ignored.

King Sinsharishken makes several efforts to surrender. Nebopolasser, speaking on behalf of the war council, informs the king that surrender is not an option.

He insists, "We are here to recover the wealth that has been taken from all of us. We are here to eliminate the city of Nineveh from the face of the earth."

Proudly, he announces to the king, "Your only option is to defeat us."

When the city is completely defeated, King Nebopolasser, King

Cyaxares, and Crown Prince Nebuchadnezzar march into the palace of King Sinsharishken, while the defeated king and his family are slaughtered.

The city's wealth, the greatest in the world, is carefully gathered and prepared for removal to the capitals of the armies. The most beautiful furniture, icons of the gods, and family heirlooms that have been preserved for centuries including gold, silver, jewels of rare beauty, and an endless list of valuables, are retrieved and prepared for removal.

The city is torched and its walls destroyed.

After the total defeat of Nineveh, a large contingent of warriors is dispatched to Nimrud. The same tactics are used to take this city where Ashurbanipal's palace is located. It is still a retreat of King Sinsharishken and is protected. Knowing the utter defeat of Nineveh, the guards fight ferociously, but with a sense of helplessness. They are totally defeated within hours.

The riches of Nimrud are also a treasure house and are slowly gathered, even as the city of Nineveh is plundered for its riches. The grave of Princess Zakutu, under the floor of the palace, is covered in debris and ashes.

The War Council meets while the riches of both Nineveh and Nimrud are being systematically identified and valued. The decision is made that the Babylonian Empire is to receive 50 percent of all valuables, with the Medes receiving 30 percent, and the Scythians 20 percent.

Each of the three capitals spends months dividing the wealth among its key citizens and ruling lords. The kings themselves receive the largest amounts of the riches to enlarge and decorate their palaces and build their armies. Every soldier receives enough riches to guarantee his future readiness to march again when the call is made.

All military hardware and weaponry are equally divided between the empire of Babylon and the empire of Medea. The royal chariot of King Sinsharishken is given to the crown prince, Nebuchadnezzar and Princess Amytis. It is a treasure of rare beauty, given for the exceptional wisdom that all the warriors of the three armies behold in this future King of Babylon. He has become the star of the entire region, and his name is already invoking fear in faraway places.

As the last wall of Nineveh is being destroyed, the city becomes ghastly in appearance. Carnivorous birds appear to be gathering from everywhere. The city that was once the richest in the world is nothing but ruins. It is torched to guarantee that nothing remains but ashes.

King Nebopolasser and his crown prince find time to be together as they travel toward Babylon. Both of them feel compelled to stay near Nineveh to witness its complete destruction. The most feared city of the world must be seen in its final hour. The honored crown prince was the first to speak.

They can talk like a father and son in private. "Father," Nabu says, "Today, I celebrate the fatherly attention you have given me and the honors we have shared. Being the warrior I have become is not an accident. I have the greatest teacher."

He continues, "You and General Sarhadden have both poured your lives into me. I will always be proud to ride into battle with either of you. I know I will be safe."

"Nabu," the king says, "a man is the most honored when he sees that his own son is a brave and skilled warrior. Together, we have ended the brutal empire of the Assyrians. Some of their warriors are in other parts of the former Assyrian Empire, and some Assyrians fled as our armies were marching toward the city. There will be action needed to finish the task, and I'm entrusting that action to you."

In a different vein, the king says, "My crown prince, your princess was very anxious as we told our family goodbye and headed to Nineveh. No one doubted that Nineveh would fall and fall hard, but only with a daring struggle.

"Amytis will be a happy young wife when she sees you march-ing down the processional in great triumph. The word has gone ahead that you have been honored as the hero of this victory. I am told that the city is electric with excitement. Receiving honor in the regal manner of a skilled warrior or even as a king demands a disciplined pride and a willingness to give that honor to those who fought with you and beside you. You must remember that some are not returning with us because they are our sacrifices of war."

The crown prince is moved by his father's tender expression and love for all the brave Babylonian warriors. They speak of their god Marduk, and agree to give special honor to the protection and direction they have received of their dedicated priest. Every-one considers this battle to be a battle of the gods, not just the people.

Everyone has heard the news. The feared, brutal city of Nineveh is in complete ruins. There is no possible way that the city can ever rule and rob the Middle East again. The city of Babylon is now the premier city of the region and of the world. They are ready to celebrate.

The king's company is not far away and the entire city and many Babylonians converge to welcome the king and his crown prince and all the victorious warriors. As they approach the city, the beautiful center gate into Babylon going directly down the processional by the grand temple of Marduk and other temples and directly to the palace is opened.

To shouts of, "Great is our King Nebopolasser! Great is our Prince Nebuchadnezzar! Great are our warriors of Babylon!" King Nebopolasser, along with Prince Nebuchadnezzar—flanked by their guards—enters through the gates. This is clearly the greatest victory of the New Babylonian Empire. Years ago, the general of the Southern Assyrian Army declared himself king of Babylon.

King Nebopolasser addresses the proud and noisy company awaiting the return of their champions, "Your sons, your husbands, your brothers, and friends have fought as the brave warriors of our empire. It was a furious war, but we won."

The roar of support fills the city as their king pauses with respect for their praise. Finally, he can speak again, "The hero and champion of this 'mother of all battles' is your crown prince Nebuchadnezzar. The future of Babylon is safe because you have the best warriors and they have the best leader."

While Prince Nebuchadnezzar stands to receive his father's honor, the city is filled with a victorious and deafening roar of approval.

Princess Amytis makes her way through the throng of people and Nebuchadnezzar sees her out of the corner of his eye. He points her out to his guards, as she is moving quickly through the crowd. They make a way for her and lift her quickly to the platform beside the prince. Forgetting his regal decorum, he takes her in his arms to the exploding joy of the crowd. It is all unplanned and clearly unparalleled to such a royal occasion. The moment becomes the happiest part of the occasion. Their future king is like all of them, and they love it. Amytis is already viewed as a goddess to all Babylon, and they are thrilled just to get a glimpse of her. She is the gift of the gods as their symbol of good will to the future of the empire. Any occasion would be perfect with her presence.

The king finishes his elegant speech and tells them some highlights of the victory. Now, he introduces the crown prince to speak.

"My fellow Babylonians," Crown Prince Nabu says, "all the warriors of this victory are champions. I desire no honor but the honor that goes to all of you. Many of you have lost a husband, a son, or a friend. Let us all pause to show you our love for your sacrifices."

Tears flow throughout the throng of people. Many of them embrace a widow or a mourning mother as they share their sorrow.

He says, "I am honored to be one of your warriors. I am honored to be the son of your king. He is the champion." Again everyone weeps, but now with love for the royal family of their Babylon.

The Assyrian Empire is but a shadow holding up in the ancient city of Haran. The king clearly charges his crown prince with the challenge of securing this last stronghold and finishing the task. Any real threat from Assyria is over.

10

Nebuchadnezzar Proves His Genius

609 BC

Crown Prince Nebuchadnezzar earns his reputation as an invincible warrior. The commanders under his leadership during the battle for Nineveh return to Babylon to herald his superior military style. They speak excitedly of him as an immortal god and all the Babylonian warriors are ready to follow him. General Sarhaddan and King Nebopolasser have witnessed his incredible techniques and his superior leadership abilities and quickly place the battlefield under his command.

After their victory over the Assyrians, the talk of all Chaldea is the telling and retelling of stories about the crown prince. The crown prince's name soars into the stratosphere and the truth of the stories is embellished to the point of the divine. Every time he and Amytis are in public view, the entire scene turns into a joyous jubilation.

King Nebopolasser and Prince Nebuchadnezzar are practically inseparable. Their relationship is still father and son. "Nabu," the king says, "We have truly won a stunning victory against the Assyrians. For years I was convinced they could never be defeated. It now appears that the death of Zakutu, followed by the death of King Ashurbanipal, had taken the life out of the empire. When they lost Zakutu, they lost the favor of their gods. I often hear how every omen after their deaths has been dark and foreboding.

"Nabu," he says, "Marduk and the favor he has placed on your life have won the victory for us. Son, I am extremely proud of you."

"Father," Nabu responds, "Do not forget that the gods did nothing for me that you did not provide in your care and training over my life."

Nabu continues, "The beautiful princess that the Medean Empire has given me is the perfect symbol and token of a favor on my life even larger than just that of our god Marduk. Our dream, which we have often discussed, is of an empire even greater than the Assyrian Empire.

"Father, my princess is the most wonderful gift you have given me. I am already planning, when the time is right, to build her a garden that will make her feel like she lives in the mountains. She often speaks of the beautiful country of Medea and its towering mountain peaks that touch the sky. Seeing her sad for even one moment is almost more than I can bear. She is a joy of life to me. Her love for me could not be stronger. She is as great to me as my mother, your Hanna, is to you."

For several days, the king and his crown prince spend considerable time dreaming and planning for their capital Babylon, and their palaces in the heart of the city.

They bring together the greatest minds available and employ Chaldean architects and builders. This team creates plans for exquisite landscapes and buildings with towering walls and temples.

King Nebopolasser addresses his son, the primary architect, and the master builder, who are to organize and lead the massive task. He commands, "Our first order of business must be the building of the towering walls to encompass the city and provide protection for the beautiful construction within. My son and I have planned walls that must be three hundred feet in height and wide enough to conduct great challenging chariot races on their crown. We will build two hundred fifty towers for our warriors that will extend fifty feet above the three-hundred-foot-walls that will be as comfortable for the warriors as the palace is for our own family."

Continuing, he adds, "The walls must be built on thirty feet of foundation beneath the level of the city so that no enemy may ever enter the city by stealth. We will leave a distance of seventy-five feet and build a second wall of the same height. The center will be below the level of the roaring Euphrates River, which will enable us to create a river of water between the two walls as added protection. The gates will all be constructed with bridges spanning the river between the walls."

Already, the plans for laying out these walls are under way and the total length has been arranged at fifty-six miles, approximately fourteen miles to either side. The great Euphrates will flow right through the middle of this fabulous New Babylon. There will be a great bridge extending over the Euphrates Rivers, along with ferryboats for crossing these waters.

Nabu speaks to his father after their architect and master builder leave for the day. He says, "I am ready to lead our warriors up to Haran and finish the task of the Assyrian dilemma. Your presence is needed here at Babylon to direct the construction of the massive walls. When you give permission, I will start mobilizing the warriors. General Sarhaddan has been enlisting and training a tremendous number of new recruits. Our victory over Nineveh has caused thousands to join the ranks. Many have heard of the wealth given to every warrior and are enthused for their own adventure."

The king puts the matter of timing and planning in Nebuchadnezzar's hands, while he begins the task of employing tens of thousands of laborers from across all Chaldea to build the walls of Babylon. The city of Babylon is destined to rise up and tower above the beautiful plains of Sumer.

Beautiful orchards already dot the countryside. Massive canals are flowing with water in every direction and the wealth of the fruitful fields makes it all so beautiful. Nothing is more breathtaking than the date farms where these stately trees produce the fruit so loved by all Chaldea. Barley, wheat, and oat fields are waving in the breeze, many of them golden in hue and ripening for harvest.

The trade routes through the Mesopotamian Valley can be viewed during the harvest season with strains of the world's tastiest grains heading throughout the empires and nations. The Chaldeans have developed a means of salting and preserving fish and water buffalo, drying dates and vintage fruits, and all their bounty is earning wealth and being used for trading.

Enormous furnaces are added for burning the bricks and ceramic tiles to build the towering walls. Artisans plan and design beautiful renderings of animals to be laid out in picturesque fashion within the walls to make this city the envy of the world. The walls of Babylon will be built like a massive tapestry to capture the appearance of the animal life that fills the Garden of Eden, where Nebopolasser has raised his son, Nebuchadnezzar. These figurines will include awesome mythological creatures that represent the theology of Marduk and the wars of the many gods that fill Marduk's pantheon.

As Nebuchadnezzar prepares to lead the massive Babylonian warriors up to Haran, Amytis gives birth to their first son. Given the name Amel-Marduk, the baby is heir apparent to the throne of Babylon.

"Amytis," Nabu says to his princess, "Our son is a beautiful gift from the gods, and he will be a king someday. I must soon begin the garden that I have promised so you can raise him to love the mountains just like yourself. The king and I are already gathering animals from every possible location so that there will be great creatures that you love filling your garden with life."

"O, Nabu," says Amytis, "you have never mentioned the animals, but what would a garden be without them?" Then, with the look of gloom, she says, "Nabu, please do not be careless as you lead the army to Haran. You are so brave. I always fear something will happen to you. Nobody will be targeted for death like you will be. Your name has spread everywhere and any warrior that kills you will be the enemy's champion."

"Remember the gods," says Nabu. "I trust my future to the design of powers greater than myself. You know we have talked of a God that is greater than the ones with which we are familiar. I have always worshipped Marduk, but maybe there is a God that has a design for the Babylonian Empire that we are yet to learn about.

"Just remain my princess," he says to Amytis, "for someday you will be my queen."

The Assyrians have set up a shadow capital in Haran and are making loud boasts against Babylon. The new king is a brother of the deceased King Ashurbanipal named Ashuruballit. The word is out that Egypt, led by the Pharaoh Necho II, is sending a cloud of warriors to help defend Haran and the city of Carchemish. Carchemish and Haran control the great traffic of traders traveling the world with riches and goods greatly needed by the exploding empire of Babylon.

The city of Haran has an ancient connection to the people of the Scrolls. The father of these people lived in Haran for many years and the city is named after his brother. Abram was his name, later changed to Abraham. At least part of the city originally worshipped Abraham's God, but some worshipped his father's god, Sin—a god of Ur. Abraham's god is known only as Lord or God. Apparently, Haran had converted from its previous worship in order to worship Ashur, the god of the Assyrians. The city's connection to Abraham is likely long forgotten.

Nebuchadnezzar quietly sets the date to march their army, trying hard to keep the wrong ears from hearing his plans. It is a massive picture as the enlarged and massively equipped company of warriors leaves Babylon. All possible communication links north toward Haran have been broken. For weeks, warriors have protected the roads leading north and turning back every possible means of news.

Approaching Haran, yet far enough away to be secretly advancing, Nebuchadnezzar meets with his commanders. "Here is the plan," he begins. "We will split into four divisions. Division one will march straight to the city directly from the south. Divisions two and three will wait for the city warriors that protect Haran to move to the south side of the city and engage company one in defense of the city. During the night, company two and company three will come in the dark of night to the east side and the west side and attack right before daybreak. Company four will circle out of sight to the north and attack on day three at the break of day. We will act carefully and slowly, staying out of reach of their arrows until they are weakened beyond recovery. It is my plan that on day six or seven we will take the city.

"Remember," he says, "We have developed arrows that reach further than anyone else has developed. Also, our feared cannon machines can cast the destructive brick balls made in our furnaces for over two thousand feet. This city cannot stand longer than seven days. We want to capture everyone possible as slaves to help build our massive walls of Babylon.

"Commanders," he says, "organize carefully your command and then rest for the night." With a garrison of guards protecting all flanks the great army settles down for the evening. The champion Nebuchadnezzar, only twenty-one years old, is being pampered like a god and is encircled with a large, specially chosen company of warriors that are only present to ensure his safety.

Unknown to Nebuchadnezzar, the army from Egypt led by the Pharaoh Necho II is detained some distance west of the Euphrates River by Josiah, the king of Zion. After a furious battle, Josiah is killed and his beaten army is heading back to Zion so a new king can be installed. His son, an evil man named Jehoahaz, is chosen to be the king of that city.

Upon hearing that Haran has fallen while he was delayed, Necho II establishes a covenant of defense with the king of Carchemish. He then returns back toward Egypt with plans to remove the king that Zion has installed and install the king of his choice, a brother named Jehoiakim.

The city of Haran falls quickly. Haran is a city with a long history and exceedingly rich. The treasures of the cities are plundered to take home to Babylon. Thousands of the able-bodied men are captured and marched to Babylon as laborers. A large battalion of warriors is placed in the previous quarters of Haran's army and a governor appointed to govern the city for King Nebopolasser. Every semblance of Assyrian rule is obliterated. The city is turned into a Babylonian city. Chosen young men from Haran are prepared to be educated to rule the city in the Babylonian style.

Nebuchadnezzar has sealed his incredible reputation with another triumph. He and his invincible army march back to Babylon to celebrate the onward progress of their new empire. A hero's welcome awaits them in their beloved capital. More importantly to Nebuchadnezzar, his princess and their firstborn wait anxiously in the royal palace amidst all the comforts of home.

The Royal College in Zion

608 BC

Ayoung man deeply respected for his unswerving faith, Daniel, hurries toward the classroom for his first morning class when his three friends come rushing up to him. The Royal College is not far from the stone walls of their beautiful city. Their temple gleams as the sun reflects off the golden pillars.

"Daniel," Azariah shouts. "Have you heard the seer Jeremiah's latest proclamation?"

"No, I haven't," says Daniel. "Is it worse than his previous ones? Our great seer friend is already in trouble with all the king's men."

"The seer says it is his last warning. He told our king that his days are numbered, and that there is little time to change his ways."

"I agree with that," says Daniel. "We have read the Scrolls. Babylon is going to be God's voice to show us that His ways are the only right ways."

Hananiah chimes in, "This proclamation is sure to land our faithful old companion in the king's dungeon. I sure hate to think of Jeremiah down in that slime to thirst and starve to death."

He adds, "He has been so faithful to the ways of God. I, for one, will surely miss his class here at the college. He is our only professor that knows the divine voice we love to hear. He has surely straightened us out in being faithful to the Scrolls, while our other teachers have made nothing but fun of him."

"Yes," says Mishael, "Yesterday, the majority of my class was making jokes about Jeremiah, and I hung my head up for scorn when I agreed with him. I almost had to leave class to save my hide."

"Mishael," Daniel says. "It is our joy to defend God's seer and to count it our pleasure; to do so is our duty.

"You do know," speaks Daniel, continuing to walk toward their classroom, "right is always right and real faith never counts the cost to obey—it just does right.

"Azariah," Daniel speaks again after a few moments of sweet silence, "what are the words of our seer, if indeed this is the king's last warning?"

"They are awesome," replies Azariah. "I memorized them in my quiet time this morning. Jeremiah said, 'And it shall be, that the nation and kingdom which will not serve Nebuchadnezzar the King of Babylon, and which will not put its neck under the yoke of the king of Babylon, that nation will I punish, says the Lord, with the sword, the famine, and the pestilence until I have consumed them by My hand.'"

"That is really final," says Daniel, as the other two, Mishael and Hananiah, join in with complete agreement.

Mishael asks, "Do you think the king will listen and save our city and temple from destruction?"

"No, I really do not," answers Daniel. "The king has grown stubborn with this faithful old seer because he is listening to the smooth voices that we have to listen to every day in class."

"Sometimes I wish I did not have to attend these classes," says Hananiah. "Yet, I know that there is purpose in my learning, and somewhere God has a plan for me."

"He sure does," answers Daniel as they enter the class and hurry to find a seat.

The teacher this morning is one of those smooth seers that the king has bestowed riches on for his wonderful predictions for the king's future. He begins the class with a warning to anyone that might disagree with him.

"This morning," he begins, "the old seer Jeremiah has made a fool out of himself. He is calling Nebuchadnezzar the king when everyone knows that the king's name is Nebopolasser. Nebopolasser is not an old man, and we have been assured that he will be the king for many years to come.

"We also know that he remembers the fate of the Assyrian king, Sennacherib, which awoke one morning outside our walls to find one hundred eighty-five thousand dead warriors. It all happened in one night, and he went back to Nineveh where his sons killed him. God is on our side," he says, "and Jeremiah will pay for taking the side of our enemies.

"Jeremiah is an old man that has become senile and paranoid. The best thing for him and us would be his imprisonment in the king's dungeon."

Daniel is not about to listen without speaking for the seer. "Professor Jeriah," Daniel begins. "I am a very young man and I know your feelings about me, but your words about God's seer and God's words are blasphemy. My parents are faithful to the Scrolls and they pay dearly for me to attend this college. They told me just yesterday that you are a false seer and that your words I am not to follow. I'm applauding my friend, the seer Jeremiah, and I believe every word will be fulfilled. Nebuchadnezzar may not be the king today, but when these words are complete he will be."

One of Daniel's friends speaks up, "Professor Jeriah, do you not remember how many times our Scrolls have named someone before they were even born? In fact, we have already learned that our people will be in Babylon seventy years—that's one day for every Sabbath that we have defiled."

"Professor Jeriah, I happen to know," says another of the three friends of Daniel, "that you do not keep our Sabbath. We saw you buying your food supply on our holy day outside the walls of our city a few weeks ago."

The professor is furious. He speaks, "I'm dismissing you four young men from my class for your disruption. I will not have my students disagreeing with me."

As Daniel and his friends walk toward the library where the Scrolls are in safekeeping, they decide to research the old sages of the past and the earlier words of Jeremiah.

First, they look for Isaiah's words from God. They read again, having read all of these Scrolls several times. Quoting Isaiah, Daniel reads out loud to his friends, "Sit in silence and go into darkness, O, Daughter of the Chaldeans, for you shall no longer be called the Lady of Kingdoms. I was angry with my people; I have profaned my inheritance, and given them into your hands. You showed them no mercy; on the elderly you laid your yoke very heavily, and you said, 'I shall be a lady forever,' so that you did not take these things to heart, nor remember the latter end of them."

"What a word in this Scroll," says Hananiah. "This seer is telling us the end of this matter even before it happens. Our nation will be destroyed because our leaders will not tell us this truth, but in the end, God will judge the Chaldeans."

"Yes," says Daniel, "but the majority would not listen if they heard the truth. Speaking for God, our seer, Hosea, said, 'they are bent to backsliding from me.'"

Azariah joins the discussion as he reads from one of Jeremiah's earlier words. "Listen to this," he says. "But, they set their abominations in the house which is called by My Name to defile it. And they erected the high places of Baal, which are in the valley of the son of Himmon, to cause their sons and their daughters to pass through the fire to Molech which I did not command them, nor did it come into my mind that they should do this abomination to cause Judah to sin."

Mishael says, "We are just young teenagers and we can see what is happening. Why do not our rulers and our king understand?"

Daniel, being the oldest, answers him, "Wrongdoing is a way

that blinds the doer. We must be careful to keep the entire book so that we never become blind."

"What will happen to us?" asks Hananiah. "Will we die in the dark things that are coming?"

"No," says Daniel, "remember the words of a good king that God chose long ago to lead us." He said, "I have never seen the righteous forsaken, nor his seed begging for bread."

It is time for the next class of the day. As they part, Daniel asks briefly, "Shall we meet tonight at one of our homes and invite our parents to talk with us and give us direction?"

They quickly agree and set the time at one hour after the hour of afternoon prayer at Azariah's home, which is closest to the temple. They have often spoken of the total destruction of the capital of Samaria and the complete obliteration of their sacred temple by King Sargon II of the Assyrian Empire. They all know it was savage.

The faithful people of the Scrolls have become very prayerful about their temple, and some of the devoted priests are secretly planning to hide the Holy of Holies.

Hananiah arrives first and begins to tell Azariah and his parents of his joy every time he is near the temple.

"I am so thankful," Hananiah says, "I learned of the pure life and can experience the pleasure of prayer and worship when we are near the Holy Place."

Even as he speaks, all the families arrive. Daniel asks Azariah's family if he can begin with prayer.

Daniel prays earnestly. "Father God," he begins, "we ask forgiveness for ourselves and our entire nation. If judgment must come, give us grace to face the seventy years determined. We pray that our king will turn rightly to hear the voice of our respected seer, Jeremiah. We pray for Jeremiah that he will be protected in his trials. We commit ourselves during the coming years to never turn from the words of your Scrolls. We thank You in advance for the promise of the seer, Isaiah, which says that all Your people will return again at the ordained time, and if this temple is destroyed, they will rebuild it in Your promised hour. Amen."

Suddenly, the door opens and Jeremiah steps quickly inside. Daniel had asked him if he would come. The four families are visibly thrilled.

"My friends," he says, "it is a dark hour and God has spoken. Our rulers are not going to obey the voice of God and our future in this beloved city will be short. King Nebuchadnezzar will soon be the king. God has spoken, and he is God's hammer to teach all men that He alone rules the affairs of men. We must not hate King Nebuchadnezzar, but serve him. And when there is true brokenness in spirit and a turning away from evil, our God will see, and He will return His mercy to us.

"I must tell you quietly," Jeremiah said, "that the true priests have already planned to hide the Holy of Holies when the hour becomes certain. I know that King Solomon prepared a room deep beneath the temple and readied a secret passage. Our God has not failed. It is our leaders that have failed. Trust the God of our Scrolls."

Azariah's mother slips out of the room as Jeremiah finishes speaking. Just before he leaves, she speaks to him. "Honorable Seer, I have made fresh barley cakes today for the families and we will be enjoying them together in a few minutes. I have prepared a parcel of them for you to enjoy in your quiet place with our God."

As she hands them to the seer, he speaks thankfully to her. "Blessings on you, dear sister," he says. "You have blessed this old man and God takes note." And he is quickly gone back to his place of abandonment in prayer and the Scrolls.

Known as the smartest in their city, these four young men are well versed in the sciences and especially dedicated to the ancient beliefs of their people. Their parents are holy people that accept nothing but the best from their offspring.

Azariah speaks, "Today, I have rededicated myself to the chosen path before me. I do not know the way, but as Abraham our father did, I will follow as He guides."

Hananiah tells about his visit to the temple. He says, "I grieve to think that our meeting place with God may be destroyed, but I have a fresh faith that He is bigger than a building of stone, cedar, and gold. I am His forever."

Azariah is flooded with tears, both of sorrow and joy. He says, "To be the servant of our God cannot be less than great in the worst of circumstances. I shall be His servant and He will turn my sorrows into joy."

The parents are happy to hear this. It is what they have spent their lives preparing them to be. Their Scroll is more than a collection of stories; it is a voice from the Divine.

Daniel's father is a scribe who has copied many sets of the covenants that they have with their God. Daniel has memorized most of them. He has watched his father painstakingly copy the scrolls. Daniel knows that his father will destroy weeks' worth of work if he finds one error he has made. Every word is precious and no word can be changed and no correction is allowed.

He is deeply moved and is already accepting the path that God might choose for him.

Daniel finally speaks, "My special friends, I am but a very young man, but I have cast my lot with Jeremiah and all of you, but, especially, with the God of those sacred Scrolls my father has copied. I know they are full of life and to do them is fullness of joy."

He turns to his parents and says, "My father and my mother, you have been my life and my joy. I love all of our friends, but I have this deep feeling from our God that my duties in life will be far from here. Remember one thing. Whatever happens to any and all of us, I will be faithful, and there is a city without foundation that Abraham told us about."

He finishes by saying, "We will all be together someday. Then and there, there will be no sorrows."

They part, agreeing to pray that their king will obey Jeremiah and save the city and their beloved temple.

After Daniel and his parents arrive home and Daniel has retired, his mother, a vivacious woman of humble purity, ever queenly among the faithful, reminds her scribal husband of their experience at Daniel's circumcision. When they had taken him the eighth day after his birth to be dedicated, the priest, a pious man, had suddenly paused as the rite was performed. Then, speaking by the Spirit, he had spoken to them in an unusual tone. His words are forever etched in her heart.

He had said, "This young lad is destined to be my servant in a strange, faraway land to be a protector of my people in their sorrows, and to receive my words of the kingdoms that shall rise and fall and of a final kingdom at the end that shall last forever."

She remembers that the priest had immediately continued Daniel's circumcision, embarrassed by the sudden inspiration from his God.

Daniel's mother then states, "Our son is a chosen young man, and we can rejoice in this dark time that he will be a voice of hope and promise."

"Yes," says his father, "and God has given him three wonderful friends that will be faithful with him.

"Jeremiah," the father continues, "told me a few days ago that these four young men are the shining lights at the Royal College. We must never cease to pray for them."

The Final Years of Nebopolasser

608–605 BC

A large company of captives from Haran quickly settles near the Euphrates River south of Babylon to work on the construction projects already at full steam. The new walls take shape, while the entire kingdom is abuzz with talk of their beauty. Achieving the many unique colors of ceramics to create the kind of beauty expected by the king and his prince is a breathtaking task. Using different colors of materials and firing the bricks different lengths of time is a demanding skill, but the result is a delight even to the laborers.

Nebuchadnezzar is content to take only a short time of rest after returning from his victory in Harran before he is at his father's side. The king and Nebuchadnezzar begin to plan the much-enlarged city. Massive streets are designed to crisscross all one hundred and ninety-six square miles of space. Thousands of Mede laborers cut stones from their mountains, while thousands of others drive carts drawn by buffalo from the quarries in Mede to locations throughout the city of Babylon. Measuring three feet by three feet and six inches thick, these stones are beautifully finished to a brush appearance on the topside. The evolving streets are creating a breathtaking city unknown in their world.

The residents of Babylon are busy building their homes throughout the city. The entire countryside sprawls with new homes as new wealth demands new building materials and decorative elements. Grain, dates, fruit, meats, and anything else that can be preserved to remain fresh is greatly desired by the traveling caravans. The brick furnaces produce beautifully decorated brick that will be sold by the trade market at almost any location on the routes. Attractive pottery is moving in both directions as the people prosper. The Chaldeans are experts in treasures of gold, silver and other precious metals. Their woodcarvings, especially from the southern marshes are extravagant. Such riches are bought quickly on the caravan's world trade. Babylon is becoming the interest of the known world as the news travels. Even the captives are allowed to prosper and are finding themselves settled to the Babylonian life. Even the captives are allowed to prosper and are finding themselves settled to the Babylonian life.

"Son," King Nebopolasser says to Nebuchadnezzar, "The wealth you brought from Harran is an incredible amount. The trade routes are bringing us a constant flow of gold and silver. Our treasury is literally full. Let's employ the best of all our master builders to plan and construct a palace for you and Amytis. It must be the most beautiful in the world and provide planned space for Amytis' garden when the palace is finished."

"Father, our empire is growing faster than I ever imagined. When our large and wise company of lords, our friends, and our appointed rulers in other parts of the empire visit us, we must entertain in a fashion to match this city's growing beauty. If we start now, by the time the walls and streets are finished, the palace can be under construction.

"I'm ready to begin that task before our warriors and I march to expand the empire into the west across the Euphrates River toward the Great Sea. Unless we extend our rule over Carchemish they are going to challenge us right here in our own capital. They are already greatly concerned about what is happening in Babylon. Many of their own people want to be part of our prosperity. They have thousands of captives that we can transfer to live among their friends from Harran. Those two cities were very close socially."

Nebuchadnezzar and Amytis decide to travel to Ecbatana in Medea. They want at least some facets of their palace's design to be Medean in style and appearance. It was also time to spend personal time with his father and mother-in-law, King Cyaxares and Queen Akkadiya, and to take their grandson to visit in their inviting palace. The trip has to be planned with care to protect the world's most celebrated prince and princess.

607 BC

Chaldea's most respected architect is employed and asked to travel with the prince and princess to Mede. Designing this palace will be the most detailed opportunity any architect has ever been given the opportunity. The royal chariot of Nineveh has been redesigned in Babylonian fashion and will be the mode of travel for this grand occasion. It is truly the grandest chariot that exists. An army of the best of their warriors is prepared to travel and they will leave secretly to enhance security.

Large crowds welcome them in Mede. The princess has not visited home since the wedding, and the occasion is a happy one for all. The crowds scream, "Nebuchadnezzar," "Amytis," "Nebuchadnezzar and Amytis," alternated with shouts of "Nabu," "Amy," or "Our prince and our princess." Slowly, the couple winds their way through the crowds until they enter the gates of the palace grounds. Then it is King Cyaxares' and Queen Akkadiya's opportunity to spend time with their young grandchild. They simply sit for hours and tell and retell the stories of success for the previous five years since the wedding. The servants of the palace are finally given time with their former princess and, now, their royal guest.

King Cyaxares and Prince Nebuchadnezzar finally move to the king's library to talk privately. The library is paneled with cedar from Lebanon and decorated with the most beautiful ivory. There is an extravagant carving of the princess that the prince has never seen. It is the king's treasure in the absence of his princess from the palace.

"Father," the prince says to King Cyaxares, "you have certainly given me the treasure of your heart in Amytis. I promise you that I love her even as you love her. She is my treasure, too. I find nothing but joy in us sharing our love for the same princess."

The king is moved to tears. "My son," he says, "she is a princess and more, she is a gift of the gods. Her presence has certainly given success to you and all of Babylon. And now the two of you have given our two families another king to someday sit on the throne.

"I treasure all three of you," the king said. The evening is given to a prime banquet, where the best cuisine of the Medes has been prepared and is served. Amytis spends as much time as possible walking among the tall, towering trees of the palace grounds and looking longingly at the tremendous mountains over the next few days. Her prince has already scheduled a surprise trip up into the highest peaks of the Medean forest. They are to spend the night at the estate of King Cyaxares' general. This is the same unforgettable place the princess had visited with her family on her first visit away from the palace when she was barely five years old.

The next day is spent planning and discussing the future palace in Babylon and every possible design. The architect, along with Nebuchadnezzar and Amytis, visit every suggested estate and wealthy house within traveling distance of the capital. They already did the same in Babylon and had stopped often as they traveled to Ecbatana. Their dream is a palace that compliments both great empires and represents the finest building technique known to their world. It must be a marvel of royalty's best as well as the most beautiful. The gleaming and finished design is taking shape in their minds.

After listening to this master designer, who was one of King

Nebopolasser's lords, describe the dream, Amytis speaks with enthusiasm, "Lord, it sounds to me that your dream is brilliant. I love those touches of my country that you have included. Building into the design of our palace a feeling of mountains and of the blue majestic sky where mountains touch the gods is beautiful. I can hardly wait to entertain my mother and father and thousands of other royal guests."

Many of the materials for this palace will come by way of the traveling traders. This will take much planning and traveling as well as a minimum of a year to start the construction. The royal couple has chosen a special stone from the northern mountains of Medea and having these quarried and moved to Babylon will take at least as long. It is a royal shade of light blue with a luster that dazzles the eyes.

Nebuchadnezzar says to his princess, "Amytis, you will have the most beautiful palace in the world where the most beautiful queen of all women will live with her king." As always, his princess simply rushes into his tender embrace.

With the palace plans complete, the rest of the trip to Mede becomes a real vacation. The master designer leaves immediately to return to Babylon and expedite the plans. The prince and princess celebrate their family and their love for each other for several weeks. They stay at several of the Medean's most beautiful estates with lords of the Medes or with the rich families of their empire. Everywhere they are seen, there is joyous jubilation!

Back in Babylon, Nebuchadnezzar is busy with his father helping lead, plan, and excite the city about its future. Three years after beginning construction, the walls are finished and the streets are paved. The grand Temple of Marduk is complete and stands right beside the location where the now expanded processional passes. The towering gate that will be the royal entrance into their city is called "Marduk's Gate."

The new palace will be at the other end of the processional from the Royal Entrance. The foundation of the palace is being prepared right on the bank of the Euphrates River. It will cover over two square miles, including the beautiful grounds to be filled with flowers and majestic trees from the country of Mede. An area of the same approximate size is reserved for the garden of Amytis.

King Nebopolasser is exhausted from administering all the affairs of state. He has visited Ur, Eruk, Kippur, Harran, and many small cities talking with his lords and governors. He is careful to give attention to every small or large center of his empire. Even his captives respect him for his effort to make one and all happy Babylonians.

As soon as every captive has spent the assigned years in free labor, they are allowed citizenship, all rights of prosperity, and their own profession or personal business. Many former captives from the Assyrian Empire, as well as his own kingship, are now leaders and a few of them are lords.

The temples of each god have received ample funds to build or expand each center of religion. The king's worship is to Marduk and that temple is the grandest temple of all but no priest or any religion feels slighted.

He guarantees to all that his crown prince will be the king of Babylon and everything will be prepared by this king for the kingdom of Nebuchadnezzar to be a golden one. The palace that is under construction for the crown prince is provided extra amounts of riches to assure its absolute perfection. The king orders large amounts of gold to assure the name of this palace is called, "The Palace of Gold." Already, the visitors to New Babylon are using the adjective of "gold" to describe the city and the Babylonian Empire.

The king and his crown prince settle in the grand library of the present palace. They can sense in their hearts the pulse of an exploding city literally towering around them and growing beyond measure. Every city wall is a picture of both beauty and massiveness. Even the gates are covered in gold.

The processional is paved and the next project is the building of the decorative walls within the city and the beautiful creatures that are going to decorate the processional and other locations. Building the bridge across the Euphrates River is a massive project. The bridge will be two hundred feet wide, a mile long, and built of great stones from high in the mountains of Mede. It will be unique in color with beautifully carved banisters of twenty feet high to allow the people to view the beauty of the river as they cross. Even the banks of the river are going to be paved and sidewalks will be provided on both sides that are the complete distance of the fourteen miles within the city.

"My son, Nebuchadnezzar, you have given yourself too many tasks of building even while you have worked closely with General Sarhadden in preparing for your next Warrior Crusade. I am delighted you are so young and strong, because your father is failing in strength."

"Father, it is certain that you have not slowed down and your enthusiasm constantly encourages me to push a little harder. I am amazed at your determination to see each task completed and the perfection that you demand of all of us."

As the king relaxes, he becomes very gentle and encourages Nebuchadnezzar in important matters. They both talk of fair treatments to all Babylonians and of ways to incorporate other cultures into the empire. The fair treatment of captives is an important matter because the king remembers the days of the Assyrian brutality. They both know that Babylon is destined to be the first truly world empire and that many dangers must be faced. They speak of their own weaknesses and the need for personal discipline.

"I know you are ready to march off from Babylon to engage Carchemish and make that part of Mesopotamia a part of our empire. We need complete control of every trade route. No empire can last without that power. We have discussed every detail and I believe you will be successful and quick. It seems you should continue right on past Carchemish and not stop until the pharaoh of Egypt and his empire are Babylonian. He has marched to Carchemish to await your coming and is determined to defeat you. Every city all the way to Egypt is expecting you and committed to stopping you. You will win, son, and I will be awaiting word every few days of each success. I hope you can leave and return while I still have strength to rule the empire."

"Father, I'm depending on you to be my counselor even when you decide to make me king. Please slow up a bit and let our wise lords carry more of the load. They are ready to do what we bid them do.

"My King and my Father," he says with love and respect, "I want to tell you about a new warriors' weapon that the general and I have invented. You were very impressed with our brick balls and casting mechanisms, but we have a new secret weapon. We have designed these brick balls with an opening inside, which we can fill with boiling tar. We have a way to close them airtight. When they are cast and hit the target, they explode and the sparks from the impact ignites the tar and it literally sets everything on fire. They are terrible and they make me tremble to watch. I want us to see a demonstration before the warriors leave Babylon."

"My Son," the king replies, fully confident in his son's abilities, "You are a genius at warfare. I sure pray you can be as wise as a king.

"Son, be careful to put the right man as king over Zion. That city is the most important. History has proven that a fair treatment of Zion is absolutely necessary to a long rule for you as king. The Assyrians learned that lesson the hard way. There are many gods among the empire, but Zion's God has the reputation of being the greatest."

Nebuchadnezzar spends several weeks as near to Amytis as he can arrange before he has to leave for battle.

The Champion Warrior Nebuchadnezzar

606 BC

The strength and size of the Babylonian army has never been so massive. They have hundreds of casting machines, along with their new baked brick cannon balls. They also have several thousand chariots, each with one driver, two spearmen, cavalry warriors, and foot warriors. They are indeed an awesome sight. Just to watch them march leaves no doubt in the observer's mind about the effect they will have. Many small towns hoist their surrender flag when the warriors arrive as news travels about their formidable force on the battlefield.

Four weeks later, the Babylonian army is within a few hours of Carchemist. Crossing the Euphrates will be their first task. Half of the army crosses several miles away and the other half continues on the East side. There is a need to defeat the Egyptians and city warriors from both sides of the river. It is the main ford of the river for all tradesmen traveling the world. The highly successful warriors of Egypt are encamped throughout the area and fighting starts at least a mile from the city walls. These warriors of Egypt have won many victories and are to be feared. It is furious fighting and there are an incredible number of deaths.

Neither the Egyptian warriors nor the Carchemish warriors know the battle they are facing. As soon as the Babylonian warriors are close enough to the city to set up the casting machine and to prepare the boiling tar, it is like hellfire raining down on the troop's encampments and the walls. No previous battle has ever known this kind of weapon. Nebuchadnezzar is kept completely out of the danger zone. He tells his commander to fight bravely but wisely and to save the lives of their highly skilled warriors. For several days they hold their approaching lines and bombard the city, but especially the camp of the Egyptians. It is a startling slaughter and the courage of the warriors is quickly decimated.

The Egyptian Pharaoh Necho II and his warriors retreat and head back to Egypt after only nine days of heavy destruction of his once feared host. As they start their march, they know Carchemish is lost, along with control of the trade routes. They do not know of the Babylonian plan of Nebuchadnezzar to follow their defeat. Carchemish immediately surrenders and gives the city over to the Babylonians. The king of Carchemish and his entire family, plus his lords are all defeated and march to Babylon to be jailed or used as laborers. After considerable conferences with the city's leading merchants and elite leaders, a vassal king is appointed. The city is committed to being Babylonian with total submission to the Babylonian rule. King Nebopolasser has a growing list of highly trained men ready to be given lucrative appointments as ambassadors in cities or large communities that are conquered. The Babylonians are ready to expand and to welcome large communities into the empire.

The ruling commander of the battlefield pauses with the crown prince to plan the march from Carchemish toward the Great Sea and down to Egypt.

Nebuchadnezzar is the unquestionable general on the battlefield. "Commanders and my brave warriors," he begins. "The victory you have won in this large and very important city of Carchemish will send shock waves throughout the world. The wealth that passes across the Euphrates at this strategic point is unparalleled. Not to pass through here on the trade routes will take months of dangerous sailing at sea and the cost will be unthinkable. This victory has doubled the flow of gold and silver into our treasury, not to name the many rich and important merchandise of the world's wealth that is now at our disposal.

"My father, our king sends words of praise. He promises great wealth when we return to Babylon. You will not be forgotten."

His first assistant, General Nergal-Sharezer, is the first to speak after the crown prince. Enthusiastically, he says, "Your leadership, General Nebuchadnezzar, makes our victories possible. The added marvels of our casting machines and brick cannons are awesome. I fear to think of the Assyrians if they would have developed such a means of warfare."

"Your honor," he says to the crown prince. "You have conceived and developed a warrior's dream for victory on the battlefield. With many other new ideas and your superior tactics, we will march to Egypt and make Babylon the empire that touches the entire world."

Nebuchadnezzar warns them against overconfidence as they plan the next engagement enroute to their ultimate dream of conquering Egypt. Pharaoh Necho II has made many boasts and absolutely expected to defend Carchemish in a massive victory against the Babylonians. His trek across the plain from the Euphrates to the border of Egypt is extremely sad in light of his many victories of the past. He is presently the ruler of all Palestine from Syria and Lebanon, including the Zion Kingdom. He cannot miss seeing what may lie ahead if Nebuchadnezzar decides to continue in his quest to the Great Sea and south toward Egypt.

With Carchemish thoroughly conquered and a Babylonian government in control, Nebuchadnezzar places a strong contingent of his warriors under a seasoned commander and heads toward Egypt with the world's most feared warriors. The warriors of Egypt are days ahead and are heading as straight as possible for their home bases to regroup, retrain, and enlarge.

One small city after another is put under Babylonian control with sufficient warriors left in command. City by city is turned into a part of the empire. Every trade post is made a Babylonian post, and the business of traders, their comforts, and tariff charges are all established as belonging to Babylon. The matter of tribute and the victory's booty for each city is left to be gathered and ready for the warriors as they march home.

Every warrior knows that the riches of each victory are a part of their pay when they are safely home. Great warriors that live and win for their king become rich in substance and are honored by everyone in the empire because Babylon's strength rests in these brave men. They often spend resting time in their camaraderie and talk of the treasures expected.

The city of Byblos on the shores of the Great Sea refuses to surrender and is under siege for several days. General Nebuchadnezzar's commanding leaders meet to decide the city's fate.

The general's first assistant speaks, "This city can easily be destroyed, but it is rich and contains treasure that we should save, both for their future prosperity and the prosperity of all Babylon. I am for waiting while they use up their food and water and willingly submit. We should send a message to the king that if he surrenders, his life will be spared and he will be allowed to continue as king under King Nebopolasser's rule."

Prince Nebuchadnezzar adds, "He must be told that he has until two sunrises to make up his mind. After that, he, his family, and his lords will be marched to Babylon as captives. If he decides to fight further, then he will be slain, along with his entire household."

His surrender comes shortly. The tribute to Babylon is heavy because of the days of delay. A strong ambassador is assigned to the city and requires all matters of government to be approved by his office. The ambassador is left with ample warriors to enforce the rules of the empire and a yearly tribute is assigned to the city. The city is a rich addition to the growing empire of Babylon.

Damascus, Tyre, and Sidon choose not to fight when they witness the entire countryside that is filled with battle-hungry warriors. The facts about the fall of Carchemish have traveled far and wide. No wise king wants to subject his city and his personal wealth to such a bombardment. They leave the kings on their thrones, but warn them of the results of rebellion. The policies are being developed and established. One rebellion means that the king will be replaced, two means the king will be carried captive to Babylon, and three means the city will be destroyed, along with the king and all his family and lords.

In each case, the king and his lords are required to come before Prince Nebuchadnezzar and present themselves as subjects of the Babylonian Empire.

A majestic battlefield palace is set up near these three cities for this ceremony.

The crown prince sits in his regal attire as each king and his lords appear. He speaks briefly as they bow in submission.

He promises, "The Babylonian Empire intends to rule fairly and honorably before all people. As subjects of this empire, you will have powers to rule by our laws and decrees. Any acts of defiance will be met with force. Any city, its king, and his lords will have all benefits of the prosperity of the whole. Our will is to have an empire where every corner is wealthy and every god is worshipped.

"Our ambassador of Babylon is present to take an oath of your allegiance and to be the Babylonian king's personal friend to you and your city or state. You will be invited to visit the capital at Babylon and, as you prove your loyalty, to share in all our wealth throughout the empire. We will make it beneficial for you to be a part of Babylon."

The ambassadors then meet and finish all state affairs with the kings and take the oath of all present for each city. In these three cities and small areas, all representatives of Egypt that had ruled them up until the present time are given safe passage to travel to Egyptian territory. Warriors are posted in each city and at other strategic locations to enforce the rules of the empire.

The city of Zion and its territory is the next major center south toward Egypt. Even the world's bravest warriors tremble as they move toward the people of the scrolls. King Nebopolasser knows the story of King Senmesherib of Assyria and the one hundred eighty-five thousand dead warriors as they camped against Zion. He warns his son to tread softly. The king of Egypt, Necho II, has replaced the hastily crowned son of Josiah after his death on the battlefield by his Egyptian warriors. A brother, Jehoiackim, has been placed on the throne and has reigned three years and has done nothing but evil.

With subterfuge and deception, King Jehoiakim moves quickly to give homage to Nebuchadnezzar. His game is politics and he plays it well. Meeting the prince from Babylon with his formidable army, he chooses to buy time while the final issue is settled between King Necho II's warriors as they regroup and return to engage the Babylonians. "Honorable Nebuchadnezzar," he begins. "I am your servant and we bow to the empire of Babylon and to King Nebopolazzer to share in the victory that has come to his Highness. The Egyptians have been cruel taskmasters, and they slew my father near the shores of the Euphrates."

Nebuchadnezzar is wise enough to allow the King of Zion to save face. "King Jehoiakin," he replies, "The Egyptians have been thoroughly beaten at Carchemish and we intend to drive them out of Palestine and to incorporate Egypt into our empire. Your entire kingdom will prosper under the Babylonian rule and we will protect your kingship if you willingly submit. There will be no leniency if you use falsehood or act deceptively."

He continues, "The king, my father, has spoken highly of your religion and your God. We want all the empire to honor their gods just as we honor Marduk the chief god of Babylon. Your temple, which we viewed from a great distance, is of excellent beauty. Your city is a jewel sitting upon these rich hills of prosperity. Your countryside, banana groves, oranges, and grapefruit trees have provided fruits that are refreshing to taste and beautiful to behold."

Assuring them of their new alliance, he adds, "Our fruitful fields of Babylon and your fields of Palestine will prosper together as our merchants travel the roads of our empire. You will be honored in our great Babylon, the golden city of the world."

"Welcome to the Babylonian Empire," concludes General Nebuchadnezzar, as the king stood before him flanked by his dominating council of lords from Zion and the land of Judea.

The conversation turns to the matter of tribute and the policies of state. The king is told that his chamberlain will soon visit Zion to choose young men to be schooled in the Chaldean laws and methodologies. A large tribute is announced and is to be collected to be transported back to Babylon. This total tribute consists of one thousand talents of gold and twice that much silver, plus an equal amount in value of spices, perfumes, and the best wines.

A large garrison of warriors is stationed for security and an ambassador is appointed to represent the interest of the empire.

Just as they finish the many matters of the state, a hurried company of warriors delivers sealed instructions from Babylon to the crown prince. The warriors are breathless and exhausted from this emergency trip. The news is stamped with the official seal of the king of Babylon to ensure the privacy of its contents.

Tense, the crown prince opens the sealed instruction. After reading the news, he simply stands before his brave commanders and close personal counselors.

Trembling, he reads, "My father, the king, is dead." He quickly moves to his private quarters and spends a few moments recovering from this great shock. It is a long way home. His mother and his princess, already considered the queen at his father's death, need him as soon as possible.

Nebuchadnezzar speaks privately to those that heard his

announcement. "I will leave for home immediately." His private warriors, the best of all, are quickly prepared. He gives instruction to his first assistant, General Nergal-Sharezer, to continue towards Egypt, while the warriors of Egypt are broken and in disarray. No one is to know of King Nebopolasser's death until he is crowned as the king of the Babylonian Empire.

At sunset, surrounded by his chief warriors, he starts for home, a journey of at least three weeks. Already ten days have passed since the king's unexpected death. He is informed that his father will lie in state until he arrives home. The son of Nebopolasser, fully prepared to be King Nebuchadnezzar, is heading home by an unannounced but planned route. In order to protect the world's most powerful man, only one special aide knows the route they will travel. He is already considered "King Nebuchadnezzar—the Head of Gold" in the hearts of all Babylon.

There is one terrifying event on the journey. A large band of warriors and robbers sweep down upon them unexpectedly. They are actually larger in number than all the king's chariots and warriors. Prince Nebuchadnezzar special guards, extremely abandoned to protect him, also knowing he will soon be the king, dash upon this company of ruffians with utter destruction. These attackers never knew whom they had endangered.

Nebuchadnezzar Ascends the Throne

605 BC

The touches of a golden empire appear throughout the city of Babylon. Gleaming gates are covered with beaten gold. The temple of Marduk, over seventy feet tall, has a golden roof and gold pillars of equal height on all sides. The new unfinished palace of Nebuchadnezzar and Amytis is quickly becoming the envy of every royal family where news of its grandeur has traveled. The palace has been labeled the "palace of the gods." The light blue granite stones from the mountains of Mede create grandeur of beauty and strength that matches the appearance of Princess Amytis. She is truly the Golden Empire's icon of divine mystery. Princess Amytis exudes a certain mysterious appeal, feeding the public's desire for a living goddess.

Crown Prince Nebuchadnezzar slips into Babylon after dark and is quickly directed to Hanna's side in the capital rotunda where the king lies in memorial. The lords of King Nebopolasser have kept all matters of state under perfect order awaiting the prince to arrive. Every Babylonian has paid respect to the king that has given them a New Babylonian Empire and no one doubts that the prince is now their new king.

Amytis rushes to be beside her Nabu and to share the grief of his fallen hero. With royal decorum, the family of King Nebopolasser prepares for his interment in an exquisite mausoleum. His burial is a private family event held within an hour of the prince's arrival. The matters of the kingdom must move forward quickly lest the enemies of the empire seek to take advantage. The coronation of King Nebuchadnezzar will occur at a sacred hour determined by the high priest of Marduk. Under the golden roof of his temple, it is announced that it will be held at 12:00 tomorrow.

Dressed in the royal attire of a king that has been prepared especially for this moment, the crown prince accompanied by his princess, go quickly to their enclosed chariot to move to the capital. Queen Hanna rides in front in her deceased husband's chariot. Upon arrival at the capital building, they descend from their chariots and enter the building. The coronation is attended by all the king's lords and invited guests. The high priest of Marduk administers the oath.

The ceremony begins. The following words are stated by the high priest of Marduk and then repeated by the king: "I, Crown Prince Nebuchadnezzar, renounce all rights and privileges of a mortal man and I embrace the divine duty of the king of Babylon. I claim the final words of all the empire. I take the duty of life and death of every Babylonian. I am the kingdom of Babylon and the life of the empire is my life. Today, I will begin the journey of walking with the gods and acting in their behalf. I am almighty, the king of Babylon."

As King Nebuchadnezzar finishes, a strange hush settles for a short span, and then the room explodes with shouts, "Long live the king; long live King Nebuchadnezzar, the king of Babylon!" Everyone in attendance bows in worship before King Nebuchadnezzar, now the king of the Golden Empire. They move quickly to the Temple of Marduk to offer worship as the custom is required of the priest. The queen of Nebopolasser now follows, both in her chariot and at each point of entrance, behind the new king and queen. She bows with the same devotion as his lords.

The high priest and his assistants conduct a worship service that continues for an extended time. Quotes that are reported to have come from Marduk are read and expounded. The music of the temple is like the sounds of gods acting in the priests and worshipers in battle. The god of rain makes sounds of thunderclouds; the god of battle fills the air with death sounds of the enemies; and the god of life fills the temple with laughter.

Satisfied that the gods have approved the new king, the priest dances and engages the entire audience in laughter, dance, and repetitious sounds of acclamation and triumph. Finally, it is time for the king to be presented to all of the empire.

They move from the Temple of Marduk to the barely finished amphitheatre. This theatre was King Nebopolasser's last project and it is beautiful to the extreme. The chariots, with curtains now wide open and the king and queen sitting in royal splendor, move slowly toward the theatre. The crowd is ecstatic, as they adore their new king and queen.

The theatre is full of people. The citizens of Babylon have loved their king since he came to Babylon with his father soon after the empire was reborn. His princess has lived in Babylon almost six years. The "palace of the gods" is still unfinished but rising like the splendor of a golden castle. When the king and queen's chariot comes into sight, an explosion of joy fills the theatre.

The king and queen step out of the chariot protected by a throng of warriors with masculine attire.

Queen Hanna presents the king to this host of Babylonians with kind and loving words. She asked for this honor and it has been welcomed. Her words are words spoken only from a mother's heart:

"To all of Babylon, I find it my joy to give you my firstborn. I remember the day that he was born and the tender kiss on my forehead from Nebo my husband. He was always a humble man and we rejoiced as I held Nabu in my arms. We knew he would be a king and named him for that purpose. He has never been less than totally loved, and now, I have given him to the gods to be one of them."

After a brief pause, she says slowly, "I give to the gods and to you, my son, to be your king."

Now, it is time for the celebration to begin. The great sports enthusiasts of the city play special games. Dances in Sumerian, Akkadian, Chaldean, and even in Medean are presented, all dedicated to the king and queen.

The entire event to this point has been devoted to the Babylon mystique, but now special guests are welcomed. The first honored guest is King Cyaxares and Queen Akkadiya, the proud parents of beautiful Queen Amytis. Their welcome is genuinely inspiring as the king speaks of his son-in-law and daughter.

"To all of Babylon," he begins, "I honor you as our special partners in building a new world of prosperity and good will. It is clear to all Mede that you receive us as partners, though we are less in strength and smaller in size. We are satisfied to share this partnership as an equal supporter of your empire and of your king. All Medea is rejoicing because our princess is now your queen. She is the most beautiful queen in the entire world and she is certainly the wife of the greatest king. All Medea is partly Babylonian today."

Also, present are other royal guests from the Scythians, the recently incorporated city of Carchemish and the many appointed ambassadors of cities like Harran, Asher, and other extensions of the two empires such as Babylon and Mede. This day will never be forgotten.

After the ceremonies are completed, King Nebuchadnezzar spends a short time with his trusted assistants. They make plans to meet a short time each day, while the king is still invisible to the city. Every report from the battlefield is to be brought to him day or night because he knows that it is exciting to the warriors in harm's way to get a letter from their king that has been written in the middle of the night. He then retires to the palace to spend time with Amytis and to rest from the strenuous trip from Zion to Babylon and the months away from home.

Nabu and Amytis establish a pattern of being two ordinary people when they and the family are alone in the palace. The servants are asked to call them, "our king" and "our queen." The family is known for their merry ways as they enjoy the rare private times they have together.

After several days, the king and queen decide to visit the construction of their palace. They are anxious to be in their new home, which is clearly the envy of the world. The news has traveled far and wide of the magnificence of this emerging castle. The promise had gone out from the king that it would be the palace of the world and every royal person would be invited to enjoy its grandeur. There will also be times of open house, where the poorest of the empire might walk within its walls.

The king and queen are thrilled with the progress visible of the palace that gives even a slight view of what the finished project will be. The centralized room is created to provide entrance and special use at different levels. The royal family will have space apart from all the other sections and will be enclosed sufficiently to be private but open to the full grandeur of the central room. The impression from this center location is like a valley in the midst of great height. This room is nearly one hundred feet to the ceiling with light pouring into every corner. There is a space for all the king's lords to gather, where he can almost secretly step from his private quarters right into their midst. A beautiful area is planned especially for royal dignitaries. Provision is made where several different countries and languages can meet separately and the king and queen can move from guest to guest. To convey the feeling of an open house, a slightly raised area with beautiful banisters is provided so the common people can walk through without disturbing any royal event that may be in progress.

The focus of this central room is a ceiling to floor waterfall with flowers, roses, clematis vines, and other mountain-like shrubs cascading from top to bottom. It is massive and extravagant to behold. Amytis is overwhelmed and weeps openly at its beauty and mountain-like appearance.

Their private quarters are expansive, covering sixty thousand square feet. While mostly unfinished, the very shape of the walls, often circular, and garnished with gold and jewels, along with the apparent beauty that each part of the room will finally present leaves the king and queen full of marvel. They can already feel a little of what life will be like in this beautiful place.

The master builder says, "King Nebuchadnezzar and Queen Amytis, this palace is without a doubt a dream house. We want all the empire to know that in Babylon at the heart of this kingdom, we see our king and queen as supreme. While your coronation was a grand event, the next grand celebration must be when we can move your family into this 'palace of the gods.'

"A large number of world travelers have walked through this unfinished building and they leave to tell the story. Without exception, everyone responds, this is going to be the most beautiful palace in the entire world.

"Your Honor," the builder says, while looking at his king, "It is for you we built this castle, and for the beautiful queen that stands at your side."

Back in their existing palace, King Nebuchadnezzar and Queen Amytis enjoy moments of private time. The king tells Amytis that this is the last quiet day before he moves quickly to care for the matters of state and the expanded work yet to be finished in the city and across the empire.

"Amytis, these days have been wonderful. Your love to me is more wonderful than life. I never want to let you forget that our empire is a happy world only as long as I have you as my queen."

Her words are simple, "I love you, Nabu, and always will."

As the retreat nears to a close, he says to Amytis, "I heard the most beautiful music I have ever heard when we were camped outside the walls of Zion in Palestine. I asked for the privilege of visiting the location of that incredible singing, but I was told it was impossible. It was coming from their Golden Temple. They said no one but one of them could go through the gates of that sacred place.

"Amytis, I am sending our chamberlain to Zion to choose young men to train and he will be instructed to bring that choir back to live in Babylon. Our music is so different. That singing from their temple has echoed in my head ever since I returned to bury my father."

Chosen Young Men of the Scrolls

605 BC

No one in Zion believes that their king will keep his word to King Nebuchadnezzar. His entire demeanor is that of deception and political opportunism. Instead, everyone whispers about the secret communication with the Egyptian king. Necho II, and the influence wielded by the counselor to the Zion king, who pressured the king to trust Egypt and not the Babylonians. The gossip suggests that the tribute is being prepared and will be sent to Babylon to buy time for the Egyptian army to regroup and explode out of Egypt. Their army has triumphed out of defeat many times before. Hatred for the seer Jeremiah grows by the day.

Azariah, Hananiah, and Mishael attend class all day. Their professor knows very well that these young men, along with Daniel, are bright students; but they cannot wait to be rid of them. Their total faithfulness to the Scrolls is nothing but a pain to these intellectuals that prefer their own imagination to the words of a seer. Professor Hilkiah speaks to the three of them before his entire class.

"I believe you young men must feel vindicated that our King Jehoiakim has pledged alliance to Crown Prince Nebuchadnezzar. It is the opinion of all our chief men that the triumph of Babylon will be short lived. There is word that Crown Prince Nebuchadnezzar left hurriedly after meeting with our great leaders. He probably left for fear of what the Egyptian lords and their king are planning. We have been partners with Egypt over many years and that partnership will not fail."

Hananiah respectfully replies, "Professor Hilkiah, how often have we been warned not to trust in the Egyptians but in our God. Our nation belongs to the God of Zion, Who has chosen us. We have our seers from Him to give us direction."

"Yes," says the Professor, "but we have young, modern seers that are well educated in our college that speak to us by modern means. We deplore those old men who think God only speaks in their ancient ways."

Azariah's heart pounds as he interjects, "Professor Hilkiah, the words of God's great seer Jeremiah, will be fulfilled. Our history proves that our God never fails. I believe you will be one of the captives marched in defeat to be a slave in Chaldea, and you are causing others among our class to believe your errors."

The teacher angrily dismisses the class and leaves out a side door. One student slams a book across Azariah's head, while another one spits in his face. These godly young men refuse to fight back and everyone quickly leaves to go to their next class.

Daniel has just left the President's office and sees Hananiah and his friends. "You look all shook up," he says. After telling him of their experience, they all rejoice together, but then Daniel must tell them the news he has just been given.

"My brethren," he begins after finding a quiet place on the campus to talk. "I just received incredible news. King Nebopolasser is dead and the new king of Babylon is Nebuchadnezzar. He left Zion in a matter of an hour when he received news of his father's death. All the talk of his fears was unfounded as we already knew.

"Just like the Seer Jeremiah spoke, the king of Babylon is now King Nebuchadnezzar. The president of the college is visibly shaken and a bit softer than I have ever seen. He even asked for our prayers.

"But that isn't all he told me. King Nebuchadnezzar's chamberlain is on his way to Zion. The king is sending him to choose the smartest young men in this college to take back and train to serve in the court of Babylon. My dear friends, we best go tell our parents what is happening and enlist much prayer. You know that the leadership and professors of the Royal College would like to be rid of us!"

Mishael speaks with excitement, "God's plan for his servants is perfect. If he wants me in Babylon to serve, it will be an appointed opportunity to represent the Scrolls and our sovereign God in a challenging place. I am ready to go."

They all agree but stress the need for all things to be done by God's decree and not their own way. A time and place to meet again is set as Daniel heads for a prayer time with Jeremiah.

As Mishael nears his home outside the walls of Zion, he sees the large caravan that is prepared for the trip to Babylon. A massive number of camels are loaded as well as a host of two-wheeled carts that are hitched to donkeys. The tribute is very large and the warriors of Chaldea are preparing to ride as escorts and provide security. The trip will be dangerous and long. A minimum of eight weeks will be required, including two weeks as guests in the Golden City that everyone is talking about. The news about the new king of Babylon is spreading like wildfire and the feeling of uncertainty is shattering. It will be a long time before there is peace in Zion again and almost everyone knows it.

Mishael arrives home at the same time as his father. After a few minutes of strong affection between father and son, Mishael asks if he has heard the latest news.

"Yes," he says. "The Seer Jeremiah has certainly heard right. If our king will obey his anointed words of warning, Zion will be spared and we can save our temple and city from the same fate as Nineveh. I fear that he is too evil and stubborn, plus his counselors are the worst of the lot. They know nothing but haughtiness against the voice of our God. Proud men never listen to the right instruction."

Michael's father is a very successful merchant and travels the world with the large and growing caravans.

"Son," he says, with hope in his voice. "The seers have declared that King Nebuchadnezzar is going to rule the world and even the animal kingdom. Nothing of the world's powers will fail to bow before this king. There will be wealth and prosperity as men, like your father, trade on a world market. If our king will submit, we will pay heavy tribute, but we can also live in relative peace and serve our God.

"I fear that the next time King Nebuchadnezzar comes to our Zion, thousands will be marched back to Babylon to build his golden city and to serve his every command."

"Father," Mishael says, "Daniel was told today by the Royal College president that the chamberlain of King Nebuchadnezzar is, even as we speak, traveling to Zion. He is coming to take the most learned men of our city back to Babylon. All four of us believe that we will be named by the college as highly educated, so they can be free of us and our constant voice for the Scrolls and our friend, Jeremiah. We have earnestly put this before our God for His will."

Daniel goes to share the news with Jeremiah. They hug each other as fellow travelers in their love of the Scrolls and even weep with joy that they know their God. Daniel tells Jeremiah of all the news from Babylon, that the king is now Nebuchadnezzar and about the chamberlain that is on his way to Zion.

Daniel says, "Brother Jeremiah, I believe I will be carried back to Babylon to serve King Nebuchadnezzar. Our God has prepared me to serve Him and to represent in His court the God that chose Him to be the Head of Gold. It will be my journey of faith in Babylon, just as your journey of faith is here in our beloved city."

Jeremiah replies, "Daniel, what is happening in our world is actually grand and even wonderful although very dark and foreboding. It is a battle of the gods seeking control of our world. As the Assyrians served Ashur their god and all the nations their different gods, the ultimate end will be a victory for the truth of our Scrolls. The true God will win and our duty is total trust and total obedience. Who knows, but you may bring King Nebuchadnezzar to believe in our God.

"You are not responsible to make him believe, you are responsible to know God and to so live, even if indeed you are in King Nebuchadnezzar's palace, that he will see Him for himself. If our God is real in you, He cannot be hid."

When Lord Ashpenaz reaches Zion, he is flanked by a superior host of warriors sent by King Nebuchadnezzar. Immediately, he meets with the councilors and lords of King Jehoiakim and tells them of his command from King Nebuchadnezzar. Everyone knows that the great warriors of Chaldea are still in Palestine establishing tribute in every city and moving toward Egypt.

"I have come for the brightest and most intellectual of your young men," he tells them. "They must be capable of standing in the court of Babylon, renowned men from the elite of your city. The king has charged me to train them in the great mythologies of the Chaldeans and prepare them to represent Zion in our empire. They will also represent your nation to us and will speak for your people living in Babylonian territory."

The Chamberlain continues, "Also, the king was greatly moved by your choir singing in your temple. He heard them in his camp outside the city. I am to bring that choir back to Babylon to make music for him and all the City of Gold. He wants them to sing the songs of Zion in Babylon."

The lords of King Jehoiakim become extremely angry but are fearful to show it to this personal representative from the man that suddenly has the entire world trembling. They ask for a few days to identify the best of their nation and secretly hope to save their temple choir.

When the high priest learns of the command for the temple

choir, they are troubled beyond measure. They ask permission to appeal to Lord Ashpenaz, and he consents to their request.

As they meet, the high priest says, "To the noble King Nebuchadnezzar and to you, Lord Ashpenaz, we petition, even beg of you, that you not require our choir to go back to Babylon. There are over one hundred choir members who sing our beautiful songs, ten play the beautiful harp, ten play the coronet, and twenty others of different instruments. They are the joy of our temple and we would be helpless to have our sacred worship without them."

Lord Ashpenaz is kind, but firm. "If I return to our capital without obeying the king's command, I will endanger my head. If you refuse, he will send his warriors and close your temple. I regret your loss but remember they will sing your songs of Zion in our city. They will be well cared for, given homes in our land, and allowed to prosper in our wealth. They are not going as slaves like numbers of your young men will be. They will serve us in Babylon, and you will be free to visit our land. Our Babylonian Empire is quickly becoming a world empire. All that submit will be free to share that wealth and all that refuse will become our captives."

Daniel, Azariah, Hananiah, and Mishael are the first four to be identified from among the young men of Zion. Several hundred more highly respected men that are strong in the skills of science, agriculture, business, and creators of innovative ideas, along with every able member of the temple choir and all the best musicians are also chosen. Seven hundred in all are required to be ready with all their personal belongings to leave in seven days. There will be no exceptions.

The City of Zion is in deep mourning. Not only is their brightest and best leaving for Babylon, but they will also be surety against rebellion in their City of Zion. It is like taking hostages to assure your faithfulness. The temple will be left with a new choir to train, and every business and almost every family is separated from loved ones. The City of Zion begins to feel the failure of obeying their

Scrolls and their unfaithfulness to their God. The warnings have been many and much of the city has often scoffed at the seers that speak for their God. If Assyria cannot escape their judgment, how can Zion escape?

It has only been three weeks since the caravan of tributes headed for Mesopotamia and now, an even greater caravan is leaving Zion. The city is thoroughly shaken, but the king and his lords are even more resolved to call for Egypt's assistance and to see the defeat of King Nebuchadnezzar.

The entire area that Babylon has conquered is feeling the effect of the One World Empire. All national interest must be sacrificed for the good of the whole. Lines of national boundaries are being removed and everyone is required to be an international citizen. The worship of all gods is allowed, except when it is in the interest of the king for everyone to bow together before him or his god.

Wives weep for husbands they will most likely never see again. Mothers are heartsick as their sons and daughters prepare for the long, trying transfer to the city called the Golden City. The temple choir sings at the different locations all across the city night after night to weeping throngs. The priests are offering sacrifices and showing some signs of belated repentance.

Daniel and his three close friends spend their time with family and at the temple. With immense joy, they relish every hour set for prayer by these lovers of the Scrolls and their deep faith. Jeremiah constantly travels among their families, speaking words of encouragement.

He addresses all four young men, who are still under twenty years of age. Daniel is eighteen and the other three are seventeen. They have spent the last four years at the Royal College and earned the highest grades in the Institution.

"Daniel," he begins, then pauses and calls all their names. "You are priceless young men that have added much joy to my life. There is no question that you are chosen to the task now before you.

Together, you four can make life more tolerable for all of us by your presence in King Nebuchadnezzar's court. You are going to this challenge for all of Zion as we endure the coming seventy years of bondage. Eventually all of our city will be destroyed because the Words of our Scrolls have made it plain. Only utter repentance can change the mind of our God and there is no evidence of such occurring. We will be separated by distance but united by prayer."

"Jeremiah" says Daniel, "I have covenanted with my God to turn my head toward Zion and bow in prayer three times every day."

"We make the same covenant," say Azariah, Hananiah, and Mishael in unison.

The walls of Babylon suddenly begin to appear on the distant horizon. The sun beams, lighting up the walls in beauty. Golden gates sparkle. Water canals are everywhere with beautiful bridges over every waterway. Babylon has been turned into an oasis of rare and unequaled beauty.

Daniel and his three friends are treated royally. They are being prepared to stand before the world's most powerful man and their decorum must be in a royal fashion. Their education has already begun and they will live in the grand "Palace of Gold" as soon as it is finished. Even the present palace is the most beautiful place they have ever lived and the food is the best of the empire. They are in a strange land under the influence of a strange god, but surrounded by the luxury that could tempt the best. However, these men will never bow to any god but the One they know. That is settled.

The rest of the massive host, numbering six hundred and ninety-six, does not fare in such plenty. The choir members and musically talented are more comfortable and well cared for with small homes and food. The rest live in tents and eat together until they can prepare homes in a special section near the city. Every captive brought to Babylon must earn the right by their devotion and skills to be given freedom and opportunities in the full society. There is little freedom and no possible escape until that time. It could be a fairly good life if they learn the life of total surrender to a foreign king and a strange god. The labor will be hard and tiring; but there is a promise of citizenship after years of unquestionable service.

The training of government officials and eunuchs is an emergency. Tens of thousands of captives, laborers, and leaders from conquered land demand leadership and require supervision. Daniel and his three companions are among those brought to Babylon for this very purpose, trained to think as Chaldeans.

Lord Ashpenaz appoints a prince to train and prepare a host of eunuchs, government personnel, for the king's enormous and growing empire. The incredible size of an administration quickly becoming a world empire is staggering. Daniel catches the attention of this prince immediately, because his character is spotless. His brilliance literally shines in his face and the quiet dignity of his life is captivating. His three friends are only a little less in their pure personalities.

The prince chooses his best assistant named Melzar, and appoints him to give these four top priorities. Their living quarters are the best available and fit for a king. Their food is served in the king's dining hall. Daniel ensures that their dinner that evening will be kosher.

"Prince Melzar," he speaks out, "our faith does not allow us a diet as your king eats. We do not eat food offered to other gods, swine meat, or any meat where the creature does not chew the cud. We do not drink strong wine. Please give us a diet with which we will not defile ourselves, so we can be the king's very best servants."

Prince Melzar is stunned. "Young men," he says, "the food we are planning for you is the best in all the empire. The wine is from your own country. Any young man in Babylon would give his heritage for such delicacies as you will enjoy."

Kindly, Daniel answers, "But our God has commanded us to eat a diet that makes one healthy and strong of mind. We stand before you robust, bright of skin, and exceedingly sharp of intellect because we have disciplined ourselves. Prove us," he says, "for the next days and watch our features and test our minds and you will see the difference."

Melzar warns them that he is placing his life on the line and also reminds them that the prince appointed by Lord Ashpenaz is doing the same.

"Do not disappoint me," he says, as the decision is made for this test of the strange diet from the Scrolls out of Zion. Ten days later, Melzar and the prince spend time with the young men. They are extremely impressed by such dedication.

"Indeed," the prince says, "your flesh is fatter, your countenance fairer, and your knowledge learned in these ten days is overwhelming. Your God must be special," he says, "as he gives full permission for a diet that matches their testimony of faith and purity."

The Hanging Garden for Queen Amytis

604 BC

*T*he magnificent palace called "the Palace of Gold" is breathtaking in the morning sun. The stone imported from the mountains of Queen Amytis' childhood create a spectacular sight. Its royal shade of blue is enhanced by the roof, which utilizes sapphire stones to accent the golden tile.

All twenty of the cupolas are covered in the sapphire stones intricately designed and layered to reflect their dazzling colors. The windows and doors are framed in gold. Each door is an artwork of gold covered cypress. The exterior of each door is gold and their interiors are beautifully designed woodwork.

The interiors of the windows are shaded with gold tapestries with different designs for every room. These golden tapestries allow maximum light but are opaque from the outside. Every window looks like a golden mirror from the exterior of this royal residence. With the golden tiled roof, gold frames on every window, gold doors, and, now, gold tapestries; this palace is clearly a reflection of its name, the Palace of Gold and often called "The Palace of the Gods."

A covered colonnade that is twenty feet deep and contains immense pillars wrapped with gold, flanks the entire front as well as both ends of this grand structure. The palace and the colonnade together measure six hundred and forty feet by one hundred and seventy feet. The columns stand over forty feet and are twenty feet apart. There are thirty-five columns on the front and ten on each end. The exterior is a magnificent sight and dazzling to behold. It is the most elaborate palace of any known empire.

This is all exterior beauty, but to step inside is to be awed. It is royalty everywhere. The king and queen's living quarters on the right side of this magnificent palace cover sixty thousand feet of floor space, thirty thousand feet on each of two levels. There is a colonnade of gold covered columns the complete width of the royal living quarters on the interior wall of the Great Room. These gold covered columns are forty-foot high with numerous large windows above that provide additional light of the Great Center Atrium.

Twenty-foot ceilings fill the living section of the king and queen. The Great Room is thirty thousand square feet and full of light. The left wing is four stories with ten-foot ceilings and provides one hundred twenty thousand square feet of space. It houses office space for his personal administrative staff and living quarters for his special chosen eunuchs, his princes, and the House of the Chaldeans. This is indeed the very center of the Golden Empire.

King Nebuchadnezzar and Queen Amytis are excited that it is time to move to this grand palace of Babylonian and Medean splendor. "Nabu," says Amytis, "We are moving into such a royal storybook life that I fear for our happiness. You have forgotten the simple things and are even forgetting me in this whirlwind world of ours. Please, let's consider what is happening and force ourselves to come down to earth. I want you as my husband even more than as my king, especially the king of the whole world."

Nabu sits stunned for what seems like a long time. Finally, he breathes deeply and speaks, "Amytis, you are so right.

"My princess," he says, reverting back to their language of younger days, "I still adore you above all else in my life. Thank you for the words you just said to me. I guess I have been living in a stupor with all the glory coming at me from every direction. No one speaks to me anymore without addressing me as a god. I guess I have started believing what they are saying."

For the rest of the evening and night, they simply enjoy their marital bliss. They both are different persons the next day. Nebuchadnezzar is so transformed by the honesty of his queen that everyone is awed by the sudden humility and kindness he exudes. The king and queen visibly care for each other with genuine concern as they have in the past and appear to care more for the people than the splendor of their surroundings.

Settling into their magnificent palace, the king and queen are very happy. King Nebuchadnezzar refuses to be glorified and treats his close administrators like friends instead of servants. The entire palace is abuzz with excitement. Royal guests are constantly being entertained in the Palace of Gold. The cuisine is exceptional.

King Nebuchadnezzar and Queen Amytis meet soon after with the master builder for the planning process of the magnificent garden immediately beside the palace. The palace and the Hanging Garden are on the banks of the river overlooking the beautiful bridge and smaller gardens that dot every open space. The palace itself is surrounded by a garden that will connect side by side to the unique "Garden of Amytis" or "The Hanging Garden." Covering a vast space, it will appear to be a mountain from a distance with cliffs, terraces, balconies, porticoes, and domes.

Enclosed in its protecting walls, there will be every animal known in both the Medean and the Babylonian Empire. Every nation blending itself into the empire will feel a part of this zoological mountain. The height of this garden will surpass the three-hundred-foot-walls that surround the city. It will be visible to the approaching world a considerable time before the walls appear.

The master builder is ready to explain his design to King Nebuchadnezzar and Queen Amytis. They listen, suggesting changes. They sit in awe as the master builder reveals a beautiful elaborate design. He says, "The bottom tier will be eight hundred feet wide, two hundred and sixty feet deep, and twenty feet in height. Each level of twenty-three levels will recede thirty feet in the length and ten feet in the width. Each level for twenty-three levels will continue to recede in exactly the same proportion to be both contoured like a ziggurat and appear like a mountain. The top tier will be four hundred sixty feet high, one hundred sixty feet wide and twenty feet deep."

He continues, "Portico will dot the walls at different levels. Domes will protect different species of animals. There will be terraces projecting over different areas to beautify the wall. Balconies will be built for viewing areas over the animal enclosures. There will be veiled areas dotting the projection to be filled with every exotic bird. Stairways with some rounded and some turning in different directions will make the entire mountain of gardens and the zoo enclosures available at every possible direction."

Lord Nergal-Sharezer, the master builder, adds, "All of this will be filled with trees, shrubs, hanging flowers and beautiful plant life. It will appear like a mountain covered with growth. Columns will be visible, with the portico, domes, terraces, and balconies. Otherwise, all the walls will be covered in nature's beauty. Most of the area under the different levels will be built with columns and open space for the animals and shade for the joy of every visitor."

King Nebuchadnezzar addresses him, "Lord Nergal-Sharezer, your explanation is superb. Let's talk of things that I'm sure you have planned."

The king begins, "Will you plan for the garden to extend over the river for a distance?"

"Yes," says Lord Nergal-Sharezer, "We have designed a projected area of twenty feet for the full eight hundred feet. This will be supported by columns of stone on the river floor rising to the floor of the first tier. Within the twenty feet over the river at three locations but hid to everyone will be three giant machines built with chains. These will reach to the top of this garden and will carry a series of buckets filled with water. These buckets will be attached every three feet and provide a constant flow of water to the very peak. They will empty at the top as they roll over and start the decline. A huge pulley turned by six strong men will operate each watering device."

Queen Amytis is delighted to hear Lord Nergal-Sharezer's plans to build small stone canals to guide the water to every area of the entire garden.

Speaking directly to Queen Amytis, Lord Nergal-Sharezer explains. "We are planning an enclosed walkway from your living quarters across to this garden just for you and guests you may invite. There will be an enclosed route and pathway all through the garden reserved for your discretion. It will be invisible to the entire city and even those that may be visiting the rest of the garden. This garden must be first and foremost the 'Hanging Garden of Queen Amytis.'"

King Nebuchadnezzar and Queen Amytis cannot say enough to show how pleased they are with the plan. "Lord Nergal-Sharezer," the king begins, "You are indeed a choice builder and I will see that you are honored above measure. Queen Amytis is certain to find this mountain as beautiful as the mountains of Medea."

Then he asks, "When can we expect it to be finished?"

The answer is simple. "As soon as twelve months or at most two years," the master builder replies. "Tell me when I can start," he says to the king.

Eagerly King Nebuchadnezzar replies, "Tomorrow."

602 BC

The dedication of the Golden Palace is planned to occur simultaneously with the Hanging Garden. The king is going to make this occasion special for his queen. He has just returned from his responsibilities in Palestine with his trained warriors. The city of Zion is still a sore spot. Tyre is full of rebels but a forced peace is in place. Tribute flows like liquid gold and riches flood the Golden city.

The caravans roaming the world find Babylon a welcome relief from both the Assyrians and the Egyptians. With tariff reduced, the trade men have quadrupled and consequently freedom in trade has served to maximize the flow of tariff's gold, silver, and rich goods into the Babylonian capital.

The News chariot riders fill the empire with the exciting facts of the beautiful palace and the Hanging Gardenss. The world of nature from every corner of greater Babylon is represented in this garden. Every king, governor, and lord appointed by King Nebu-chadnezzar plans to attend. No one wants the "Head of Gold" to notice their absence. Every house is full of guests. Every temple is primed for their mythological worship. The temples to Ishtar and Marduk have acquired hundreds of sacrificial animals.

Thousands of the highest-ranking officers are invited to stay in the Golden Palace. Despite the summer heat, the building stays remarkably cool. A unique system built into the palace, fills the entire structure with cool refreshing air from beneath the building where tunnels allow the flow of water from the river beneath and behind the palace. The air draft out of the cupolas pulls the water-cooled air from the tunnels. The Garden of Amytis has the same system to imitate a mountain breeze rising among the animals, trees and the beautiful flowers.

The crowds from all over the world move between temples, games, theatrical events and satisfying feasts of the delicacies of the world. The city is a bazaar of goods, foods, and drink.

The dedication of the palace and Hanging Gardens is the crowning event. As the crowds walk through the palace and climb to the top of the mountain garden, they are overjoyed by the beauty of their surroundings.

At the announced hour for the ceremony of dedication, the highly decorated theater is packed. The king and queen of the empire are the center of attention. Toast after toast is offered to celebrate the couple. The Empire of Gold must have a Head of Gold and King Nebuchadnezzar is that Head. King Cyaxares is asked to give the dedicational speech.

The King of Medea is dressed royally. He announces, "This is the Palace and Garden of the Medean Princess now the Babylonian Queen. To King Nebuchadnezzar, the greatest king of all times. To Queen Amytis, the most beautiful queen I dedicate the words I will speak today.

"The world is at peace and there is wealth unknown before this time. Treasures are flowing in every direction. A king that sets over this empire is wise. He is first a husband and a father and he is rightly named, 'The Head of Gold.' The warriors of this empire are brave and daring. The Chaldeans that divine are mindful of the gods and they provide wise words to this king.

"He seeks wisdom of many lesser men than himself. I can testify of that for myself. His lords are wise and welcomed by him. I applaud the king of Babylon, King Nebuchadnezzar." The applause and adoration erupts and lasts for nearly an hour.

"Finally, I must speak for the queen. She is a wonderful wife to the king and a wonderful mother to my grandchildren. The king tells me of her wisdom of words to himself and often times that she helps to warn him of danger. She is the most beautiful woman on the earth; I applaud your queen, my daughter and always my princess." Again the applause and worship is deafening. She is still the princess as well as the queen and she of all the inhabitants of Babylon is the Crown Jewel and gift from the gods and the roar of the crowds proves her position.

"Now," says King Cyaxares, "I dedicate the Palace of Gold and the beautiful Hanging Gardens to Marduk, to Ishtar and to all the gods, to the empire, to all Chaldeans and to all the people where this empire touches, to King Nebuchadnezzar and to Queen Amytis."

Dancing fills the theatre, spilling into the streets. The celebration spreads to every nook and corner of the city, lasting into the early morning. Everyone is exhausted. Finally and slowly the roar ended, the dances stopped and everyone found their way to their sleeping quarters.

Quietly one could hear from every part of Babylon, "This is the greatest celebration and the golden city of the world." Everyone had been made to feel royal themselves.

17

The Golden City of Babylon

603 BC

When the sun's rays reflect upon the golden bull that sits on top of the Hanging Gardens, it is visible for miles. This garden mountain is four hundred and sixty feet tall and this glimmering symbol of Babylon adds thirty additional feet. It has become the sight to watch for of any one traveling toward the capital of the empire. At night, thirty burning torches decorate the entire top level of this king's gift to his queen. These huge torches with flames ten to fifteen feet high cast a light over the entire city. Babylon is a marvelous sight in the night hours.

Azariah, one of the four Eunuchs chosen from the Royal College in Zion, hears that his father and mother are traveling with a trading caravan that is passing by Babylon on their way to the East. The king learns of this matter as well and invites Azariah's parents to stay at the Royal Palace. Azariah's mother will stay in Babylon with her son until the caravan returns back. She will be staying in a special guest room for chosen visitors. It is a special occasion for Daniel, Azariah, Hananiah and Mishael. Azariah sent word for them to plan on arriving in the evening after the torches were lit on the Hanging Gardens upper level and throughout the city.

In the early morning, one day before their arrival, Hilkiah and Huldah share their excitement to see their first-born son. Suddenly Hilkiah gets a glimpse of the golden bull in the distance. They are still a days' journey from Babylon.

"Look" Hilkiah says, "I see the symbol of the city that we have been watching for."

"I see it," Huldah says excitedly. "My son, my son," she adds with tears flowing freely down her cheeks, "I will see my son again. It has been three painful years."

"Tomorrow evening," Hilkiah adds. "I am told by our guide that we should arrive some two hours after the dinner meal. It has all been planned to arrive in the early night when the golden city is at its most beautiful picture. It's been three years, mother, since we saw our firstborn. It will be a happy evening."

"Yes," she says, "I am so delighted that you are a business man trading on the world market. I would be so happy if Daniel, Hananiah, and Mishael's father and mother could be with us. They were weeping heartbrokenly as we left them standing outside the city walls. They almost did not get to see us because of the curfew in Zion and the tension with the Babylonian warriors that guard the city. Father, when will it all end?"

Hilkiah and Huldah talk freely as they travel out of hearing distance from the great host of the Caravan.

"Huldah," Hilkiah responds, "we know the Scrolls have made it all plain for us and Jeremiah has spoken personally that the city could have relative peace if King Jehoiakim would freely submit to King Nebuchadnezzar. He believes he will soon be disposed and someone put in his place. Maybe the new king will hear the words of our seer. If not we will probably be exiled to Babylon ourselves."

Hilkiah continues, "It appears that King Nebuchadnezzar is overly patient with our city Zion and our temple where we worship. Other cities have been totally destroyed for less reason than I see evidence among our city fathers and our king.

"Our hope is in our God whom we trust and pray to three times every day. Remember it is with our son and his wonderful friends in Babylon that we have made a covenant."

The flaming torches on the enormous walls of Babylon, across the city and on the top of the Hanging Garden, create a formidable and inspiring sight that overwhelm Hilkiah, Huldah and other travelers. They slow down as they absorb the sight of the city. The walls gleam under the glow of the torches. Special torches light the golden gates. News has been sent ahead and the well-guarded gates are opened for the caravan to enter.

Azariah and his friends have an honored place at the gates because of their positions with the king's court. When he sees his parents arrive, he weeps as he moves quickly to be at their side. Huldah and Hilkiah are delighted to see their son and show kind affection to him and his friends Daniel, Hananiah and Mishael. The donkeys and their carts along with Azariah's camels and helpers are carried aside to be cared for by servants of the Palace.

The parents of Azariah with their son and Daniel, Hananiah and Mishael move quickly to the Palace. Dinner has been held ready for a quiet meal and a happy reunion. As they eat and rejoice, Prince Melzar and several close friends enter the special dining room reserved for this occasion. The prince offers a special welcome from the king and queen. Azariah's parents will be happy guests in the grand Palace of Gold.

"Father, mother," Azariah says, "It will be my duty; along with my dear companions to begin as soon as you can rest a bit to show you the 'Golden City of Babylon.' You know how much we love Zion, but this city is where God has put us and we are duty bound by the decree of our God to honor authority that He has established.

"Until we return, we will show nothing but respect to the city where we are men under the king's authority. Remember what Jeremiah wrote in the Scrolls. 'Seek the peace of the city where I have caused you to be carried away captives and pray for it.' It is a remarkable and grand city," says Azariah. "We pray soon there can be a temple to our God in this city, in God's time."

Eager to explore, Hilkiah and Huldah get ready the next morning to see the Golden City and hopefully be able to describe everything to their many friends back in the City of Zion. They would be the first from the city of Zion to visit Babylon and return to describe the condition of those that had been exiled. Hananiah, Mishael and Daniel's families are desperate for information and news about their loved ones.

Azariah speaks in confidence to those that will tour the city with him and his companions as their guide. He whispers, "Our names have been changed and you must use the names we are known by here in Babylon. As eunuchs of the king it will be offensive for us to go by our given names. Daniel is Belteshazzar, Hananiah is Shadrach, Mishael is Meshack, and I am Abednego. We have prepared name tags for all of us and that will prompt you to remember as we converse together and to others.

"The queen has given us a rare invitation to bring all of you into their private living quarters. We have never been ourselves so this is a treat to us. I have permission for us to go immediately. The queen herself is waiting."

Queen Amytis is dressed especially for her guests from the City of Zion. The king had spoken to Amytis about the choir he heard and had shown special feeling about their temple and its absolute beauty. She meets them at the main entrance always used by the king's guests. Azariah is the first to speak.

"Queen Amytis, your Highness, we are honored to have this invitation. This is my mother, Huldah, and my father, Hilkiah. They are the most special people in the world."

Azariah's mother, a gracious and lovely lady herself speaks first to the queen. "Your Highness," she says, "You are indeed most beautiful as my son has told us. We are honored and thrilled just to meet you personally. To see you and King Nebuchadnezzar's personal living area of this Palace is like a dream. Thank you! Thank you!" Such simple and kind words take the queen by surprise.

She guides them as they move slowly through the immense

living room, see the king's private library, their huge bedrooms and even are privileged to speak with the children. Everything is exquisite; from carved panels of fir and cedar to Persian rugs of exceptional beauty and paintings that appear to be alive. There are special rooms for the entire king and queen's separate family members when visiting. There are rooms where special servants create the king and queen's grand wardroom from the world's richest fabrics.

The dining area is extremely large and the furnishing is elaborate. Delicious aromas float out of the warm kitchen as servants busy themselves in readiness for the next meal.

Queen Amytis takes time to explain everything.

As Abednego leads the way, they spend time enjoying the Hanging Gardens and then move across the beautiful bridge over the Euphrates River. Abednego invites Belteshazzar, Shadrack, and Meshach to join him in describing the grand sights of the city.

"The vast amphitheatre covers many acres and can accommodate well over one hundred thousand seated spectators," Belteshazzar says as he joins Abednego. "Some of the activities of this towering structure I will explain to you. The games are usually life and death games that we are careful to avoid. Prisoners who have been sentenced to death are often brought and fed alive to the lions, tigers and cougars. We have often heard the screams as these animals tear their victims apart. The crowds roar their approval. The longer and louder the screams become, the greater the roar of approval. It is vicious; something we would never tolerate in Zion."

"It is sad," says Hilkiah, "that such beauty is marred by man's thirst for violence."

Hananiah mentions the sport of chariot racing both in the amphitheatre and on the enormous fifty-six mile wall around Babylon. "Almost weekly, there is a chariot race on the walls," he shares. He points out near the theatre where there is an incline to the top of the wall and a decline coming from the opposite direction.

"Four, sometimes eight and sometimes as many as sixteen will line up here in the theatre and race to the incline and around the walls fifty six miles. Of course the winner is the first one to race down the incline and to the finishing line here at the center."

He continues, "They win large prizes so often they get deadly with one another. Several times a year a chariot will run off or be driven off the wall to their death. Life is not respected here in this city as we have been taught to believe in Zion."

Huldah motions for their attention and says, "Please that is enough of the dark side. I want to see the processional you spoke of last evening." Quickly they moved back across the bridges to the very front of the Golden Palace. They had come into the city by the entrance of the World Traders and Caravans and entered the Palace from the area where the eunuchs and Chaldeans had a special doorway. Now they stood at the center of the great columned porch. Looking directly toward the Ishtar gate they were almost smitten with the glory before them.

They see the golden temple on the right and Meshach describes it to them. Their Seers forbid them to enter a temple as this.

Meshach explains, "The mythological sounds that come from the worship of Marduk are so different from our worship and music. Often you can hear the gods represented in the priest or a worshipper warring and debating their position. Each god believes he or she is greater so they often sing, dance or dramatize their struggle for supremacy. When the rain has failed and the waters of the Euphrates recede they will sacrifice animals and even children of some poor family to appease the gods. It's chilling to hear, even the sounds of these events!"

They marveled at the extravagance of the Marduk temple and the gold lavished everywhere, from the doors to the roof and golden statue of Marduk visible from their viewpoint. This is the largest temple throughout the land of Chaldea and covered a huge area of the Royal Enclosure.

"The entire Procession Way stretches from the Palace center to the Ishtar gate, as you can see," comments Shadrach. "Over on the left is the large bastion of our warriors, and General Nergal-Sharezer office. It is the living quarters and barracks for well over one hundred thousand warriors. They train both here and in Uruk where there is a much larger bastion. Altogether we have over one million warriors preparing to take the world for Babylon."

Abednego speaks up again, "On the right is the Palace of Nebopolasser where his queen and her large staff and servants live. King Nebuchadnezzar loves his distinguished mother. She is still queen Hanna to everyone.

"There are over fifty temples to different gods. Several of them are the temples of Ishtar, greatly loved in the Chaldean areas of the Golden Empire. One temple is the temple of Sin that was originally the god of Abraham's father. Abraham was trained to worship Sin before he heard the voice of the God we love."

Daniel, named Belteshazzar in Babylon, asks Shadrack to let him describe the "Procession Way." He explains, "This enormous stretch of beautifully paved and decorated area is the Entrance Way of Royalty when they enter Babylon. King Nebuchadnezzar does not leave the city or arrive except by this famous ceremonial way. It is paved from end to end with huge flagstones of lime stone."

"It is six miles long and can stand well over one million Babylonians. The sidewalls are slabs of Rebecca stone with veins of minerals cascading through the slabs. You can see the many projected pillars built into the walls. This manner of construction makes the walls appear massive and beautiful.

"Look," he said, "at the grand lions and other mythological creatures that are imposed in these walls as all were marching toward the palace. The lions always represent Ishtar while the bulls represent Marduk. Whenever the king returns with our massive warriors everyone is required to fill the processional and welcome him home. This is the ceremonial entrance of the Babylonian Empire."

Belteshazzar, Shadrach, Meshach and Abednego have shown the

Golden City proudly to Hilkiah and Huldah. They are already anxious to share the whole story back in their City of Zion.

As they arrive back at the palace, Master Ashpenaz is waiting for Belteshazzar. He goes quickly to Master Ashpenaz' office as requested.

"Good news, good news," Ashpenaz announces to Belteshazzar. "We have arranged for the choir from Zion to sing tomorrow night at the Amphitheatre. The three ceremonial years of Chaldean cleansing is finished and this will be their first performance. The entire city is being notified and the king and queen will be present."

Belteshazzar reminds Master Ashpenaz that their three years on the ceremonial diet are also finished.

"Yes," says Master Ashpenaz, "We will announce at the event your entrance to the 'House of the Chaldeans' and you will become counselors to the king."

The choir has trained for three years in private. These years are required of all captives that are brought to Babylon from conquered territory. The choir members are fully prepared to sing again before an audience, if only it could be in Zion.

The king and queen are in their Royal box flanked by warriors with drawn swords and flashing spears. Belteshazzar, Shadrach, Meshach and Abednego with Hilkiah and Huldah are nearby in the seating area of Eunuchs and Chaldeans.

The stage is set for the performance. All Babylon has been told of the king's love for the music of Zion. The choir members shed tears like rain because they are about to sing Zion songs in a far away city and in captivity. They know better than to shed these tears on stage so they pray earnestly, wiping their tears and prepare to perform. As the curtain rises, the harps begin their melody, while the sweet sounding clarinets and other instruments slowly merge their sounds together. The most beautiful music Babylon has ever heard wafts through the air, changing the mood of everyone present and touching every tender heart.

For two hours, the choir sings Zion's songs because they know no other. From, "The Lord is My Shepherd," to "Who is the King of Glory," they sing of their Scrolls and the God of Zion.

Standing ovation after standing ovation interrupts almost every ending tune. Queen Amytis is in tears and Queen Hanna will never forget the evening. The people of this capital city have heard happy music and will be ready for the next performance.

Master Ashpenaz steps to the podium. He says, "Four men among us have finished the ceremony of introduction to the House of the Chaldeans." He introduces Belteshazzar and his companions. He continues, "They are now counselors to our king and to all Babylon." The crowd roars approval even while there are jealous Babylonians in the House of the Chaldeans that are troubled by Zion's presence and refuse to join the applause.

Then he announces that the members of Zion's Choir have also finished their years of Chaldean cleaning and are now full citizens of Babylon. They can build homes, become businessmen and pursue the life of full citizenship.

The Golden City has been touched by the influence of the Scrolls and the God of Zion. These captives are different, their faith is unusual, but something rings true to everyone that listened to them sing and play.

A Dream in the Palace

603 BC

It was a terrifying night for King Nebuchadnezzar. Amytis and he had talked long with much concern about the Babylonian Kingdom and especially the warnings from his Chaldean wise men. For nights, he has been plagued with startling dreams. Unknown to him, his sorcerers, soothsayers and other eunuchs were extremely unhappy and very jealous of the four members of his House of Chaldeans that were from the province of Zion. Rumors were flying of bad omens and plots to assassinate him and his beloved queen. Extra security was posted everywhere the king and queen ventured. It was an unhappy period in Babylon.

King Nebuchadnezzar awoke the next morning with a startling apprehension. He had dreamed what seemed like the entire night and he was drenched in sweat and raging with fear.

"Call all the Chaldeans, also the magicians and all my astrologers and sorcerers," the king screamed.

"They have not eaten their morning meal," said his Master of the Wise men.

"I do not care about their morning meal, I have not eaten either and neither could I eat," cried the king. "Send for them immediately."

When they wait in the huge court of religious affairs, the king enters with haste. He appears confused, his clothes and hair in disarray. They are all startled by his appearance.

He begins, "I have dreamed a scary and overwhelming dream. It must be from the gods. It is awesome and bigger than life and it is your purpose, the very reason I feed you and provide you with Babylon's best to give me the interpretation. I am deeply troubled and you are the representatives of the gods."

"Tell us the dream," said the entire company of religious scholars, "and we can easily divine for you the answers." They continued, "We are your fellow Chaldeans and the brightest of the lot and we have the wisdom of the gods and the ages."

"O," said the king, "but I have forgotten the dream. It was so awesome that it fled from me. The greatness of this dream was beyond my ability to recollect its substance. You are my servants of these gods and you will know both the dream and its meaning."

The king saw their haughtiness and their blank stare and he added with anger, "If you will not make known unto me the dream, with the interpretation thereof, ye shall be cut in pieces and your houses shall be made a dunghill.

"But if you show the dream and the interpretation thereof, ye shall receive of me gifts and rewards and high honor. Show me both the dream and the meaning and you will be the highest honored in all Babylon."

In desperation, his entire houses of the religious elite pleaded, "Let the king tell his servants the dream," as they feigned their humility "and we will show the interpretation."

The king is filled with fury at their response, replying, "I know your game, you would gain the time to devise a dream and supplant me with your scheme. I will not give you the time to make your plans and deceive me. You will prepare lying and corrupt words before me until times are changed, therefore today, this morning and before you eat, before you leave my presence, I must have your answer."

Now with desperation they cry out, "O, King, live forever,"

and then they make a fresh appeal. "There is not a man upon the earth that can show the king's matter, therefore there is no king, lord, or ruler that asks such things of any magician, or astrologer or Chaldean. It is a rare thing the king asks, and none except the god whose dwelling is not with flesh, can show such a matter to a king."

In desperation he commands, "Kill them all," and flees back into his private chamber.

All the diviners are quickly moved into a secure location and prepared for slaughter. Four members of his house of the Chaldeans are not presence. The king sends Arioch, his captain of the guards to go find them. The Chaldeans had not invited Belteshazzar and his three Zion companions.

"Belteshazzar," says Arioch the Captain, "Come with your companions, all four of you, no delay, you are sentenced to death by the word of King Nebuchadnezzar."

With tender wisdom, Belteshazzar asked to know the reason for his condemnation and for that of Shadrach, Meshach, and Abednego. Because of his wise inquiry, he is told of the king's dream and the whole matter. Then Belteshazzar asks for the honor of appearing before the king to make his appeal.

"O, King Nebuchadnezzar," said Belteshazzar, "I know the God that reveals secrets and He has given you this dream. Give me just hours to go before Him and I will tell the dream in such a manner that you will remember and then I will interpret the dream for you. The dream is unto you, O, King Nebuchadnezzar, and peace will return to your sleep."

While all the rest of the king's Chaldeans and religious wise men waited expecting death, Belteshazzar enlists the prayers of his three companions and God answers him in that very night.

Belteshazzar goes quickly in the morning to Arioch to save the lives of the wise men and to announce his readiness to inform the king of his dream.

Arioch proudly brings Belteshazzar before the king and announces, "I have found a man of the captives of Zion that will make known unto the king the dream and the interpretation.

The king was quick to ask, "Art thou able to make known the dream which I have dreamed and the interpretation?"

Belteshazzar answers before King Nebuchadnezzar, "The secret which the king demanded cannot the wise men, the astrologers, the magicians, and the soothsayers show the king. But there is a God in heaven that revealeth secrets, and maketh known to the King Nebuchadnezzar, what shall be in the latter days. Thy dreams and the vision of thy head upon thy bed are these.

"Your dream, O, King, is from the God which is above all flesh and all gods and all religions and is the God that ruleth in the affairs of men. He has established you for His purpose. O, King, He ruleth in the light and in the darkness and nothing is hid from Him.

"King Nebuchadnezzar, this God has revealed to you, the future kingdoms of all the earth. You saw a great image whose brightness was excellent and the form thereof was terrible. The head of the image was gold and that head of gold is you. There was a breast and arms of silver and that kingdom will follow but will be inferior to you.

"Then there was a belly and thigh of brass and that World Kingdom is third and inferior to the second. There will follow a fourth which is the legs of iron and the fifth which is the feet, part iron and part clay. The ten toes represent the sixth and then a great stone, without human hands shall smite it all to establish His kingdom on this earth. O, King, you have been shown God's battle for this earth and with the gods of men. The God that gave you this dream will rule in the end."

Then King Nebuchadnezzar falls on his face and worships Daniel. He commands that all the wise men, Chaldeans, astrologers, sorcerers, and soothsayers and all Babylon should worship Belteshazzar and offer an oblation and sweet odor unto him.

King Nebuchadnezzar now knows that there is indeed a battle of the gods and that Babylon was in the thick of that battle. He declared to Belteshazzar, "Of a truth it is that your God is a God of gods and a Lord of kings and a revealer of secrets."

The king wants to cast himself on the side of this God of Belteshazzar so he makes him a powerful man, giving him many gifts and making him the governor over the whole province of Babylon and chief of the governors over all the wise men.

"Governor Belteshazzar," the king said, "I am placing you over the entire region of our capital city, the City of Gold of the empire of God, to rule in your great wisdom. You may worship your God only seeing he is the God of gods."

"What shall we do?" asked the governor over the House of the Chaldeans to the captain over the astrologers. "The greatest honor of the Babylonian Empire except that of the king himself has been given to a faithful keeper of all the laws of Zion, the city we have begged the king to destroy."

The captain over the astrologers said, "As we read the signs, we will continue to read the warning of impending disaster if anyone forsakes the temples of Ishtar and the temples of Marduk. The king knows of the fury of the high priest of these temples if he fails to show for their celebration and to appropriate the gold and silver demanded of these priests."

"All the captives from Zion must be required to worship our gods," adds a leader of the soothsayers. "We must carefully plan awesome events where the king himself is worshipped and convince him to make decrees that allow no exceptions. If we fail our gods we will all pay the price of their rage."

The king has honored all the royalty from his far-flung empire. They speak to him as the Head of Gold. His warriors are winning territory and stretching the boundaries. Many kings and governors volunteer to join the Babylonian Empire to receive his honor and escape his wrath. No king of any city or nation wants to see the warriors of

Babylon outside their walls. The huge casting machines of flaming tar have sent a chill throughout the world. The kings, queens, and lords of the world march to Babylon to bow at the feet of this Head of Gold. The expansion of Babylon brings the entire world to King Nebuchadnezzar's Palace.

Governor Belteshazzar now requests of the king to appoint Shadrach, Meshach, and Abednego to high positions to rule the provinces of Babylon.

The king answers, "You may appoint all three of them to rule under yourself over every affair of this province, but I want you, Governor Belteshazzar, to sit in the gate of the king to give me your divine wisdom and to protect the kingdom for me. Of all my wise men you are the protector over this kingdom of Gold because your God has set it in place as He has designed."

Human Empires and Babylonian Politics

602 BC

Rumors about the king's dream and the narrow escape from death for the respected masters of his religious affairs have sent shockwaves to the farthest corners of the kingdom. The beloved Chaldeans, all the soothsayers, astrologers, and even the magicians had failed their king, and a captive from Zion had come to the rescue. The future and the talk of the gods was the captivating conversation of every political event.

The priests of the gods, represented by the disappointed wise men, are angry. The ancient Epic of Gilgamesh is suddenly the favorite study of learned men. The works of such noted men as he and now called Nimrod by the students of the Scroll, are followed with interest. King Nebuchadnezzar is being compared to that famous warrior and builder. An epic about Nebuchadnezzar had been written and circulated to the ends of the empire, which tells the entire story and exalts the Head of Gold.

In the Province of Zion

In Zion, King Jehoiakim meets with all of his lords and chosen seers. Jeremiah is invited so the court can mock him for his support of Daniel. The news of Daniel's interpretation of King Nebuchadnezzar's dream is the topic of discussion and the pronouncement by

Daniel that the King of Babylon is the Head of gold has angered them beyond despair. All of this company know well of Jeremiah's full support of Daniel's interpretation.

The meeting is held in the outer court of Solomon's Temple. The king intentionally tries to bring spirituality to his rule. Passing beyond the golden pillars and through the beautiful temple doors, the group enters the richly decorated temple. For King Jehoiakim, it is all a show of religious pomp.

Nevertheless to Jeremiah, just to be near God's temple, although compromised and far from the spiritual life of the past, the thrill of the God of Zion fills his soul. His face lights up with the joy of his faith, making his enemies even angrier toward him.

The king's seer Aholibah is the first to speak. He says, "We all know that Jeremiah, who is present at the king's invitation, has betrayed his own nation and is in complete support of the empire of Babylon. Daniel is now the governor of the capital province and Azariah, Hananiah, and Mishael are over all of the affairs of the same. Their triumph is of short life," he declares, "because I have a word from God.

"Listen," he said, "Thus declareth the Lord of hosts. 'I have broken the yoke of the king of Babylon. Within two full years will I bring again into this place all the vessels of the Lord's house, that Nebuchadnezzar, King of Babylon, took away from this place and carried them into Babylon.' "

The seer Jeremiah taunts him by saying, "Amen, and when the words are fulfilled you will know it is from the Lord."

Aholibah approaches Jeremiah quietly and then grabs the yoke of his anointing off Jeremiah's neck suddenly and breaks it. He says, "Thus saith the Lord, 'Even so will I break the yoke of Nebuchadnezzar from the neck of all nations within the space of two full years.' " Jeremiah quickly leaves the meeting, and goes to his private place of prayer.

King Jehoiakim stood up to speak. unaware that one of his

princes is now a watchful eye for the King of Babylon and will quickly report to his contact. He says, "I am in full support of our seer Aholibah and in constant contact with the King of Egypt. His army is retraining and greatly enlarged and preparing to recapture the whole of Palestine. We must consider King Nebuchadnezzar's entire dream as belonging to his gods Marduk and Ishtar. There is nothing to fear, for soon we will be free of the Babylonian warriors stationed outside our walls. We are the chosen nation and people and our modern seers and priests are faithful to this nation."

Everyone present discussed in detail the Epic of Nebuchadnezzar, debating and interpreting the meaning of future empires.

In Medea, King Cyaxares meets with his lords and discusses the dream of his son-in-law. They are in their mountain retreat, high in the loved Elburtz Mountain Chain, not far from the Caspian Sea, hidden away from prying eyes. The poplar and pistachio trees are in full bloom. Roses and clematis blossoms light the path to the retreat. A large flock of herons suddenly rises from the landscape and heads toward the open space of the gleaming waters in the distance.

King Cyaxares cannot help but think of his princess Amytis and the joy she would feel just to be there.

"I fully support the dream of the King of Babylon and commit myself and our nation to be a part of the extended empire of Babylon. The prosperity of the empire is sweeping the world and we are partners in this great wealth. The One World Empire will end all wars and unite the nations for incredible prosperity," says King Cyaxares.

His General Kumrama declares, "We are joining our warriors with the warriors of Babylon. Even as we speak, one hundred thousand of Medean's best are marching across the Euphrates into Palestine to join the Babylonian forces set in array against the land of Egypt. The forces of King Nebuchadnezzar have closed up this past center of world trade for four years and slowly it is falling into defeat. Its once enormous wealth will soon flow into Babylon and

Ecbatana and the wealth of all world trade will become centered in our Empire of Gold."

The conversation turns to discussion of the frightful dream that had captivated the world. One of King Cyaxares' richest lords says, "The next vast empire that was represented by silver sounds like a joining of the Medean and Persian powers. We talk often of the fact that the Persian Nation is really part of Medea. Our mountains are one and our people are spread by families from one end of Medea and Persia to the other. It would be natural for the next grand center of power to flow from the Medean and Persian Mountains."

"Are you a seer?" asked another of the lords.

"No," he said, "but our present unity is between the families of our loved king and his daughter. We have great leaders among ourselves and soon the powers of politics will swing. Even the dreams of King Nebuchadnezzar warn us of that fact. We should never again give up our future to one political direction. The world is ours also."

"Yes," says the king, "I agree that there are great men among our Medean and Persian Nations and the future is for all of us. The World Empire must belong to one and all. The great king presently is my son-in-law, but the future will shift and all nations must learn to give honor to each other. The strong whom the gods will choose will rule in the end."

In the province of Egypt, King Necho II has suffered one humiliating defeat after another at the hand of the Babylonian warriors. His borders have been violated over and over and any effort to launch an attack back toward Palestine, Syria, or Lebanon has failed. King Necho II has constantly assured King Jehoiakim that he would come to his rescue but each new thrust north has been driven back in defeat. He summons his council of Lords to a retreat in Southern Egypt on the west side of the Nile River far below the areas that have been violated by the Babylonian warriors. Nearly half of Northern Egypt has been raided and stripped of its wealth by their forces. The king knows that all of Egypt is in danger. The Egyptian palace on the Mediterranean Coast has been sacked. Even the gold that was upon the pillars and doors has been removed.

The news of King Nebuchadnezzar's dream and Daniel's interpretation has left his army even more broken in spirit. Every effort to move north has been defeated as the warriors of Syria and Lebanon have joined forces with the warriors of Babylon. The trade routes thru Palestine into or out of Egypt have been closed completely. The news of an additional reinforcement of one hundred thousand Medean warriors has been confirmed. Any nation that allows trade with Egypt is being warned of future consequences. Egypt is thus forced into isolation and her people suffer.

Turning to his gods and soothsayers, Pharaoh Necho II pleads for advice, "I must hear from our god Horus or Isis, your silence is causing our nation tremendous fear. My warriors are living under dark omens and clouds of disappointment." He threatens, "Divine for me the future or I shall slaughter you and your households."

Trembling, the Master of all the wise men answers, "Every sign among our priests and sorcerers is presently foreboding but the times will change and our gods will triumph. We all know of the wars that rage between the many gods but Horus has prevailed before. Marduk and Ishtar may be strong now but all will pass. The news from Babylon shows us that it was the God of Zion that was triumphant in interpreting King Nebuchadnezzar's dreams. Maybe Zion's God is confusing the gods of Babylon."

A lord of the Pharaoh's Council of mighty men responds, "We have word from Zion that the king's seer has promised that the yoke of Babylon will be broken within two years from the neck of all nations. We must wait while we build our warrior's strength. Egypt will triumph soon. We must not forget that the king's dream spoke of another man and empire that would replace the Head of Gold. I believe that will be Egypt when our gods are strong again."

The Scroll Believers are comforted by the news that Daniel is now the Governor of Babylon. Jeremiah has gone quickly to the home of Hananiah where all the families of Azariah, Mishael, and Daniel were meeting with Hananiah family. A few trusted friends that also loved the Scrolls had been invited. Each of them had acquired a copy of the Epic of Nebuchadnezzar and had read of the great dream. They knew immediately that the same God that inspired their Scrolls had inspired this dream and Daniel's interpretation. Everyone was ecstatic with joy.

"God is in control," were the first words of Jeremiah. "We live in a dark time and judgment fills our land but when you know it's all the work of our God, it is comforting. I have assurance that King Jehoiakim will be removed from the throne here in Zion within days and Zedekiah will be placed in his stead. He will be better only for a short time because our princes will force him into their mold. It's all politics!

"It's evident that our sons and fellow believers are truly impacting Babylon. The report by Hilkiah and Huldah of their strong faith and acceptance with the king and queen is encouraging. The temple choir, now in Babylon, only serves to enhance the strength of Daniel and the others. They are doing what our God told me to write for us all."

Hilkiah, Azariah's father, says, "My fellow believers, my opinion is we will all soon be captives in Babylon. The politics of Zion is corrupt and that will make it impossible for King Nebuchadnezzar not to destroy our city. Solomon's temple has been stripped within to pay tribute and buy time but as Jeremiah and our other seers have declared, the temple itself will be destroyed. None of us will live long enough but it will be rebuilt when all have learned to obey the Scrolls. Our God is worthy to be praised."

Hananiah's father mentioned the king's dream. "I'm overwhelmed with the great future picture in this dream that Daniel interpreted. We have no idea of the time frame but to think of the final kingdom when God shall end human empires is grand. Remember Abraham spoke of a city with foundations. Our human empires are all built on sand but the future day is coming when the gods will cease their warring and the God above all flesh will establish an empire that will never end. Zion will certainly be at the center of that empire."

In the province of Babylon, the Babylonians read the Epic of their king, now called the "Head of Gold." Mostly they live for the present and talk only of the grandness in which their lives are filled. Their homes are rich and decorated with the treasures of the world. Celebrations and pleasures are daily delights and the whole city is full of flesh. King Nebuchadnezzar is careful to see that every Babylonian gets a share of the vast river of riches that is flooding the capital.

As two Babylonians are walking down the breathtaking sidewalk of the Processional with enormous lions of colored ceramics towering beside them, the Epic of the king is the main topic of conversation. "It is wonderful to know that Babylon, right here in ancient Sumer, is again the center of the world," states an older gentleman proud to be a Babylonian. "My grandfather told us of long ago when everyone knew that our marshes and the Garden of Eden were the birthplace of man. The south of Babylon is still rich in nature but he told us of a harvest time far greater than the present. It's like the world of Chaldea has been born again."

His friend responds, "King Nebopolasser, and now his son King Nebuchadnezzar, have given us new life. The temple of Marduk and the temple of Ishtar are surely responsible. But why did the wise men out of our temples fail to interpret the dream? Governor Belteshazzar, from the temple in Zion that we have often feared, saved all of them from death. I'm glad we Babylonians worship all the gods. If one fails, another can help."

"Yes," answers his friend, "But we are told by the wise men that Belteshazzar will not worship our gods, and the king is so relieved that he can sleep again that he gave him permission to worship only his God. Maybe they are just jealous and that is why they are warning us about the danger of people from Zion. Even the warriors have become political and mistrust the four powerful young men that the king exalts so openly."

The elderly gentleman responds, "But everyone admits their impressive abilities as administrators and the fairness of everything they do. They are so different from the other wise men, called Chaldeans, who are talking all the jealous talk. Everyone knows that Governor Belteshazzar calls their king the 'Head of Gold.' How can he be an enemy if he is the king's friend and choice to govern Babylon for him?"

The Epic of Nebuchadnezzar has exalted the king throughout the Golden Empire. Even his enemies are careful to give the king no reason to distrust them. Their negative talk is always anonymous. Arioch, the Captain of the King's Guard, is a fan of Belteshazzar and his three vice governors. Carefully, he restricts the wise men that failed the king and their political cronies from any opportunity to do harm to the king.

To Belteshazzar, Arioch promises, "Governor, you have proven your faithfulness to Babylon and to the king and I am extending guards over you and the vice governors. Even the Crown Prince Amel-Marduk bears watching, but he must never know of my suspicion. The queen has spoiled their children and they are not being prepared to rule when their father is gone. Queen Hanna often reprimands her, and even begs Queen Amytis to be tough and to force the children of the king to grow up in wisdom and royal abilities."

He continues, "In this amazing interpretation of the king's dream, the next empire was announced as inferior to the present. Do you imagine that the dream suggests that his sons will fail or that another great empire will destroy Babylon and rule the world?"

Belteshazzar simply answers, "Only God that rules can answer that question. My duty is to serve King Nebuchadnezzar and protect his kingdom as long as I live."

Worship Before the Golden Image

594 BC

Leaving Babylon to travel south is a picturesque experience for all Babylonians. The fertile fields and groves with their marvel of constant canals flowing with water from the Euphrates River create abundance. Tall palm groves bearing their abundance of sweet dates are most often swaying in the desert breeze. Banana and pineapple plants in perfect rows by the thousands line the roadway. Passion fruit trees are in abundance as well as papaya and many others. Southern Mesopotamia cannot be called less than the Garden of Eden. The countryside of Babylon is where the life of plenty found its source. The residents in Babylon often said, "What good is gold if there is no food."

The many rural communities along the southern route are home to tens of thousands, especially captives from Haran, Carchemish, Syria, Lebanon, and Zion. Their homes were mostly brick from the leftover abundance rejected by the quality demands of the walls and buildings in Babylon. There were plenty of life's necessities, although a very simple life. One such large community was home to the captives from Zion. The members of Zion's choir had been provided with the better homes and living conditions although placed in this rural area a short distance from the city.

Every captive could eventually earn the right for self-expression in his or her choice of profession and build his or her own home in the higher-class communities. The members of the choir had finished this period and were quickly acquiring professional standings in the Babylonian life.

The wise men of Babylon were planning a religious celebration and had received permission to create a staggering statue. They chose an area called Dura that was adjacent to the Zion community. This choice of location is clearly connected to their distaste for the God of Zion. These men are utterly jealous of Belteshazzar, his friends, and the Zion Choir loved by the people of Babylon, especially the king and queen and Queen Hanna, the king's mother. They are extremely fearful for their temples and its ideas of religion being forsaken by the people of Babylon.

Governor Belteshazzar plans a visit with the key leaders in the Zion community to address their concerns. Samuel, a devoted lover of the Scrolls, has been chosen to supervise their community. His leadership has turned their little city into a model of discipline, order, and prosperity. Loved by everyone in the community, Samuel quickly gains respect throughout the province.

Samuel says, "Governor Belteshazzar, our community knows that the wise men have chosen this area because they dislike our God and our faithfulness to Him alone. They also have promoted a whispering campaign against you and your three assistants over the entire province. Please help us know how to remove the distrust and prove our loyalty to life here in Babylon. We want to be neighbors to everyone and obey the words of our Scrolls at the same time. This huge statue of worship is going to tower over us day and night."

Governor Belteshazzar wisely answers, "My fellow worshippers, the world has many gods, many temples, and makes many religious pronouncements. Our duty is to fear none of that and not to react to anything that is done or said. Anyone can believe and do right when they are near our temple in Zion and surrounded by believing friends but the real is as wonderful when we are surrounded by something so different."

Looking at Samuel, he says, "You have already earned a good

reputation by your example; teach everyone in your community to do the same and in the end of all things right will prevail. There is no reason to fear a statue that neither moves nor speaks. Those who know God also know that there are no accidents with Him.

"Remember what our seer Jeremiah said to us: 'Build ye houses, and dwell in them; and plant gardens, and eat the fruit of them; Take ye wives, and beget sons and daughters; and take wives for your sons, and give your daughters to husbands, that they may bear sons and daughters; that ye may be increased there, and not diminished. And seek the peace of the city whither I have caused you to be carried away captives, and pray unto the Lord for it: for in the peace thereof shall ye have peace.'"

After Governor Belteshazzar leaves to return to the palace, Samuel meets with his entire community to encourage them and read again those words from Jeremiah. After reading these words to everyone, they took heart and enjoyed a peaceful evening. Samuel says to the people, "We are strangers here in Babylon, yet we are prospering greater than many of our friends in Zion. Our king is still defiant against the faithful seers. We have learned that Ezekiel is being removed here to Babylon to live among us. We will have one of the highest respected of all the seers right here teaching us the way of our God. Turn your eyes from all that disturbs and look away to the promise. Be model citizens and soon you will all be greatly blessed because it always happens to anyone from Zion."

The area of Dura is suddenly alive with workers. In the center of at least twenty-five acres, the statue will be built and the foundation is under construction. The platform is first finished at least twenty feet in height. The feet are formed and the legs begin to take shape. A mound of earth is laid around the entire statue so the workers can be raised and the material brought up a ramp. Only a few feet of the statue can be seen and then the mound is raised. It is evident that the work is a work of art and Babylon's best are hurriedly following the design of the wise men.

A leader of the Zion community approaches Samuel and asks, "Do you know of whom or what god this statue will represent? It is clearly a very rich undertaking and unforeseen honor is planned for someone."

Samuel remarks, "I believe it will be of King Nebuchadnezzar because the soothsayers, Chaldeans, and the other wise men are trying to greatly impress the king. They are still angry over their failure, and are jealous over the governor's interpretation. Men who think themselves wise and that have been embarrassed never give up trying to even the score. It is evident we will know very soon."

In a few weeks, the statue is fifty feet high and appears to be only near the waist. The mound is now very large and growing and nothing of the statue can be seen. An enormous amount of materials is brought by the captives. Every new group of captives is made to work long hours and given little time to think about home. Once a captive is broken in spirit, the hours are reduced and the food is both increased and improved. A few months serves to condition the captive to his surroundings and Babylonian citizens are developed out of them. The ways of the Chaldean sorcerers is captivating to the people. Queen Amytis opens her heart to her king. "Nabu," she says and immediately the king scorns her for using the name from the past.

"Queen Amytis," he said, being very proper and dominant. "I am your king also and we will not use the names of our youth. I am the Head of Gold and by great wisdom, I rule the Babylonian Empire."

"King Nebuchadnezzar," she responds with a bit of sarcasm in her voice, "I love you as I always have and always will, but I hate the new king that I'm living with. You are letting the voices of jealous men push you toward some idea of the gods. I do not want to live with a god—I want to live with my sweetheart." The king humbles himself for a moment but regains his strong will and moves into his library and shuts the door.

Queen Amytis sits for an extended time alone with her tears. Finally the king returns to their sitting room.

He comes and sits beside her and tenderly touches her hand. After she dries her tears they treat each other once again as Nabu and Amytis, recognizing that the king's enemies and his own pride are forcing him to be someone he is not.

The startling statue is complete behind the ramp of earth and stands ninety feet tall. The mound of earth now covers a large tract of land and completely obscures the image except the head and top of the shoulders. Now the task is to cover the entire statue with solid gold from the top to the bottom as the earthen ramp is slowly removed.

Artisans of the highest quality must melt gold and carefully plate this exceptional statue. Every design of the person's features and appearance must be replicated. Weeks are spent in transforming a statue of brick and molten stone into a statue covered in pure gold. Once the head is finished and the shoulders are covered in the gold, it is clear that the imposing image is King Nebuchadnezzar.

As soon as the queen learns of this effort of the Chaldeans and other classes of the wise men, she is starkly afraid for the king. Her warning to him is being ignored as his pride and haughtiness grows. Even his children are unhappy with a father that has come to believe what his manipulators are saying to him.

Now that the statue is practically finished and the word is being spread to the farthest ends of the empire, the king invites the princes, governors, captains, judges, treasurers, counselors, sheriffs, and all the rulers of the provinces to come to the capital for a celebration. As the time arrives to unveil this artistic statue, no one dares to miss the occasion.

That idea that had begun with his Chaldeans, soothsayers, magicians, astrologers, and sorcerers has now become the king's impetus for greatness. The only man absent at this special occasion from among all his administrators and rulers is Belteshazzar. The king had made a decree with him that he would never be asked to serve or bow before another god but the One that gave interpretation to his dream. Belteshazzar was satisfied that his absents would not be questioned.

Gathered around the gleaming gold statue of King Nebuchadnezzar are his appointed vassal kings and governors from his worldwide empire. Each is attired in the royal apparel of his appointed province. King Jehoiakim from Zion and his lords are present, and all their pomp is a picture of political showmanship.

His judges and sheriffs are dressed in their court robes and caps, and appear ready for the trial of everyone's allegiance. Captains and princes represent a multitude of his officers and appointees. The Empire of Gold and all the exceptional rulers of the world create a spectacular sight. Standing at an extremely visible location and ready for their test are Shadrach, Meshach, and Abednego.

The crier with the king's script in his hand stands to issue the decree. He announces, "To you it is commanded, O, People, Nations, and Languages, that at what time ye hear the sound of the cornet, flute, harp, sackbut, psaltery, dulcimer, and all kinds of music, ye fall down and worship the golden image that Nebuchadnezzar the king hath set up: And whoso falleth not down and worshippeth shall the same hour be cast into the midst of a burning fiery furnace."

Music planned for this occasion was not joyful music but awesome in its power, planned to instill both fear and awe. The entire assembly falls down to worship the image of King Nebuchadnezzar. The worship lasts for hours and no one moves until the music stops.

Immediately, certain Chaldeans approach the king and accuse Shadrach, Meshach, and Abednego of disobeying the worship of the king. They were in their appointed place where the jealous Chaldeans had planned for them but they did not bow or bend. The Chaldeans remind the king: "Thou O, King, hast made a decree, that every man that shall hear the sound of the cornet, flute, harp, sackbut, psaltery, and dulcimer, and all kinds of music, shall fall down and worship the golden image:

"And whoso falleth not down and worshippeth, that he should be cast into the midst of a burning fiery furnace.

"There are certain Jews whom thou hast set over the affairs of the province of Babylon, Shadrach, Meshach, and Abednego; these men, O, King, have not regarded thee: they serve not thy gods, nor worship the golden image which thou hast set up."

Furious, King Nebuchadnezzar sends for the three vice governors of all the province of Babylon. "O, Shadrach, Meshach, and Abednego, do not you serve my god, nor worship the golden image which I have set up?" He asks in frustration. "Now if ye be ready that at what time ye hear the sound of the cornet, flute, harp, sackbut, psaltery, and dulcimer, and all kinds of music, ye fall down and worship the image which I have made; well: but if ye worship not, ye shall be cast the same hour into the midst of a burning fiery furnace; and who is that God that shall deliver you out of my hands?"

It is evident that the king recognizes their names and the abilities of these men. He wants to save them from his own decree without compromising on his part. He offers them a second opportunity.

Their answer is an unflinching expression of their faith in their God. "O, Nebuchadnezzar, we are not careful to answer thee in this matter.

"If it be so, our God whom we serve is able to deliver us from the burning fiery furnace, and he will deliver us out of thine hand, O, King.

"But if not, be it known unto thee, O, King, that we will not serve thy gods, nor worship the golden image which thou hast set up," declares the accused men from Zion. The king was full of rage; a vicious rage like he had never manifested before. Being defied was not one of his virtues and especially before every mighty name under his kingship.

The king commands the furnace to be heated seven times hotter than before. It becomes an inferno of unbearable heat. The three vice governors are taken, still dressed in the royal garments of their high offices. They are bound, hands and feet, and prepared for death. There is no doubt that the great company of the Babylonian Empire's elite is aghast. The three men that his royal court in Zion considered the worst of enemies were about to be eliminated. They asked why Daniel (Belteshazzar) was not included with the three but the question was lost in the hurry to execute the offenders.

King Nebuchadnezzar is before the entire leadership of his worldwide empire, and three young men in their twenties had defied him. The strongest men of his army are called to prepare and cast the three in the furnace. The king's reputation has been challenged and he will act to restore order to the celebration.

His best and bravest warriors take Shadrach, Meshach, and Abednego and approach the furnace entrance. The heat is unbearable. They keep trying to get close enough to cast the bound victims in, but it is impossible. Finally at the king's command, they make a dash to the entrance. As the best of the king's men throw the men into the furnace, their clothes burst into flames. Right before the eyes of the king's world leaders, they are cremated and turned to ashes. It is a critical moment for King Nebuchadnezzar and the Golden Empire.

The Fiery Furnace Epiphany

594 BC

An intelligent young man of uncommon stature named Sinbabel, who possessed broad shoulders, strong arms, and high cheekbones, and was a nephew of the king, is one of the six warriors dead. Nahrin, Sinbabel's father and the king's brother-in-law is grief stricken. He is also furious with his brother-in-law, the king, but knows better than to react. Sinbabel, who has been trained from his youth to be a warrior of the highest quality, and who could have become the general, is now dead.

Another young man of the six dead warriors was the son of Arioch, the captain of the king's guards. His name was Shufnan, the firstborn, and was an exceptionally brave warrior. His complexion was dark, and he had black hair and a quick smile. He was the pride and joy of his parents. The faithful captain, one that the king could trust with his life, is now overwhelmed with sorrow!

While the king tries to salvage the celebration, the families of these six young men try to keep their sanity. The priests of Marduk and Ishtar offer counsel and promise huge honor from the gods for the sacrifice these families have been forced to make. Priest Barshlama, the High Priest of Marduk offers his consolation.

"Marduk is supreme and these three young men from Zion were blaspheming our god when they refused to bow to the king chosen by Marduk to rule Babylon. The unplanned sacrifice of your sons earns them and you grand honor from every god we worship in Babylon."

He promises, "They are already in the realm of the gods." He begs them to be at peace. It appears evident that defending the king was Priest Barshlama's first priority.

Queen Amytis rushes to be at the side of the distraught and troubled king. She had been unhappy from the moment she learned of the statue and the plans of the Chaldeans and the large company of wise men. She is no longer sure the name "wise men" was a proper name for them. So she did not hide her resentment for their troublemaking tendency. She is faithful to defend her man in public even if she considered him at fault. She also tells him her opinion in private regardless of his attitude.

Immediately at his side, she is like a rock of strength. She silently prays, "O, God of Belteshazzar, I do not know you but I honor you. I pray for my husband the king. I believe that you have put him on his throne and I beg for him to recognize that fact. Reveal to him again your power as you did by his dream. If I can know you, I will serve you and honor you as my God. Belteshazzar is your servant and these three men slaughtered by the king were also. I believe and I pray for their souls."

For several hours the red-hot furnace has roared. Finally it is cooling and can be approached to remove the ashes of the six warriors sent to death by their king. The king must display his sympathy for Babylon's best that had died because of his unbending rage.

The queen has tempered his anger and helped him clear his head. Belteshazzar stands beside the king and has received the king's regrets and sorrow. The king now sees what his religious elite have done to him in their misguided zeal to appease and regain his loyalty. Belteshazzar is devastated, weeping for the loss of his loyal friends of the Scrolls. It is a terrible moment for Governor Belteshazzar.

King Nebuchadnezzar arises from his royal throne that is located in a beautiful concave at the highest level near the golden

statue. As he starts to move to be near the ashes of his slain warriors, astonishment fills the king's face. For minutes he cannot speak
but simply gazes into the entrance of the huge furnace that is still
exceedingly hot on the inside. He then arises quickly and speaks
loud enough for the entire elite of his world empire to hear. He
turns to his chosen counselors, the very best of Babylon, including
Governor Belteshazzar. He asks, "Did not we cast three men bound
into the midst of the fire?"

They answer him in unison, "True O, King."

He then says to them and all of the company of his empire, "Lo,
I see four men loose—loose—walking in the midst of the fire, and
they have no hurt." Belteshazzar's heart leaps with overwhelming joy
and excitement, but he cannot disrupt the king.

"And the form of the fourth is like the Son of God." He repeats
it again with amazement. "The form of the fourth is like the Son
of God." The king forgets royal decorum and moves hastily toward
the very mouth of the furnace. It is still a burning fiery furnace but
now reduced from the sevenfold level of heat the king demanded in
his fury.

Standing near the furnace, he cries out toward the entrance,
"Shadrach, Meshach, Abednego, my celebrated governors of the
Babylonian province, ye servants of the most high God, come forth
and come hither."

The eyes of every person present are suddenly watching the
entrance as they stand in amazement. It is unbelievable! Every religion in the world talks of miracles and paranormal events, but few
have seen them. The king's demeanor leaves no doubt that something has occurred that cannot be explained.

Shadrach, Meshach, and Abednego quickly walk out of the
flames right before the multitude, fully dressed and untouched by
the fire. The king's princes, governors, captains, and counselors, still
gathered together, see that the fire has no power over these men. Not
a single hair of their heads is singed, nor were their coats changed,

nor the smell of fire had passed on them. They had been totally protected from the flames.

This God of Belteshazzar has upstaged the king before and now again. Yet without hesitation, King Nebuchadnezzar declares, "Blessed be the God of Shadrach, Meshach, and Abednego, who hath sent his angel, and delivered his servants and that has changed the king's word, and yielded their bodies, that they might not serve nor worship any god, except their own God.

"Therefore I make a decree that every people, nation, and language, which speak anything amiss against the God of Shadrach, Meshach, and Abednego, shall be cut in pieces, and their houses shall be made a dunghill: because there is no other God that can deliver after this sort."

The next act of the humbled king is to promote Shadrach, Meshach, and Abednego in all the province of Babylon. His decree above will, at least for a season, stop the whispering campaign against the servants of the Scrolls and the God of Zion. King Nebuchadnezzar realizes that every act of man relates to the god he serves. The battles of the world are the battles of the gods being fought on the human plane and which god a man serves, determines his actions and character.

Later that day King Nebuchadnezzar and Queen Amytis are finally alone in their palace sitting room. "Amytis," the king says, "Your grand wisdom that you spoke to me days ago was very wise and I am honored that you are my queen. I have such a tendency toward a proud and haughty heart and it will be my defeat unless I can overcome. I remember when we spoke years ago about the gods and we mentioned learning of other gods and even of a God that is above all gods. I am certain that we saw the action of that God today that is above all gods."

"Yes," she says, "As I sat beside you in the concave prepared for your honor and near the statue I prayed to Belteshazzar's God. I was heartsick over the three celebrated vice governors I thought were destroyed and I am still full of grief over the talented warriors you sent to death. I prayed to that God that I do not know. I must tell you, my Nabu that this is the God I plan to serve. I will not grieve you in being outspoken about it, but I respect Belteshazzar and Shadrach, Meshach, and Abednego. They are the kindest men that serve you and they are protectors of your empire behind your back."

"Amytis, how can I repay my brother that lost his son, Sinbabel, or my captain of our guards that lost Shufnan, both whom we loved so dearly? They have visited our sons since they were kids and they often played together. As teenagers they hunted, fished, and spent time at our home in the marshes."

"My king, Nabu," Amytis answers, "First, let's plan a great banquet here in the palace for all six families and open our hearts and let the grief pour out. Also we must set up a memorial of all six in a special place beside the Processional so that we will never forget them. We must ask their families' forgiveness for our failure."

"I agree," he said.

Belteshazzar, Shadrach, Abednego and Meshach spend the next day in the Zion community beside Dura. The word has started to spread through the empire of the great miracles and the king's decree that Zion's God can no longer be spoken evil of by anyone. It will take days to reach Zion itself and the complete extent of the kingdom.

Governor Belteshazzar appears to tower above everyone. He is required to wear the royal attire of his high office and everywhere he goes the people are quick to bow. The same honor has been bestowed on Shadrach, Meshach, and Abednego. As they enter the Zion community, the response is breathtaking. The four governors of the Babylonian province are simple men and immediately receive their honor but then request to be treated as fellow believers in the Scrolls. Belteshazzar starts first and opens his heart to everyone, "I want all of us to pause and honor the six slain warriors of our Babylonian best. They were brave men and their families are grief stricken."

Everyone stood silently and then Abednego prayed, "O, God of our fathers, we pray for peace in Babylon and in Zion. We pray for the six families of the slain men. We pray for our king and queen here in Babylon as well as our king and queen in Zion. We trust You, O, God of heaven, for Your wisdom in all of our lives. Give our King Jehoiakim and his princes in Zion wisdom to submit and save our city and our temple. Amen."

Belteshazzar continues, "Yesterday, our God gave our friends one of the sovereign miracles that our Scrolls tell us about. Remember when you were so worried about the statue and I told you that right always prevails if we do right. What a wonderful thing has occurred that will inspire all of our Scroll families back in Zion.

"The 'Son of God' that the king saw in the furnace was really the eminent Deliverer to come that all of the faithful lovers of the Scrolls look and wait for. Remember Isaiah, one of our seers that wrote of His day in the future. He said that His kingdom would be an everlasting kingdom. King Nebuchadnezzar's dream told of a celebrated Stone cut out without hands that would end all empires to establish an everlasting empire ruled by that 'Stone.' The fourth man that he saw yesterday was that 'Stone,' the head of the corner."

"Here we are in Babylon," says Belteshazzar. "And our God is revealing the future to us. I'm going to write about it so everyone can read God's plan for the future. Where God's revelations are being revealed there is always peace, and we must be at peace right here in Babylon."

Shadrach speaks, "Yesterday was my first moment to be in the literal presence of God. As we walked and talked in the furnace, the Son of God told us of His glorious day in the future. We were instructed to never doubt what He gives His seers that are true to Him. He also reminded us that when we walked out of the furnace, He would stay inside for everyone that must enter because of their unbending faithfulness, He will always be there waiting on us. Remember the burning bush and Moses, or Elijah that ascended in a whirlwind of fire. Our God is a consuming fire.

"Our hearts were greatly saddened when we heard King Nebuchadnezzar's voice calling to us to come out of the furnace. We could have stayed with the Son of God in that place of His revelation forever."

The location of Dura becomes a favorite spot that almost every visitor to Babylon comes to visit and see. The Zion community is appointed the keeper of all of Dura and provided guides to give visitors the official tour with the true story of their God's faithfulness. It came to be known as the Dura Gardens. It will be filled with flowers and trees from the hills of Zion. The Zion communities immediately begin to plan a beautiful Zion temple where regular prayer and worship will occur to their God.

When the news reaches the city of Zion, the Scroll lovers are full of the joy of their God. King Jehoiakim has returned and is still determined to resist Jeremiah's words and to expect an end to the Babylonian control of his kingship and of the city of Zion. King Nebuchadnezzar's watchful eye over King Jehoiakim through one of his princes has convinced the king that Jehoiakim must be replaced. When the King Jehoiakim was in Babylon for the celebration, he shunned Belteshazzar, Shadrach, Meshach, and Abednego, and when the three vice-governors were delivered out of the furnace the Zion king made light of it.

King Nebuchadnezzar consults with Belteshazzar about King Jehoiakim. Belteshazzar has labored tirelessly to save Zion and the temple from being destroyed. The King of Babylon honors his governor and has acted patiently to save Zion himself. No other city has been given so many years to end its rebellion.

The warriors of Babylon march with their king himself toward Palestine. After the death of six of his beloved strong warriors, the king wants to be with his men. Everyone speaks of their deaths as such a waste, especially when Shadrach, Meshach, and Abednego were found to be alive. When he reaches Zion, he immediately calls for King Jehoiakim and puts him in chains. He replaces the king with his sixteen-year-old son Jehoiachim, and then marches for a foray into Egypt with all of the warriors that came with him and those already stationed in Southern Palestine along with the one hundred thousand from Medea.

While King Nebuchadnezzar and his warriors are deployed near Egypt, King Jehoiachim hears a false report that Egypt has defeated the Babylonian warriors, driving out the large contingent of Babylon's warriors that were enforcing the rule of King Nebuchadnezzar. When Nebuchadnezzar is leaving Egypt after the defeat of Egypt's warriors he hears of King Jehoiachim's rebellion and returns to Zion to replace him. He is replaced with an uncle named Zedekiah, a strong prince in the city.

King Nebuchadnezzar speaks directly to the new king. "Honorable King Zedekiah," he says, "I am giving you a grand opportunity to save your city and your breathtaking temple, but this is my last act of patience. I am taking your seer, Ezekiel, greatly respected, and ten thousand of your best men and their families. This is my warning and proof that your city will suffer total destruction if I march across the vast desert to return again to settle your defiance."

The families of Daniel, Azariah, Michael, and Hananiah are all removed to Babylon along with Ezekiel. The condition in Zion grows worse by the day and the faithful lovers of the Scrolls prefer life under Daniel and their friends in full control of Babylon rather than life under the rebellious leaders and king in the city of Zion, their own city.

It is clear that the center of the Voice of their God has shifted to Babylon. Now that Ezekiel is headed to Babylon, at least some of the Scrolls are going to be written in this strange land where many gods are vying for control. The Scroll lovers know that being in the middle of true history in the process is challenging to anyone listening for the Voice of God.

As they trek along at a hurried pace Daniel's father Ithamar starts the conversation. "We have expected this forced move to Babylon for months. It's a relief to be on our way where our sons have made such an impact for our God. Only eight years of the seventy years determined for our nation to be in bondage have passed. I'm ready to begin life in this strange city and make the best life possible for my family and make sure they are prepared to be faithful until the promised day."

Hilkiah, Azariah father, says, "We have not had an occasion to pray together and thank God for our sons' deliverance. That was a wonderful miracle and even greater is the revelation of our future Deliverer. The 'Son of God' that appeared in the furnace with our sons will someday appear to all of us. Our faithful seers have promised that triumphant day when all shall look upon Him."

As they converse together, traveling with ten thousand of Zion's most prosperous and talented citizens. They are being hurried across the arid desert with every possession they are allowed to carry. Children weep from exhaustion and empty stomachs. It is a miserable situation but only slightly worse than circumstances had become in Zion. They have been promised that they are headed for a city of gold and a new life of plenty.

The friends of the scrolls make every effort to be close together and are trying hard to encourage every one of the captives. The families of Governor Belteshazzar and the vice governors, Shadrach, Meshach, and Abednego have been identified to the warriors and they are careful to give preference and comfort to them. These families show respect and appreciation for the kindness but request to be treated the same as all the other captives. They desire no difference between themselves and the rest of the ten thousand captives.

22

Zion's Choir Singing in Babylon

596 BC

When King Nebuchadnezzar arrives back in Babylon after placing Zedekiah on the throne in Zion, he calls for a notable celebration of peace in the Golden Kingdom. Governor Belteshazzar and his three vice-governors have organized an impressive financial system and gold fills Babylon's treasure houses. The entire Babylonian Empire has a single currency and wealth increases to every province. Far away kingdoms join the Golden Empire; some with delight and some out of fear.

The governing system that Governor Belteshazzar developed in the Babylonian province is quickly imported to every part of the empire. A college institution is established under the Babylonian governors where the financial and governing principles can be taught throughout the world. Nebuchadnezzar is the king and Belteshazzar is the governing brain of his one world Golden Empire.

Governor Belteshazzar is out for a stroll and, as always, is flanked by awesome appearing guards. He has found the Zion Choir gathered by the river of the Euphrates. The Choir just left the practice of the day to picnic together in a beautiful park on the bank of the Euphrates River. As they were practicing and singing the songs of Zion, a spirit of gloom had sweep over the entire crowd. They are at the "Willow Tree Park" and their musical instruments are hung on the willow branches while they picnic and talk of the temple in Zion.

After encouraging the choir, the Governor continues to walk along the edge of the river on the beautiful stone path. The choir director Mahalath follows him. The willows are breathtakingly beautiful. The towering walls of the city pass nearby and the water rushes under the wall from outside and almost explodes through the city waterway. Stopping at a bench, they talk about the coming "Celebration of Peace." The choir director says, "Governor Belteshazzar, our choir and musicians are having a tough day. When we begin to practice for the celebration we cannot help but think of Zion and our temple and the growing poverty among those still trying to survive. With the splendor that surrounds us, we still long for the rolling hills of Palestine. We think of the figs, of the pomegranates, and the beautiful vineyards of grapes.

"Governor," he continues, "We are terribly homesick. These dear Babylonians love our music and our songs about our God and His Words, but they are still so different from us! They love our music because it is happy music and our lyrics and musical sounds touch deep in the human soul, but they still fear our God that we love so deeply."

The Governor opens his heart to his friend, knowing his words are confidential. He replies, "I understand your homesickness and I, just like all of you, will never allow myself to forget Zion. My heart longs for home and to simply look on the beautiful stone-walls carved out of our hills. Yet I know that I will never see those walls until the day of the eternal kingdom. I often weep and three times every day I open my windows west directly toward Zion and pour out my heart to our God that chose that city." The two grown men, Governor Belteshazzar and the excellent choirmaster of Zion's choir weep together as they talk about their longing for the City of Zion.

Suddenly, Governor Belteshazzar has an idea. "I'm going to write a song about our home and heritage and especially about Zion. At the grand 'Celebration of Peace,' I will dedicate it to all of those that love our scrolls and honor our City of Zion. I will be careful to honor everyone in Babylon that has been brought as captives and make mention of their home also. I will also speak of Babylon lovers and make the song honorable to everyone. Home is where the heart is and this song can be the most memorable of all at this grand celebration."

Master Mahalath leaps from the bench where he sat in enthusiasm. He declares, "Governor Belteshazzar, the choir will be ecstatic! We will learn the song, write the most beautiful music, and sing it with mirth in our hearts. I have learned that every sorrow that births a song is worth the tears we shed. I promise you that our choir will not disappoint." The governor hurries to his living quarters while the choirmaster goes quickly to give the good news to his great singers and musicians.

Mahalath rushes up to all of them and shouts, "I have big news for you! The governor is going to write a song about us, and our sadness for home. He has experienced the same tears you and I are shedding and he also longs for Zion. He just shared with me that he opens the window of his prayer room toward Zion three times a day and pours out his heart to his and our God. It's thrilling to know that our governor right here in Babylon is not just from our home but he is one of us in his heart."

The choir has labored for weeks to perfect their concert to all of Babylon. From the picnic in Willow Tree Park, they have been encouraged and determined to sing their new song written by the governor and to absolutely touch every heart. The music is perfect and cannot be sung without shouts and praise filling the practice hall. It is a song worthy to be sung by every homesick person for ages to come. They already knew that this song would someday be listed in the Psalms of their Scrolls.

The celebration begins with much fanfare. Every temple had its special event. The huge stadium hosted event after event and the city was one giant bazaar with every delicate food available to all. The arts and drama lovers sponsored many expressions of interest most often dedicated to one of the gods worshipped in the empire. The closing event in the Stadium was announced as the "talented Zion Choir and Its Master Musicians." With the gods being promoted in almost every event, no one could complain when the choir expressed their love for the God of Zion.

The grand stadium is filled to capacity. Small groups of the singers and musicians had conducted short skits announcing their concert and presenting a taste of their superb talents.

King Nebuchadnezzar and Queen Amytis arrive early so as not to miss a note. Queen Hanna sits with the king and his family. The king has asked the governor to sit with him so every word of the songs and comments of the choir could be interpreted.

Harpists open the event with melodious music that teased the ears of every person. Following the harpists is a cornet selection that brought the crowd to their feet with earsplitting applause. Selection after selection from skillful choir numbers to special music, to solos, is played and sung. Miriam dance songs taken from the celebration she led following triumph at the Red Sea were favorites. It thrills the Babylonians when the choir sang of their victory against Egypt. Each number is tastefully presented to inspire, even convict, but never to condemn.

When the time comes for the grand song written by the governor, he asks the king for permission to present this song as his tribute to all the captives of his beloved home and City of Zion. The king is delighted to agree.

"As your governor of all of Babylon," he begins, "I am proud to serve our king and his queen and all of you, to make our city and community a very wonderful place in which to live. It is the most beautiful city in the world; there is no doubt.

"But as all of you know I came to Babylon as a captive of Zion. It is the city of my birth and the location of the temple of my God. I have loved the City of Zion and always will remember the golden temple where I delighted to worship my God.

"This talented choir that you are enjoying is singing the songs of my temple in Zion. It's not easy for our choir of master musicians and remarkable trained voices to sing our temple songs in a strange city. All of us were taught from our very first memory to never forget Zion and our heritage. We cannot forget.

"Therefore with the king's permission I am dedicating a new song that I wrote for this choir to every captive from my homeland. I also dedicate it to those of you from other famous cities and lands because you grow homesick for those places of memory. I dedicate it to every Babylonian that embraces this place of your birth and who loves to call this Babylon your home always. No memories are greater than our childhood ones.

"I found this celebrated choir weeping in your park called Weeping Willow Park. Their musical instruments were hanging on your willow trees and I penned this song to remember our Homeland that we call Zion. It is dedicated to everyone that loves home, father, and mother, grandparents, and just to walk where we walked as children.

"This choir calls this song 'A Masterpiece.' I call it 'Home.'"

"Sing it choir," Governor Belteshazzar says, and with tears, he walks to his seat beside King Nebuchadnezzar.

As they sing, they act out every line and every emotion and the large crowd is filled with memories and joys of the past.

"The Masterpiece"

By the rivers of Babylon
There we sit down
Yea, we wept, we wept
When we remembered Zion

We hung our harps
Upon the Willows thereof

For there they that carried us away captives
Required of us a song

And they that wasted us
Required of us mirth
Saying, saying to us
Sing us one of the songs of Zion

How shall we sing
How shall we sing
The Lord's song
In a strange land

If I forget thee
O, Jerusalem, O, Jerusalem,
Let my right hand
Forget her cunning

If I do not remember thee
Let my tongue cleave
To the roof of my mouth
To the roof of my mouth

If I prefer not Jerusalem
If I prefer not Jerusalem
Above my chief joy
Above, all, my chief joy

The choirmaster Mahalath speaks to the audience at the end,
"We sing of Zion because of home and because of our God. We
invite you to put the name of your home place when we say Zion
and to sing with us your memories. Sing of your mother and father,

the paths you walked as a child, the visit to grandfather's house and the special days when all of you gathered with uncles and aunts."

As the choir sings again, the stadium is filled with voices. You could hear the shouts of people from Samaria, Egypt, Damascus, Haran, Carchemish, and others. It seemed that everyone sang of home and their loved ones and the memories of childhood. There was not a dry eye present as the choir gave them a long and loud encore, over and over again.

The large crowd lingers long as the applause continued to fill the stadium. Captives from many parts of the empire finally believe that someone had thought of them and shown respect to their sorrows and separation. Both relief and sadness fill the stadium.

As soon as Belteshazzar could leave the king's presence, he moves quickly to the practice quarters assigned to the Zion Choir. The king and queen show much interest in the choir and because of the concert; rumors circulate and reach Belteshazzar that every member must receive a liberal stipend from the royal treasury on a regular basis.

Rushing into the practice room with shouts of praise, he exclaims, "You did it! You did it!" He proclaims, "You brought our Zion right into the midst of Babylon." The room erupts with tears of joy and celebrations of praise to the God they know is real.

One King Rules the World

590 BC

never has so much power been in the hands of one man. He could not step out of his ornate world on the north side of the palace without everyone bowing on their faces. His singers serenaded him at every function of the empire. His every dictate is instantly obeyed. He is indeed the "Head of Gold," and the splendor is dazzling.

This world of King Nebuchadnezzar had become a constant contradiction. On the positive side, there was Governor Belteshazzar and his three vice-governors. The Zion Choir was the king's delight, and Queen Amytis was a faithful lover of Belteshazzar's God. His kingdom is now ordered by the dream interpreted by Belteshazzar.

But there is also another side. It is the warring of many gods in a daily struggle for supremacy. The wise men of Babylon never give up their battle to unseat the governor, who is master over all of them. The High Priest of Marduk, Barshlama, is an avowed enemy of every lover of the Scrolls, and his regular proclamations declare death to all of them. Life in Babylon might have been festive on the surface, but it is also unsettled and dangerous in unseen dimensions.

King Nebuchadnezzar meets with his master architect, whose firm of Babylon employs dozens of noble designers. He is one of the king's famous lords, and has been made wealthy by the Golden Empire.

He says, "Lord Neriglissar, our wealth is bulging from our treasury houses and it belongs to all of the empire. I want you to identify the needs of every city in Chaldea, the needs for temples, government buildings, city walls, and paved highways. We must also build a large city and seaport on the gulf to serve the world traders. Tyre has submitted to our empire and her huge ships are now our ships and trade can be expedited and greatly enlarged.

"It's important to me that you start with Uruk and rebuild the temple of Inanna Rebuild the city walls of that ancient city and any other need you find. Appoint a designer over each location and present me the identified needs, the cost, and the laborers needed. Since Babylon's walls and structures are complete there are several hundred thousand captives that need employment to earn the small salaries for their daily needs. I'm assigning you to start moving them into the areas of construction where the workers are needed. All of Chaldea must be a model for the entire world to see."

Lord Neriglissar responds, "I was in Uruk recently and met with the city lords. They shared a number of emergency needs. May I start on the temple and walls immediately, without further delay?"

"Proceed," said the king. Lord Neriglissar then adds, "There is a beautiful location on the coast not far from your father's immense estate. It will be a grand location for a teeming city and a vast seaport." The king understood the exact spot of the site and gave permission to begin. A paved highway was to start at this seacoast town, pass by Uruk, and come straight to Babylon.

King Nebuchadnezzar reminds the Lord, "Do not forget Kippur and Ur. Those cities, and, indeed, every city in Chaldea, must be treated equal. Our wealth is for one and all and I want to be remembered as a defender of all of the boundaries of Mesopotamia. That's what my name means that our celebrated King Nebopolasser, my father, gave me. My mother Queen Hanna spends most of her time at the estate. She will love the seaport city so close to home and the paved highway from there to the capital."

Soon after, Governor Belteshazzar meets with the king in an extended session to discuss Zion. "The news from Zion is very troublesome," the governor declares. "King Zedekiah will not accept the words of Jeremiah, my faithful friend and a reliable seer. He knows every word of the interpretation from your dream, but his political seers are constantly giving him false information. As we talk, Jeremiah is in a dungeon where he will die in a few days if someone does not rescue him. Zion must be the most troubled city in the Babylonian Empire."

"Governor," the king says, "I have been extremely patient with Zion because my father warned me of the powers of your God. Also, I want to save your city for you, Shadrach, Meshach, and Abednego. Your choir has become my favorite, and I respect your God."

The king becomes extremely serious. "Why is it that what I see in you and all the Scroll lovers in Babylon is so different from King Zedekiah and the Scroll lovers that believe in your same God in the city of Zion? Your seers from Zion war with each other just like our priests do in Babylon. How can we believe that your God is any different?

"My Queen Amytis has declared to me her faith in your God and I am pleased because she is so happy when she reads from your Scrolls, especially your Psalms. She has pleaded with me not to touch the city of Zion, but my warriors and our new General Nebuzaradan are disagreeing strongly and demanding that something be done."

The king adds, "I would not allow an illustrious man like your Jeremiah to be left to die in a dungeon because I did not agree with his pronouncement, neither because he has enemies among my lords. You certainly have enemies in Babylon, but I will never allow them to touch you for harm.

"If it comes to pass that we march again to Zion to end the resistance, I will make special provision for Jeremiah and he will be protected. I have already given word to our new General Nebuzaradan that he is to provide for him and let him choose whether to come to

Babylon where you can care for him or to remain in Zion among those of the poor. There is yet a margin of time to save the city if there is something you can do."

The Babylon News Agency is a massive entity. Vice Governor Abednego has been put in total control and trusted by the king to report to him daily of the state of the empire. A massive news office and structure towering over the banks of the Euphrates River is home for this important function. The king issues an edict to be read throughout the empire at all citizens' meetings. It declares "Anyone that dares to harm, impede, or disrupt the free travel of the chariots carrying the news and messages from the king or to the king will be immediately put to death."

Those special chariots carry one personnel from the agency and two warriors and they moved like lightening. Watching them pass so smoothly and swiftly throughout the Golden Empire is both awesome and fearful. Everyone gets the sense that the Head of Gold knows every secret of the massive world of the Golden Empire.

Vice-Governor Abednego has faithful staff members, well paid and respected in every corner of the world. These capable and trained couriers are news savvy and allowed to employ secret representatives that watch every ambassador and government person. They are fully protected by the contingent of warriors in each province. As a show of force often two or more chariots with armed warriors will travel with the news chariots. Stations for changing horses have been established throughout their paths of travel.

The Babylonian Warriors under the new General Nebuzaradan now number over two million strong and growing. These warriors are some of the richest of the empire and always ready to plunder where the least infraction is reported. When they put down rebellion, they also reduce the area to sheer poverty. This is the bonus of their profession.

Well-trained and disciplined, these men are fearsome. When there are rumors of trouble, they move through the area with such a show of efficiency and power that usually the trouble vanishes.

The talk of all the warriors is of Zion and the constant rumors and actions of this rebellious city. Every warrior fears being appointed to this charge. They fear and often hate the God that the enemies of Zion say resides in the golden temple that is visible throughout the city. Most of them long for the day they can destroy this province and the temple. The world of the gods is full of rage.

Unknown to Governor Belteshazzar, Jeremiah is delivered from the dungeon in Zion. King Zedekiah takes Jeremiah secretly out of the prison and brings him to his palace to inquire of the Lord. The warriors of Babylon are encamped about the city and the king was stricken with fear. King Nebuchadnezzar has not yet given permission to attack, but hopes instead to instill fear by their mere presence alone and thus accomplish the goal of complete surrender without use of force. The full forces of the Babylonian warriors are yet to be dispatched from their barracks in Chaldea.

King Zedekiah asks of Jeremiah, "Is there any word from the Lord?"

Jeremiah answers, "There is, for God said, 'Thou shalt be delivered into the hand of the King of Babylon.'"

Then Jeremiah asks of his king, "What have I offended against thee, or against thy servants or against this people, that you have put me in prison?"

The king then commands that Jeremiah be given food as long as there was bread in the city for the city was shut up by the embargo of the Babylonian warriors.

King Zedekiah's princes believe every word of the false seers and actually expect the warriors of Babylon to be found dead each morning. They rise early and secretly look at the warrior camp for signs of life, expecting the false words to be fulfilled. They consider Jeremiah and his proclamations the work of a fool.

When the nobles hear his latest proclamation after he left the palace and is being herded back to prison, they demand his death in the dungeon.

Jeremiah stops the guards that lead him to prison as they passed the temple. There he proclaims the words from God: "Thus saith the Lord, This city shall surely be given into the hand of the King of Babylon's Army which shall take it."

The nobles demand his slow death in the dungeon and the king gave him to their hand.

King Zedekiah says, "Behold he is in your hand for the king is not he that can do anything against you."

These nobles want the most painful death possible for Jeremiah so they lower him into a pit filled with mire. He sank down to his armpits and is unable to sleep or rest. With no water and no food, he will die a miserable death. While all of this was happening, the lovers of the Scrolls were praying in Babylon. Governor Belteshazzar opened his window toward Zion and crying out for deliverance for Jeremiah. The city and the temple are no longer the objects. All was lost because the moment of hope had passed. Jeremiah is their burden.

A slave of King Zedekiah hearing the plight of the seer of God is determined at any cost to deliver him. He goes to the king before all the city and his princes and says without fear, "My Lord, the King, these men have done evil in all that they have done to Jeremiah the prophet, whom they have cast into the dungeon; and he is like to die for hunger in the place where he is: for there is no more bread in the city."

The king must have known that all hope was gone for he says to this Ethiopian slave called Ebed-Melech, "Take from hence thirty men with thee, and take up Jeremiah the prophet out of the dungeon, before he die."

This compassionate black man went swiftly to the dungeon. Knowing that Jeremiah was near death and his skin would be like paper from dehydration, he took old rags and sent them down to Jeremiah to put under his arms. Then he passed down a rope to put under the rags and took the famous old seer up out of the dungeon. Carefully he washed and bathed Jeremiah and fed him his own last piece of bread and small amount of water.

The City of Zion and the Temple of Solomon were lost. The king had dispatched a massive number of his best warriors with their large tar ball machines and chariots without number. The treatment of Jeremiah moves the God of Zion to fill the heart of Nebuchadnezzar with wrath against King Zedekiah. The King of Babylon installed him as his vassal king with instructions and warnings and he did not listen. There can be no further delay. The warriors of Babylon are consumed with rage as they march toward Zion.

The City of Zion in Ruins

586 BC

The walls of Zion are totally surrounded with the greatest army of human history. Governor Belteshazzar, is fully aware that he cannot defend Zion or even try to convince King Nebuchadnezzar to be lenient another day. The placing of the seer Jeremiah, in a pit of mire to starve to death is the last moment for patience. The nobles that rule Zion with King Zedekiah are as vile as the worst of the wise men in Babylon.

Zion is completely closed and has been for months. The city is near to starvation. There is a horde of gold, furniture, and possessions in the homes of the wealthy that the warriors desire to save from destruction and for themselves. They know that an abundance of riches awaits them inside the walls of the golden temple glimmering in the sunlight.

The guards watch every morning for the sign of death in the camp of the Babylonian warriors. The warriors of Babylon themselves have heard the famous story of the Assyrians' utter massacre, and are fearful, even anxious, to end the standoff. Any sickness at all in the camps is treated like an emergency. The whole camp calls upon their gods, Marduk and Ishtar, for protection. The warriors believe that the gods are battling and they wait for the notable omens.

King Nebuchadnezzar arrives at the makeshift headquarters set up at Riblah in the land of Hamath. He immediately takes charge of the battle plans with his General Nebuzaradan. After a full report, he gives direction.

He orders, "Tomorrow at daybreak we will begin to bombard the city with our red hot tar ball machines. Target only the walls to begin. Stay clear of the golden temple and the section where the wealth is most likely to be. After a short time retire for the day after setting a watch for anyone trying to escape.

"On the third day fill the city with arrows raining down relentlessly on them. Do this for the same short time and retire to wait. Do this day by day at short intervals and at different times so that no one dares to be in the opening.

"At interval days renew the bombardment of the walls with the tar ball machines until the walls are weakened and can be beat down by our large battle-rams. This will take some weeks but I want to save our warriors from death.

"While you are slowly destroying the walls and incurring death in the city, set up tents all around the city to roast huge amounts of food for all our warriors to enjoy. Do it at a safe distance from the city. This will have a huge effect upon the morale of the inhabitants.

"Invite them to come out and eat and feed them when they do. Suggest they leave the city to save their own lives. Have our criers who speak Hebrew continue to warn everyone in the city and let anyone leave in peace that desires. All that leave must be stripped of everything but the clothes they wear. Their possessions are for our warriors."

King Zedekiah calls for a meeting with his nobles. He has finally accepted the ultimate. "Where are the promises of Aholibah and all his young seers that continue to bear good news? What good are promises when our city is slowly being destroyed? The walls will soon begin to fall. The Babylonians are wise and are saving the riches of the city for themselves. Hundreds have left to eat their food and then flee to the countryside."

The Seer Aholibah stands to defend himself. He replies, "My words cannot fail because we have the unanimous agreement of all of the seers except for the ancient Jeremiah. Even the nobles of the city begin to jeer him, and suggest they have been fools for listening to him."

The master of King Zedekiah's nobles speaks, "I believe that our city is lost. We should slip out of the city before sunup tomorrow morning. All will surely be destroyed if we stay and fight. Maybe the temple will be spared and further destruction stopped if we leave. The warriors of King Nebuchadnezzar are encamped as far as the eyes can see. We are no match for them. Our God has failed us or else we have failed Him. I vote to leave tomorrow morning—slipping out by the king's garden and the gate between the walls. It is a secret gate and we can escape and return when the warriors have sacked the city." The vote was unanimous and Aholibah slipped out with his head bowed low in defeat.

The high priest, one of the nobles of the king, quickly moves to the temple to hide everything possible. Only he and one other priest know of a secret passage deep beneath the temple. It is the plan created from Solomon's day to protect the temple and its priests. If one of the two died, another faithful priest is chosen. For several hours he and the temple priest remove the most valued of temple possessions. First, the famous Ark of the Covenant is carried by the priest appointed, as prescribed by the Scrolls to this secret location.

They put the grand Altar of Sacrifice, the beautiful Seraphim that overlooked the Ark and every vessel of gold or bronze that was left into hiding. Many of the valued temple possessions had already been used to pay tribute to Babylon. When they had removed everything possible, the secret location was sealed with a special provided closure. Every trace of this secret location was obscured so that anyone coming inside or beneath the temple could not possibly know of this place. Solomon in his remarkable wisdom had planned for such a possibility.

Those that knew of the plans to slip out of the city met at the appointed time and escape. But when the escape of the king is discovered, the warriors of Babylon pursue them with a fury. They are overtaken by Babylon's great chariots and horsemen in the plain of Jericho and immediately captured to stand before the "Head of Gold," King Nebuchadnezzar.

It is a pitiful sight for the lords of Babylon to look upon. Standing before King Nebuchadnezzar is King Zedekiah, all his sons, all the nobles of Judah, and their families.

"King Zedekiah," King Nebuchadnezzar said, "I appointed you carefully to be my king in Zion. I thought I saw nobility in you. Talented men of your city are exceptional leaders of the Babylonian Empire. Your seer, Ezekiel, is faithfully serving your God in Babylon. Your temple choir is composed of the most celebrated singers and musicians in the Golden Empire. Why could you not honorably serve me as your own God has told you to? I have had your Scrolls read to me and I know of their dictates. You are a disgrace to your city and have caused great harm to your own people. What you have done to Jeremiah is vile and I have come to deliver him from your dungeon if he is still alive. I must judge you today and I take no pleasure in doing so."

To his guards, he states, "Slay the nobles of Zion first. Let the king that has failed them watch." As the King of Zion stood the nobles were, one by one with their families, slain before the king's eyes.

He commands, "Slay his sons that they have no opportunity to deceive us as their father did." As King Zedekiah watched, his sons and their families were, one by one, put to death.

Lastly, the king says, "Take this man that is pathetic to me, put out his eyes and put him in chains to march to Babylon when the task of destroying his city is finished." He was quickly blinded and bound and Zedekiah was removed to a garrison of prisoners.

King Nebuchadnezzar gives instructions to his general concerning Jerusalem. He orders, "The lives of everyone in the city are to be spared except in cases of defense. The gold in the city treasury and the temple belongs to the City of Babylon. The riches of the temple are to be placed in the House of Marduk. The immense homes and treasures of the people belong to our warriors. Allow them to freely gather everything of value and then the city must be destroyed. We have been patient and no additional opportunities can be allowed for sedition in this city."

To those noble lovers of Zion, it is a heartbreaking occasion. They are bound and prepared to march to Babylon but required to watch as the warriors of Babylon moved from one house or building to another and loaded large carts with the treasures. It is a time for celebration for the brave warriors that had spent months outside the walls waiting for victory.

The temple walls are slowly stripped of their gold. Huge pillars are dismantled and loaded for someone's mansion in Babylon. Cedar wood is carefully removed to be sold on the world market. Everything from this temple known over the world is sold as a treasure from Solomon's temple.

After days of plundering, the city is emptied and ready to be burned. The people of Zion had been prepared as captives, kept bound for days, and made to sleep in the open. Their last sight before the long march could begin was the burning of Zion and the temple of Solomon. The temple that was the richest structure in the world now lay in ruins, replaced by the enormous palace and Hanging Garden in Babylon.

The huge tar balls and machines of Babylon are put to use as the city is blasted. Every place a tar ball landed bursts into flames. For hours the large machines blasted, one after the other, as fast as they could be loaded. The distinguished Zion is aflame until it is in total ruins. The captives, bound and tied together, including thousands of fathers, mothers, and children, are all gathered at a distance, weeping as they saw their former life come to an end.

As the thousands of Zion families march off toward Babylon, the General Nebuzaradan did not forget the king's instructions. He moves among the captives that were chained together until he finds Jeremiah. He is frail and hardly able to walk. When the general finds him, he has him immediately removed from his bonds and freed.

"Seer Jeremiah," the general said, "King Nebuchadnezzar has personally given instructions to care for you. Your captivity in prison and the placing of you in the pit of mire was for our king the final defiance of King Zedekiah. He did not know of your deliverance from the pit until he was told after King Zedekiah was captured. Our warriors were moved with haste to Zion, hoping to save your life for Governor Belteshazzar's sake. The king was relieved to know you were safe.

"I shall personally tell him of your destination. You may go to Babylon and be greatly cared for or you may return to your estate in Zion country to live among the poor and the farmers that are left. Let me know of your choice and I will appoint someone to care for your trip to Babylon or your return home."

Without hesitation, Jeremiah said, "It is God's will for me to go home to my family and to fulfill my charge before my God. Thank you, Master Nebuzaradan, for your kindness. I appreciate greatly someone helping me in my much weakened condition to reach my desired destination. Please thank King Nebuchadnezzar for his excellent kindness. Please tell him that he and Queen Amytis will be regularly in my prayers to the God of the Scrolls."

Nebuchadnezzar has traveled from Riblah to Zion to watch the final destruction of this troublesome city. He could not help but remember the words of King Nebopolasser, his father, to tread softly toward this city that he said was sacred. Tears actually stained his cheeks as he watched it consumed by fire. If for no other reason, he was sad for Belteshazzar, Shadrach, Meshach, Abednego, and the Zion Choir. They were more faithful to him than many of his own countrymen.

The news arrived in Abednego's office that Zion is in total ruins and the temple destroyed. Abednego goes quickly to see Governor Belteshazzar to share with him the news. The news also includes the safety of Jeremiah and that he is going to his country estate to serve the poor left in Zion Country. Included in the dispatch is a rough count of the captives marching toward Babylon. There are at least fifty thousand, not including children, babies, and the elderly. The only ones left in Zion are the poor. Already, the word was out that any future captives would be placed in the cities where skillful works of improvement were occurring. Also, the new city and seaport on the gulf prepares for several thousand workers plus families. Life will be hard for those that could endure the several weeks crossing the desert on foot chained together. The people struggle, with broken hearts and lives, toward the strange land of Chaldea.

The Zion communities in different locations as well as many Babylonians begin instantly preparing and building small houses and even preparing their own homes for extended guests. By the time the captives arrived, there would be somewhere for them to live. The governor would use his earned respect to give time for rest and recovery before they were worked as slaves in the Babylonian Empire.

Nebuchadnezzar Goes Insane

584 BC

*T*he atmosphere in Babylon is very different now that Zion lay in a ruinous heap. A spirit of deep competition between Babylon and Zion that was evident from the moment Belteshazzar interpreted the king's dream, now intensifies. The wise men representing the many gods of the Middle East are always in battle with the God of Zion, and with Zion destroyed, they believe they have won at last.

However, no one doubts the impeccable leadership ability of Governor Belteshazzar. The endless flood of riches into Babylon forces an uneasy peace. King Nebuchadnezzar and Queen Amytis could attend celebrations in every corner of the empire while the governor and the excellent palace staff kept the empire humming with efficiency. Every city in Chaldea experiences needed improvements. The seaport town on the gulf becomes the world's center for import and export and Babylon is constantly filled with royal guests, entertainers, and business tycoons.

King Nebuchadnezzar and Queen Amytis have just finished a six-month tour celebrating the expansion of the Golden Empire. In Ecbatana, the capital of Medea, they spend days being serenaded and toasted at incredible events with Queen Amytis' parents, the king and queen. The progress in the kingdom of Medea is second only to that of Babylon. The capital city is awash with improvements and filled with the riches of the empire.

King Cyaxares and Queen Akkadiya take their daughter Queen Amytis and King Nebuchadnezzar on an exciting trip into the mountains. This great retreat center of the king near the Caspian Sea becomes the center both of rest and festivity for three days. Medean crowds came in droves to see their princess of years ago and to celebrate the Golden Empire that everyone rejoiced to share. The queen of Babylon, Amytis, still as vivacious as ever spends every moment possible enjoying the beauty of the mountains that she loved. Often she is near to being transported back to the days as a little princess dashing from flower to flower and swooning under the pull of nature's living creatures and exotic birds.

Finally back in Babylon, they visit cities, exploding with progress and full of pride in their king and queen. At the seaport province there is a grand welcome celebration for the boyhood king remembered as Nabu. The king and queen stay at his mother's estate where the king was born. Vast wealth has been poured into the estate just to prepare for the event. The stone paved super highway from Babylon passing by Uruk has been filled with travelers for days.

The food of the king's childhood is prepared for everyone. Water buffalo, fresh seafood, venison, quail, and roasted duck is prepared for tens of thousands of guests. Queen Hanna, retired to her estate, is quite old but was still alive with her happy disposition. To her son she spoke at the important closing moment of the celebration.

"King Nebuchadnezzar," she says, "I remember the day you were born. I knew you came from the gods because I saw the divine in your eyes. My husband was such a wise man and he chose the name Nebuchadnezzar. He was determined that you would bring life back to Chaldea. We had been subject to the Assyrians for so long, and prospered in spite of the tribute and taxes but we wanted to be free.

"My king, you have picked up where your father left off and today I declare you to be the greatest king of all history. Never can there be a king like you again. I honor you, my son and my king; King Nebuchadnezzar."

The praise from his mother causes the king's heart to swell with incredible pride.

Back in the palace at Babylon, the king rejoices in his empire for days. The king and his queen can travel in a style that is beyond description. Their new carriage, totally layered in gold, which had recently been delivered by the finest carriage and chariot building enterprise of the empire, is too marvelous to describe. They prepare to visit every area that has been improved in all Chaldea. The warriors traveling with them are dressed in royal decorum for escorting their king. Crowds gather at every possible location by the thousands and worship him like a god. He is at the height of his glory.

Despite this splendor, the king becomes troubled and sleepless. Queen Amytis grows concerned. Governor Belteshazzar has always been totally open and honest with his superior. He has warned him for days that his sense of pride and self-exaltation could not bring him lasting happiness. Too much honor has pushed the king into a self-centered stupor. Troubled beyond his own ability to understand, he dreams a disturbing dream that fills him with fear.

King Nebuchadnezzar called for his wise men and personally asked for the magicians, astrologers, Chaldeans, and soothsayers. He tells them the dreams, but they could not make the king to know the interpretation. They know that the dream was a dark affair and a dream to excite every enemy of the king. The king's first dream they could not interpret because it was of his glory. This dream they want no part of because it was of his demise.

Then the king sends for his governor of Babylon. "O, Belteshazzar," he says, "Master of the magicians, because I know that the spirit of the holy gods is in thee, and no secret troubles' thee, tell me the visions of my dream that I have seen and the interpretation thereof.

"Thus were the visions of mine head in my bed; I saw, and behold a tree in the midst of the earth, and the height thereof was great.

"The tree grew, and was strong, and the height thereof reached unto heaven, and the sight thereof to the end of all the earth:

"The leaves thereof were fair and the fruit thereof much, and in it was meat for all: The beasts of the field had shadow under it, and the fowls of the heaven dwelt in the boughs thereof, and all flesh was fed of it.

"I saw in the visions of my head upon my bed, and, behold, a watcher and a holy one came down from heaven;

"He cried aloud, and said thus, 'Hew down the tree, and cut off his branches, shake off his leaves, and scatter his fruit: let the beasts get away from under it, and the fowls from his branches:

"'Nevertheless leave the stump of his roots in the earth, even with a band of iron and brass, in the tender grass of the field; and let it be wet with the dew of heaven, and let his portion be with the beasts in the grass of the earth:

"'Let his heart be changed from man's, and let a beast's heart be given unto him; and let seven times pass over him.

"'This matter is by the decree of the watchers, and the demand by the word of the holy ones: to the intent that the living may know that the most High ruleth in the kingdom of men, and give it to whomsoever he will, and setteth up over it the basest of men.'

"This dream, I, king Nebuchadnezzar, have seen. Now thou, O, Belteshazzar, declare the interpretation thereof, forasmuch as all the wise men of my kingdom are not able to make known unto me the interpretation: but thou art able; for the spirit of the holy God is in thee."

Belteshazzar is astonished and for one hour listens to the voice of God concerning the dream. He is troubled for the king and the consequence of what he is about to interpret.

Approaching the king, Belteshazzar replies, "My lord, the dream is to them that hate thee, and the interpretation thereof to thine enemies.

"The tree that thou sawest, which grew, and was strong, whose height reached unto the heaven and the sight thereof to all the earth; whose leaves were fair, and the fruit thereof much, and in it was meat for all; under which the beasts of the field dwelt, and upon whose branches the fowls of the heaven had their habitation:

"It is thou, O, King, that art grown and become strong: for thy greatness is grown, and reaches unto heaven, and thy dominion to the end of the earth.

"And whereas the king saw a watcher and an holy one coming down from heaven, and saying, 'Hew the tree down, and destroy it; yet leave the stump of the roots thereof in the earth, even with a band of iron and brass, in the tender grass of the field; and let it be wet with the dew of heaven, and let his portion be with the beasts of the field, till seven times pass over him.'

"This is the interpretation, O, King, and this is the decree of the most High, which is come upon my lord the king: That they shall drive thee from men, and thy dwelling shall be with the beasts of the field, and they shall make thee to eat grass as oxen, and they shall wet thee with the dew of heaven, and seven times shall pass over thee, till thou know that the most High ruleth in the kingdom of men, and gives it to whomsoever he will.

"And whereas they commanded to leave the stump of the tree roots; thy kingdom shall be sure unto thee, after that thou shalt have known that the heavens do rule."

King Nebuchadnezzar has no better friend than his governor and he knows well that he speaks the truth. Yet it is not easy to hear these words.

"Wherefore O, King, let my counsel be acceptable unto thee. Break off thy sins by righteousness and thine iniquities by showing mercy to the poor; it may be a lengthening of thy tranquility."

Twelve months later, after no change or brokenness in the king's heart, he walks in the midst of his glory. He can only think of his greatness. He has forgotten the words of the first dream that his empire was the work of the eternal God. The king begins to talk to himself and anyone listening.

"Is not this great Babylon that I have built?" He takes all the credit for his magnificent city and forgets the captives from many cities on whose backs the great walls and ornate buildings have been built.

He continues, "That I have built for the house of my kingdom by the might of my power and for the honor of my majesty."

While he speaks, a voice fell from heaven saying, "O, King Nebuchadnezzar, to thee it is spoken, Thy kingdom is departed from thee."

The same hour, his mind convulsed and he becomes totally insane. All of his reasoning departs and he flees Babylon like a beast. Amytis screams at him to return to the palace as he flees on foot like a wild man. Within minutes he is lost in the crowd. Throwing off his royal garment, he could not be recognized in the derangement of his action.

Amytis sends for Governor Belteshazzar, and he comes with haste. "Governor," she says, "his dream has come to pass. I have pleaded with him to be my friend and husband again, to humble himself and recognize the great men that make this empire so golden. The worship of the excellent people of this empire has driven him mad.

"Where will he go—what will he do? Will someone kill him,

or will he be slain by the wild beasts that roam Chaldea?" She asks in terror.

Governor Belteshazzar tries diligently to counsel the queen while an impressive host of faithful guards are searching the city for the king.

He explains, "Queen Amytis, the dream was from the God that I serve and that you have embraced. The promise that was connected to the dream said he would return in humility and give glory to the exalted God that orders the affairs of men. You can believe that he will be forgiven when he has been tried and found broken."

Rumors of every shape were told and retold. Governor Belteshazzar calls the princes and lords of the empire and takes skillful pains to secure every government function. Guards, faithful guards, are posted at important gates and offices. The notable General Nebuzaradan of the warriors gathers his commanders and secures every post.

The empire is in faithful hands and everyone was compassionate for their queen. With Governor Belteshazzar's help and support, Queen Amytis takes charge of the empire, since she is well prepared for the time of crisis.

Several warrior catch glimpses of the king, but he slips through every safety net they establish. As a boy he had roamed all of Chaldea, and knows every hideout and waterhole.

He finds a great stallion of one of his warriors all bridled and saddled. As soon as it is dark, he heads for the marshes where he was born. By morning he was miles away, and finds an excellent hideout to spend the day out of sight. Again, at dark, he rides toward the playgrounds of his youth. The business of the empire has left him depleted, and he immediately puts it out of his mind.

By morning he arrives in the edge of the marshes. Another night of riding and he will soon know every inch of the terrain. He spends the day beside a running brook and catches fish with a makeshift hook. Somehow he has managed to carry tools to help him build fires quickly. He looks and acts like a wild madman.

Again he rides during the night, and is soon in sight of Queen Hanna's estate. Nobody can know of his presence. In a few days his beard obscures all recognition. Indeed, his nails grow long and hard and he resembles a gruesome creature. The marshes become a welcome sight to him as he lives in his hideouts and evades every person he sees.

When Queen Hanna receives the news, she spends the day weeping and then begins to search as she did when he was a boy. She knew his hideout and almost found him on several occasions. His recognition of his circumstance would come and go. At times he would recognize himself and spend days remembering his Amytis and longing for her comforting presence. Then he would slip back to the mind of a beast of the field and awake to find himself eating grass because he had briefly forgotten how to catch a fish.

Queen Hanna begins to visit places where he played as a boy, and leaves food for him. She would secure it from the wild beasts and when she returned he would have eaten it and left his secret code as he did when as a boy he played games with his mom.

She knew he was always near and became a regular supplier of food and clean clothes. Then he would revert back and the food and clothes would go untouched for weeks.

Queen Amytis spent weeks too heartsick to leave the palace. Daily she met the efficient staff and cared for the empire business. Royal guests were treated as always. Governor Belteshazzar became the voice of the king for Queen Amytis when the sadness of the king's condition drove her into seclusion.

Governor Belteshazzar slipped unnoticed out of Babylon to spend time at Queen Hanna's estate. "Queen Hanna," he says, "Your faithfulness to watch and be here near the king's hideout is extremely important. I know that this is the darkest moment of your life, but it will turn out right.

"Your son's condition," he said, "is the result of the frailty of all of our lives and how easy it is to trust in ourselves. When he sees how truly weak and helpless is our flesh and he looks beyond that flesh and self to the fact of a mighty God in control he will return and you will have your son back."

Queen Hanna took hope. "Yes, Governor, I have heard the splendid Zion Choir sing of this truth you teach me and I have read this in your Scrolls. My son will be back in the palace."

The guard that stood before the carriage house heard someone inside and quietly slipped around and opened a side door. Immediately, without the queen seeing him, he saw her sitting in her seat weeping profusely. She was there for hours, praying to the God of the Scrolls. She had always prayed and addressed her prayers to the God of Belteshazzar, but something had changed. Queen Amytis, in her utter sorrow, now released her faith and called Him, "the God of the Scrolls." While she prayed in the magnificent golden chariot of the king, she knew there was hope and her Nabu would return. She decided that she, too, with Queen Hanna, would go looking for him at the right time.

The Throne Protected

584–577 BC

Babylon has become a metropolitan city, spread for miles in every direction. The Golden Empire is so well organized and efficient that the absence of the king has no effect on daily affairs. The brilliance of the governor and his three vice governors' organization allows no room or vulnerable cracks for mutiny or revolt. The Golden Empire is in good hands.

Queen Amytis slowly gets a grip on her own emotions and proves to be an effective administrator. Her prior princess reputation was so attractive and inspiring that the empire could easily accept her as a long-term queen. She knows that her role will end as soon as her love is back on the throne. Her son, the crown prince, is helpful, although too young and weak to ascend in his father's stead. Her young daughter, Princess Kima, is attracting inspiring attention for the queen.

Governor Belteshazzar is the queen's shadow. Although fully capable of being the king, he has no interest in moving beyond his appointed role. He is totally aware of the Divine design for King Nebuchadnezzar, and will be a rock for the queen until the king comes home.

Medean's exceptional king, the father of Amytis, comes with his queen and her mother for an extended stay in the palace. He is a welcome sight to the entire city, and certainly offers the company much needed by Queen Amytis. King Nebuchadnezzar has often spoken fondly of King Cyaxares, and it is easy to see him as one of the powers behind the throne. He moves among the lords and princes of the city with ease and support. While in Babylon, he attends all the important meetings of both the queen and the governor. He respects the business acumen of the men from Zion. He has great leaders and financiers that are men out of Zion from two to three generations back.

While King Cyaxares is close by his daughter, Governor Belteshazzar plans a visit to the seaport on the Gulf, with a personal visit to Queen Hanna. Being seen as indispensable to the empire, he travels under heavy security with a large contingent of warriors. He is welcomed at each stop with royal treatment. All of his actions and his demeanor leave no question that his loyalty is to the king, even in his absence and to his queen, who acts in the king's behalf. His entire purpose in every action and statement is to create peace and assurance that all is well as everyone waits for their king to be healthy again.

The city lords of the seaport spend time with the governor. The governor addresses them with the air of complete authority, saying, "I am here to compliment all of you for the splendid administration that is evident in your new city. As I traveled from Uruk, the ancient city called Erech by my father, I was overwhelmed with the beauty. The super highway was literally lined with towering palms and beautiful flowers. Your effort to make all of the construction and improvements nature friendly was impressive. My chariot almost collided with a majestic lion rushing from the marshes into a grove of trees on the opposite side. The natural world is visible everywhere, and I loved it."

They discuss the most efficient method of loading and unloading the ships, and the order of record keeping the governor had designed. The city governor Adad expresses his delight to the governor.

"Governor Belteshazzar, I am delighted at such an organized

way to make the port more efficient and to be careful with account-ability for all the cargo. Everything you planned for us has been implemented, and we are hearing much appreciation from all con-cerned. The port is described by every trader passing through as the best organized in the world. Everyone knows that you have been the source. Thanks for your wisdom, Governor Belteshazzar."

Belteshazzar replies, "Governor Adad, your hard work and capa-ble administration will be fully reported to Queen Amytis. You and your lords are commendable leaders, and the Babylonian Empire is proud of this seaport and the welcome that is shown to everyone."

There is a huge banquet in the evening to celebrate the visit by the governor. It is a state affair, and one of the first such banquets given in honor of Governor Belteshazzar. He is honored, but careful to speak of Queen Amytis as the final authority for the present, and to promise that she would be planning a visit at an early date. When her name is mentioned, the entire banquet explodes in applause and adoration.

The governor states, "Queen Amytis is proving to be a woman of exceptional ability. She has always been strength behind the scene for her king, but at present she is your queen in full charge."

Governor Belteshazzar leaves early the next morning for a visit with Queen Hanna. He planned an unannounced trip into the marshes in search of the king. The majority of his security would wait for him at the seaport. He has been careful to choose men he could trust with total confidence, and they traveled through the extra ordinary garden-like marshes to the fantastic estate of the for-mer king, the father of King Nebuchadnezzar. Everyone esteemed these marshes, and to visit them was like a trip into an unspoiled paradise.

The majesty of the chariot ride to the point where small prows were waiting was too remarkable to be true. The moss on many of the trees created an atmosphere of secrecy. Heavily armed security had been stationed in a complete circle of the area where the king was believed to travel. The security and moss filled trees together made you think of a long lost garden that was forbidden to the world. Somewhere in this boundless maze was a deranged man that no one could find, and who moved more like a tiger than a man.

When the queen saw Governor Belteshazzar, she bowed in respect and love. "Welcome to my world and my garden," she said as the governor carefully stepped out of the prow.

"Blessing and favor to you," he said to the queen as he carefully embraced the adored wife of the deceased King Nebopolasser.

Queen Amytis had sent several items that she loved. The governor also purchased a beautiful oriental rug to be used at the location chosen by the queen. She blushes in simple appreciation for the kindness.

After a brief time of assuring the queen that everything of the empire is secure and without danger, the governor asks for information, if there was any, concerning her son, the king. Then he asks for the privilege of spending a few hours in the marshes near her home where everyone believes the king is hiding.

As tears flowed down her cheeks, she says, "Governor, I am told that you believe the king will be well and return to all of us. You must know that those words from you are all I have to hope. I have spent hours, hundreds of hours, prodding my way all over these marshes. I see many proofs of his presence. One time I saw him fleeing like an animal. He has eaten many times of what I left, and he always leaves evidence that only he and I would recognize. He is out there, but he does not want to be seen or bothered.

"He respects you so highly, maybe it is better that you do not look for him or see him. That might be too much for him to handle in his present state of mind."

"I agree," he says. "Will you let me go with you to leave food there for him? I also want to leave something that he will know came from me alone."

Together they go deep into the marshes. The warriors are asked to stay behind at the mansion. Queen Hanna takes a change of clothes, a new coat for the cool night, and plenty of fresh food. The governor had been given an expensive gift by the king that he loved greatly. It is a very expensive covering that the governor used, with the king's knowledge, as a kneeling place for prayer. The governor had often suggested to the king that he begin to have a regular prayer time. The governor had earlier purchased the king a rug for that very purpose.

Governor Belteshazzar believes that the king would get the message leaving the rug would send. No one has a covering like this one. The king could not have forgotten the joy that his governor had expressed at this gift. It is left with the food and a simple note signed, "To the King, from Governor Belteshazzar."

Returning to the magnificent house of Queen Hanna, the governor bids her farewell as he leaves for the return trip to Babylon. As he steps into the prow, the queen stands in the doorway with tears flowing freely down her cheeks. Only a mother can hurt like the queen is hurting.

As a safeguard for the Golden Empire, Governor Belteshazzar and General Nebuzaradan plan several months of exercises for the Babylonian warriors. The news went out to every corner of the world that the greatest warriors on earth would be conducting exercises to sharpen their skills and demonstrate their weapons. The warriors are divided into groups of approximately one hundred thousand men with five thousand chariots assigned to each formation.

Five companies would cross the Euphrates near Carchemish and perform exercises in different locations of the area between the northern tips down to Egypt. The other five companies would exercise throughout Chaldea to the northern area near ancient Nineveh. The rest of the warriors—comprising over one million strong men—

would conduct planned exercises around Babylon and south to the seaport while maintaining strong security.

There would be chariot races, staged battles between the chariot warriors, and displays of the great tar ball machines. Every possible example of the skills of the warring Babylonians would excite all that viewed them. Arrow shooting contests and hand to hand battling would be demonstrated. Every technique of these warriors would be on display and witnessed in action.

It grows immediately evident that there had never been an event so anticipated by everyone. The cities near each planned demonstration promote the events. The local cities and communities plan food, and it becomes a celebration enjoyed all over the empire. The unmatched skills of these warriors will send a message to every corner.

The absence of the king is completely overshadowed by the warriors of the Golden Empire demonstrating their skills and showing good nature with each other. Young men and local children are brought into the mix and taught great lessons of personal discipline. It is a triumphant time throughout the Empire of Gold. Nothing like this has ever happened before.

At the palace, Queen Amytis is learning the value of her presence throughout the Babylonian Empire. No one can represent the king as well as her. Dressed in her queenly attire she is too lovely to ignore. Her charm is in the ordinary way she steps right into the middle of the people. She has no fear, but feels completely protected by her own faith. She is careful to save her crying for private times in the palace.

She and the family decide to spend a few months moving across the empire in the golden carriage that had not been seen in three years. Her daughter, as beautiful as her mother, has been shielded up to this time. The queen knows that the Golden Empire needs a fresh inspiration and has decided the young princess is the right choice. The entire family will spend several weeks preparing themselves to inspire everyone everywhere they travel. The word went out across the News Channels as Governor Belteshazzar carefully planned the security with Arioch, the king's guard.

When the golden carriage leaves Babylon it is to a roaring send off. It is awesome to see the beautiful carriage in the midst of hundreds of guards dressed in their royal attire, which is worn only when guarding the king and queen. They will travel north to Carchemish and cross the Euphrates River at the new bridge. It is a marvel of beautifully designed stone with a strikingly Babylonian flare. The bridge is to be dedicated by the queen herself, and then together with her family in the golden carriage, she will be the first to cross it. No one will ever forget watching the queen and her family in the carriage surrounded by the highly trained guards.

The queen announces, "I am here, representing our King Nebuchadnezzar, to dedicate this stately bridge to our Babylonian Empire. This bridge cost a huge sum, and the empire is proud to make this contribution to the unlimited people that it will serve. Local people will be greatly served and the world traders and dedicated businessmen that serve us all will save valuable traveling time.

"The flood seasons can no longer impede or slow up those on a schedule to deliver the riches to this area. Let's call it, 'The Queen Hanna Bridge' in honor of a woman we love so much and that is highly esteemed by one and all. She is suffering so intensely at the present because of her son's sickness." The roar of approval leaves no doubt that all is well. Princess Kima touches every heart with her charm, and stands beside the queen with the crown prince and all the family of five children. It is an unforgettable sight.

The honor given to Queen Amytis at this event is indeed a royal homage. The family travels in Palestine for three weeks visiting Damascus, Tyre, Sidon, Aleppo, and Byblos. Every community in route is given the privilege of seeing the queen, the crown prince,

Princess Kima, and the family and they all proved up to the task of showing the beautiful side of a royal house.

As they pass back across the new bridge over the Euphrates, they travel on to Haran, across Mesopotamia, and visit every major city and many small communities. Kippur, Ur, and Uruk are all visited as they traveled south. The family has never seen the seaport town nor watched the magnificent ships come and go. Staying with Queen Hanna and being close to where the king is in hiding offers both joy and sadness to all of them.

Princess Kima charms everyone in the seaport community and gives out her hugs and childish giggles wherever she went among the people. A fresh and beautiful sense of the Golden Empire hangs over this family, especially when they sit in the golden carriage surrounded by the royal guards.

A welcome home festivity is planned for Queen Amytis and the family's return to Babylon. They arrive after dark, as planned by the governor, to a city in waiting. The walls are lighted double to the normal. The royal family sees the glow from an imposing distance away.

When the carriage enters The Marduk Gate, the city explodes into revelry. The Zion Choir she loved waits on a tower stand with its instruments of music. The choir bursts into a most glorious welcome song written by the governor himself. For hours, they celebrate. Foods have been prepared for the entire city and the queen's most loved delicacies are ready for the family at the palace.

The city lords and exalted leaders are present in the banquet hall to give Queen Amytis her most memorable moments of appreciation.

Queen Amytis Searching the Marshes

577 BC

It has been over six years since King Nebuchadnezzar fled the palace in Babylon. Queen Amytis has been a rock of strength to her family, the noble lords, the princes, and the Golden Empire. But she is exhausted and lonely. She misses the love of her heart. She decides that it is now time for her to go into the heart of the marshes and stay there until she finds him or he finds her.

Meeting with Governor Belteshazzar, she informs him of her intent and asks for total confidence. She signs the proper documents so that the governor can affix the king's seal on anything that comes before him. He will act as king until she returns. No one will be told where she will be, not even the family.

The next morning she simply fails to come into the king's throne room. As he has done numerous times before, the governor proceeds with the business of the empire. Everyone has come to expect the same. Everything appears to be business as usual. She dresses incognito and catches a public carriage to the seaport. She actually enjoys traveling as an ordinary person and makes friends with the other riders.

Without the trappings of royalty, she can enjoy the natural beauty that appears. The date trees line the highway. Orange groves are in full bloom and the farms are green and growing. She marvels at the canals full of water and the farmers busy at work. Carts carrying workers to the field and oxen pulling plows amaze her with childlike fancy.

Whenever she had traveled in the country before, everything had stopped and the crowds had lined the roadways. Now, she sees life in the natural and it is breathtaking to her. The carriage stops at a roadside bazaar and she purchases fresh figs and a cold container of orange juice. She is like a child on a picnic.

As they reach the edge of the marshes, she begins to think of her Nabu somewhere in the depths of this beautiful but dangerous world. She considers the kind of environment he is enduring. Wild beasts literally fill this world. Poisonous creatures are numerous and a place to sleep when one is in the wild appears non-existent. She intends to dress as best as she can, take only what is necessary for survival, and thrust herself into the world of her lost love. Can she survive? She is not sure, but do this she must.

In the seaport, she loses herself for two days. She watches just in case Nabu might come sometime to the city to search for food or just to wander idly among the crowds. It is thrilling to Amytis to walk along the water's edge and watch the ships come and go. She almost longs just to be a Chaldean living a normal life.

A carriage is hired to take her to the estate of Queen Hanna. She loves the normal ride toward the depths of the marshes, but finds it difficult to pass the security established for protection of the king. She convinces the guard to send someone to get Queen Hanna without revealing who she is. The queen expects Amytis and comes quickly to the checkpoint. Without a word, the queen identifies her as family and the guard lets her pass.

Queen Hanna, feebler than Amytis expected, is delighted for her to visit. As they sit in the mansion deep in the grand estate and a good distance from the busy world, they share their hearts and their love so needed by both of them.

Queen Hanna reveals, "Queen Amytis, my daughter, our Nabu is out there, so very close. He never misses his food that I leave for him anymore, but not one time have I been near enough to speak to him. Recently, I found a tiger that he had killed. It was evident that the tiger had attacked him and he was able to break his neck with those enormous arms I so well remember. My workers said that an incredibly strong man had broken the tiger's neck. No one on our estate staff would be capable of such a feat."

His mother weeps as she tells of several times when she has seen him at a distance. "Amytis, he is as wild as the animals. We find places where he eats the same grass and foliage that the water buffaloes and the tigers eat. I can tell that his hair is matted and long and his face is beastly. The tiger he killed was clawed and huge slices were ripped on his neck and shoulders. It appeared that he ate some of the raw meat. Why did the gods so attack him and make him so wild and beastly?"

"Mother," Amytis says, "The gods that did this to him are the warring gods that our world has experienced throughout almost all of history. When men become proud and boast of themselves as our Nabu had come to do, they make themselves vulnerable to dark powers and beings that destroy human lives. A haughty person is not far from insanity. We have known many who did such foolish things in their pride and selfishness.

"I am reading in the Scrolls that Governor Belteshazzar reads. It says that there is a beast in all of us, and left to ourselves and our haughty ways, we can lose our mind. The second dream that our Nebuchadnezzar had was a warning to quit glorying in self and to give glory to the high and holy God that rules in all of human affairs. He was warned to break off his sin and to care for the poor on whose backs we have built this golden empire.

"Let's pray and believe that your son and my love will remember that dream and obey the revelation that the governor gave to him.

"Tomorrow, I am going deep into the marshes to look for him. I may not return until he comes with me."

"My darling," Queen Hanna says, "You do love him so much. I am so proud you are his queen."

The stately estate of Queen Hanna has many employees. Her

estate master is a gentle man, totally faithful to the queen and deeply concerned for King Nebuchadnezzar. He had seen the tiger after he had been killed and knows that the king is dangerous and has the strength of a beast. Often he warns the workers to never encounter the king if they see him and to do nothing to provoke him to anger. The queen convinces Amytis that the master must know she is out there in the marshes and watch out for her as she is looking for Nabu. She consents.

Dressed in common clothes, the beautiful princess, the queen of Nebuchadnezzar, leaves early the next morning and heads in the direction his mother had last seen him. It is not long before Amytis is drenched in the waters that cover at least half of the queen's estate. Moving slowly, carrying food and the necessary provisions for nighttime, she travels at least two miles into the depth of rare nature and breathtaking beauty. If the circumstance of her action had been to enjoy the wild it would have been a wonderful experience.

Being near the center of what she perceives as the queen's estate, she establishes for herself a camp, a kind of base to go in different directions. The queen has given her a map that Nebopolasser once drew as a young father and she can see the basic direction toward the mansion. She had tried hard to learn a little about survival in such a place and sets up the camping location both for protection and to hopefully draw the king to herself.

Exhausted, she settles down to rest. She has a Scroll of the Psalms to read and arranges for herself a place for prayer. Berries of different kinds are everywhere. The water is extremely clear and teeming with fish. Eating will be no problem and the dry ledge that she can sleep under appears comfortable. She will find her love or he will find her.

The time alone is refreshing to a princess and queen that have always lived in a glass house. The first days are uneventful. A few wild animals frightened her, but keeping a strong fire causes them to stay clear.

A few times she calls out, "Nabu, Nabu, its Amytis. Where are you? I have come to see you. I cannot take our separation any longer." Twice she hears noises that she knows are that of a man but they fade away quickly.

The second week she begins to take a hike for approximately a mile or less in different directions. Almost every day she sees where someone has been—animal or human. Twice, she knows that it is a man and she is convinced it is her king.

At the end of the second week, she finds where Nabu is living. It is under a large rock overhang and in the very back she finds a covering she recognizes. It had been a gift to the governor that the king had so proudly given him. The question of how it got there is overwhelming to her. Did he bring it with him? It is neatly placed and appears to be placed in a way that someone would use for resting, praying, or thinking. She takes hope, as she is careful not to disturb anything or leave any evidence that he has been discovered. It is so well hidden that no one has found this place but Nabu and herself.

She must not surprise him or discover him. He must come to her and she now knows that he is aware of her presence. She slips back quickly to her camp and waits. She is anxious and knows she will encounter him soon.

The frequency of voices or noises that appear human grows day by day. Each time she speaks loud enough to be heard. The moment she speaks all movement ends. Her words are always the same. "Nabu, Nabu, it is Amytis. I have come to see you. I cannot take our separation any longer."

Amytis will never forget this moment. She has been over three weeks in her camp. After she says "Nabu, Nabu," she hears him say, "Amytis, Amytis, is that you?" That is all, and he is gone. She weeps until she is totally exhausted.

The next day it happens exactly the same way. This time he says, "Amytis, Amytis, neither can I stand our separation any longer," and he is gone. Now, she knows the power of destruction is breaking and it will not be long until she will see him.

Two days later, as Amytis waits, she hears his movements and calls out, "Nebuchadnezzar, is that you?" For several minutes she hears nothing, and then he speaks.

"Amytis, you cannot see me as I look now. I have talked to the awesome God that we once talked about. I have admitted my pride and haughtiness. I feel clean inside and my reason and understanding is returning.

"Please go to mother's house. Tell her to leave the guesthouse open tomorrow night. Put clothes there for me to wear, scissors to cut my hair, and a razor to shave with. I must prepare myself before either of you can look at me, I'm a mess. Please go quickly. You have been out here too long. Amytis, I love you more than words can express. Please forgive me."

He hears her weeping profusely and begs her to please stop. "It's too much for me," he says. Amytis immediately leaves for the mansion. When she approaches the house, Queen Hanna is waiting for her. She says, "Amytis, Amytis, I have stayed here every day watching. O, how happy I am to see you. I have feared the worst."

"Mother," Amytis says, "Our king is back. He finally opened his heart from a hiding place and told me to come to you. He wants the guesthouse ready for him to slip into tomorrow night. Nobody can watch for him. He does not want to be seen until he cleans and shaves himself. O, Mother, the God of Belteshazzar has heard us!"

Amytis herself is a mess. She is a queen in rags and spends the day bathing, refreshing herself, and eating civilized food. Exhausted, she does not remember going to bed and sleeps most of the next day. The guesthouse is made fit for a king. Everything he needs is waiting. His favorite food is prepared and on the table. The master of the estate is careful to clear everyone from seeing distance for that location of the estate.

Sometime after complete darkness, Nebuchadnezzar comes quietly to the guesthouse. After midnight, the queen sees the lamp burning and knows her son is home. Amytis hears the door of the guesthouse open. She, too, sees the light and has to utterly resist running to him as he is. After hours of trying to shave his tangled beard, to cut the knots from his hair, and to bath; he falls asleep on a bed for the first time in seven years. He does not awake until later the next day.

When he opens the door of the guesthouse, Amytis is sitting on the patio waiting for him. She is dressed in her most beautiful, feminine dress, and simply says, "Nabu, I love you." He almost leaps on the patio and sweeps her into his arms. "Amytis, I love you, please forgive me." After holding her in his arms for a long time, he holds her face and they laugh together again.

Queen Hanna is standing in the doorway when he sees his mother. Hugging her as only a son can do, he begins to tell her how much every piece of food, every piece of clothing meant to him. He tells her how each time he saw the evidence of her presence, he had a few minutes of peace and understanding. "Then," he says, "Everything would go dark again. Mother, you kept me from total chaos and darkness. I love you, Mother."

Amytis has to ask him, "Nabu, how did you get the covering I saw in your hiding place? You gave that to Governor Belteshazzar."

"I do not know," he answers, "but, one day I realized that it was the gift I gave him and that he used it to pray on and I began to do the same. In my mind, though foggy to me, it seems that it was the time when I began to recover."

King Nebuchadnezzar Returns to Babylon

577 BC

A News Chariot races toward Babylon. The driver is wild with anticipation as he carries the latest news about King Nebuchadnezzar. Some rumors that had circulated about the king's whereabouts and his state of mind declared him a beast while others said he had died. This driver however, had the real facts.

As he rode into Babylon, he began to announce for all to hear, "Good news about our king! Good news!" But it was not his job to tell the rest of the story. Vice-Governor Abednego is the master of the news bearers of the empire, and it is his story to release. The coming announcement has spread like wildfire, and the news is immediately dispatched to the city and throughout the world:

"The king has returned to Queen Hanna's home in the marshes and has recovered from his loss of reason. Queen Amytis went several weeks ago into the wild of those marshes without protection or weapons. She went to find the king or be found of him, and intended to stay until her beloved returned with her. Our queen has proven herself the unfailing princess and queen of the Babylonian Empire.

"Our king will remain at the Nebopolasser's Estate until his strength has returned. The beautiful home of Queen Hanna will be the capital for the next short time until he is well enough to travel to Babylon. Governor Belteshazzar and a number of his chosen princes will travel immediately to meet the king and to plan his return to the palace." The city went ecstatic and parties continued all evening and night. The sun was rising as the city fell into silence.

The king's carriage of gold is seen leaving the city as the last sounds of rejoicing fade away. The crown prince, princess, and their entire family ride in a second carriage, for no one could ride the carriage of gold without either the king or the queen. The governor and the chosen lords leave, accompanying the family. Later in the day the City of Babylon awakens to a new day for the Golden Empire. King Nebuchadnezzar would soon be at home in their palace.

Life at Nebopolasser's Estate is a whirlwind of activities and royal happenings. The king and queen spent days romancing and enjoying one another. They were like the youngsters they both remembered; just happy to be together, to laugh, to talk, and to plan. Nabu, as he now encourages Amytis to call him, has asked her forgiveness over and over. Once again, they talk of the gods and they freely speak of a God that is higher than the heavens and a ruler over all the affairs of men. Both pledge to lead their lives by faith and to invite Governor Belteshazzar to teach them all God's ways.

Queen Hanna, the king's mother, is frail and spends most of her time in her private quarters away from the incredible activities. Her private time with her son is a breath of fresh air to a mother whose strength is swiftly ebbing.

"Son, please tell me what you understand about your terrible experience. From your youth you have been a challenging young man to your mother. I remember how careful and free you roamed this estate, and the joy you always brought to my heart. We had a way with each other, and you have always been my champion. The things you have accomplished as our king have never been realized ever before. The Assyrian Empire was a success, but never like this Golden Empire, of which you are king. Your father would be so proud of you," she says.

"Mother, the things you and father taught me and that I learned from your wisdom are a wonderful part of my life. You taught me to trust other people; to give them a challenging task and to let them succeed. Our empire is absolutely full of men and women who have succeeded beyond imagination. That is one reason for this Golden Empire. You taught me many such ideas," he replies warmly.

"My survival in these marshes for seven years was because you and my father both taught me and released me to learn the skills of the wild. I know now that my pride—even a haughty pride—brought me to despair. The idea that a king is a god, as believed by so much of our world, is a horrible mistake. I am without excuse, but this very thought has been attributed to me by the multitudes and it made me insane. The idea itself is insane. We are mortals that live and die, and I will never believe that false thought again nor will I allow it to be assigned to me.

"Mother, I am already writing *The Epic of the Insane King: Nebuchadnezzar*. When it is released you will understand my seven years of hell perfectly."

"Son, I will never forget you fleeing from me like an animal. But I remember how you would take the food or clothes and my token of love, and always leave your token in return. I know you remembered this from your youth, and it gave me hope. The little hearts you would take a fresh branch and shape were as exact as we did when you were my little spoiled lad. For that one moment of action you seemed so normal."

"Mother," the king says. "Every time I made that heart for you I would seem so okay for a few minutes, and then I would be wild again. Now I believe those very acts of telling you how much I loved you, and you doing the same, kept me from going totally over the edge. Mother, you are one of the big reasons I am back."

They weep together as they had done many years ago. "Son, your mother is ready to die in peace," Queen Hanna quietly replies.

It's an overwhelming moment for King Nebuchadnezzar as he sees the chariots approaching. The crown prince, Amel-Marduk, comes straight to his father and treats him exactly like it is normal to treat royalty. The father accepts his honor, but then treats him as his son.

"My Son, thank you for being the strength to you mother that she needed. She has told me of your constant respect and your daily effort to be as a father to the family. Your royal action during the trip throughout the empire has been explained as a display that all was well in my absence. My son, I must spend time with you as my father did with me. I have failed, but I will correct that weakness. When I'm back in Babylon we will work together on some fantastic projects for the empire."

His little princess is now ten years old and beautiful beyond measure. She is a perfect image of her mother. When she sees her father, she leaps into his arms. Nabu weeps as he holds her in his grasp. His entire thoughts and mind rushes past the years and back to the time he would see Amytis as the little Medean princess, and know she is the love of his heart. It was a grand family reunion. Governor Belteshazzar, the Lords of Babylon with him, waits in the Great Room for the family to be united.

King Nebuchadnezzar asks to see his Governor of Babylon first. Belteshazzar steps quietly and gently into the magnificent library and study of King Nebopolasser where the king is going to conduct the affairs of state. The king is seated in his father's old recliner, but stands to welcome his trusted friend. They embrace in a royal manner and remain standing while tears flow freely down each face.

The Governor says, "King Nebuchadnezzar, my friend, I'm the happiest governor and lord in your empire. Having interpreted your dream—that you have now lived—I never doubted your return. The God I serve does not play games with people and He has preserved you to fulfill the design of this Golden Empire. Now you can do it for Him instead of doing it for yourself. It will not always be easy. There are many watchers, and you have seen some of the good ones. There are also dark ones that claim to be gods, and they will all battle until that "Stone cut out without hands" establishes the eternal earthly kingdom."

"I do not understand it all," the king says, "but I am writing *The Epic of the Insane King: Nebuchadnezzar*. This will warn men everywhere of the danger of haughtiness and self-will. I owe the wonderful people of our empire my honesty and regrets. They must know that I faced my failures and changed my ways. I want them to love their king, but I do not want to be worshipped.

"My Amytis has personally cleaned the exquisite covering I gave to you years ago. I did not remember how I came to possess it in my hideout, but I recognized it as the place you knelt to pray. Somehow I began to pray while kneeling thereon, and now I know that a change slowly began to occur. The little hearts my mother and I made for each other and the covering where I prayed prepared me to hear my Amytis' voice and then to emerge from the dark cloud. It all seems like a nightmare. You, my mother, and my queen are champions in my life.

"I want to go personally and invite my lords into this library. They must know immediately that their king is humbled and ready to serve." The king walks from the ornate world of his father's paneled study into the Great Room where his lords were waiting. Most of them have never seen the mansion of Nebopolasser, and especially his private hideaway filled with mementos of his reign. The spacious room with the vaulted ceiling is overfilled with gifts and expensive expressions of his years as King of Babylon.

"Welcome into my father's home," he says. The queen is now beside him, at his request. "You have been faithful to my queen during these years of my failure and extreme sickness. I do not know how to thank you enough. She has told me of your strength and patience; how the empire has remained strong—and even growing—because of wise men like you standing tall. I offer you my regrets and my promise to repay everyone fully. I intend to serve you as you have served me and my queen."

As they move back to the library, tears stain the cheeks of strong men. It is now evident that their king was both going to be their friend and their king. Every affair of the empire is addressed lightly until the king has a peace that nothing of importance has suffered. The date of his return to the palace is set, and a vast celebration is planned. The City of Babylon will be given its time of reuniting itself with its much loved and missed monarch.

After each lord is given a few minutes to speak to King Nebuchadnezzar, he announces the release of his current epic. "I have written in the first person the story of my fall into the dark night of despair. It tells the story of my failure and return. It will be sent to the farthest reaches of our empire. It will put to rest the rumors and farfetched stories that blame others instead of me. It will be rightly named, *The Epic of the Insane King Nebuchadnezzar*. Before I ride the golden carriage and live in our magnificent palace, I want the world to know the truth of my folly and forgiveness."

As Governor Belteshazzar and the king's lord's return to Babylon, the epic is released to the news agency to be dispatched to the world. It reads as follows:

The Epic of the Insane King Nebuchadnezzar

Nebuchadnezzar the king,
        Unto all people, nations, and languages, that dwell in all the earth; Peace be multiplied unto you.

I thought it good to show the signs and wonders that the high God hath wrought toward me.

How great are his signs!

And how mighty are his wonders!

His kingdom is an everlasting kingdom.

And his dominion is from generation to generation.

I Nebuchadnezzar was at rest in mine house, and flourishing in my palace:

I dreamed a dream, which made me afraid, and the thoughts upon my bed and the visions of my head troubled me.

Therefore, I made a decree to bring in all the wise men of Babylon before me that they might make known unto me the interpretation of the dream.

Then came in the magicians, the astrologers, the Chaldeans, and the soothsayers: and I told the dream before them; but they did not make known unto me the interpretation thereof.

But at the last Daniel came in before me, whose name was Belteshazzar, according to the name of my god, and in whom is the spirit of the holy gods: and before him I told the dream, saying:

O, Belteshazzar, master of the magicians, because I know that the spirit of the holy gods is in thee, and no secret troubleth thee, tell me the visions of my dream that I have seen, and the interpretation thereof.

Thus were the visions of mine head in my bed; I saw, and behold a tree in the midst of the earth, and the height thereof was great.

The tree grew, and was strong, and the height thereof reached unto heaven, and the sight thereof to the end of all the earth:

The leaves thereof were fair and the fruit thereof much,

and in it was meat for all: the beasts of the field had shadow under it, and the fowls of the heaven dwelt in the boughs thereof, and all flesh was fed of it.

I saw in the visions of my head upon my bed, and, behold, a watcher and a holy one came down from heaven;

He cried aloud, and said thus, Hew down the tree, and cut off his branches, shake off his leaves, and scatter his fruit: let the beasts get away from under it, and the fowls from his branches:

Nevertheless leave the stump of his roots in the earth, even with a band of iron and brass, in the tender grass of the field; and let it be wet with the dew of heaven, and let his portion be with the beasts in the grass of the earth:

Let his heart be changed from man's, and let a beast's heart be given unto him; and let seven times pass over him.

This matter is by the decree of the watchers, and the demand by the word of the holy ones: to the intent that the living may know that the most High ruleth in the kingdom of men, and giveth it to whomsoever he will, and setteth up over it the basest of men.

This dream, I, king Nebuchadnezzar, have seen. Now thou, O, Belteshazzar, declare the interpretation thereof, forasmuch as all the wise men of my kingdom are not able to make known unto me the interpretation: but thou art able; for the spirit of the holy gods is in thee.

Then Daniel, whose name was Belteshazzar, was summoned for one hour, and his thoughts troubled him. The king spoke, and said, Belteshazzar, let not the dream, or the interpretation thereof, trouble thee. Belteshazzar answered and said, My lord, the dream be to them that hate thee, and the interpretation thereof to thine enemies.

The tree that thou sawest, which grew, and was strong,

whose height reached unto the heaven, and the sight thereof to all the earth;

Whose leaves were fair, and the fruit thereof much, and in it was meat for all; under which the beasts of the field dwelt, and upon whose branches the fowls of the heaven had their habitation:

It is thou, O, King, who art grown and become strong: for thy greatness is grown, and reacheth unto heaven, and thy dominion to the end of the earth.

And whereas the king saw a watcher and an holy one coming down from heaven, and saying, Hew the tree down, and destroy it; yet leave the stump of the roots thereof in the earth, even with a band of iron and brass, in the tender grass of the field; and let it be wet with the dew of heaven, and let his portion be with the beasts of the field, till seven times pass over him;

This is the interpretation, O, King, and this is the decree of the most High, which is come upon my lord the king:

That they shall drive thee from men, and thy dwelling shall be with the beasts of the field, and they shall make thee to eat grass as oxen, and they shall wet thee with the dew of heaven, and seven times shall pass over thee, till thou know that the most High ruleth in the kingdom of men, and giveth it to whomsoever he will.

And whereas they commanded to leave the stump of the tree roots, thy kingdom shall be sure unto thee, after that thou shalt have known that the heavens do rule.

Wherefore, O, King, let my counsel be acceptable unto thee, and break off thy sins by righteousness, and thine iniquities by showing mercy to the poor; if it may be a lengthening of thy tranquility.

All this came upon the king Nebuchadnezzar.

At the end of twelve months he walked in the palace of the kingdom of Babylon.

The king spoke, and said, Is not this great Babylon, that I have built for the house of the kingdom by the might of my power, and for the honor of my majesty?

While the word was in the king's mouth, there fell a voice from heaven, saying, O, King Nebuchadnezzar, to thee it is spoken; the kingdom is departed from thee.

And they shall drive thee from men, and thy dwelling shall be with the beasts of the field: they shall make thee to eat grass as oxen, and seven times shall pass over thee, until thou know that the most High ruleth in the kingdom of men, and giveth it to whomsoever he will.

The same hour was the thing fulfilled upon Nebuchadnezzar: and he was driven from men, and did eat grass as oxen, and his body was wet with the dew of heaven, till his hairs were grown like eagles' feathers, and his nails like birds' claws.

And at the end of the days I Nebuchadnezzar lifted up mine eyes unto heaven, and mine understanding returned unto me, and I blessed the most High, and I praised and honored him that liveth for ever, whose dominion is an everlasting dominion, and his kingdom is from generation to generation:

And all the inhabitants of the earth are reputed as nothing: and he doeth according to his will in the army of heaven, and among the inhabitants of the earth: and none can stay his hand, or say unto him, what doest thou?

At the same time my reason returned unto me; and for the glory of my kingdom, mine honor and brightness returned unto me; and my counselors and my lords sought unto me; and I was established in my kingdom, and excellent majesty was added unto me.

Now, I, Nebuchadnezzar, praise and extol and honor the King of heaven, all whose works are truth, and his ways judgment: and those that walk in pride he is able to abase.

King Nebuchadnezzar
To All the Golden Empire

As the world reads this startling story, the king and queen of the Golden Empire left for the capital city. Their destination is the beautiful palace sitting on the Euphrates River edge. The city is fully prepared to receive them in the evening. King Nebuchadnezzar, with his queen, returns home after seven years.

Peace in the Golden Empire

577-563 BC

As the golden carriage enters the Ishtar Gate, the city of Babylon explodes with joy. Seven years with the cities and empire's royal family in disarray because the king had lost his mind had left a deep wound. Everything was golden in wealth, but the grandeur of royalty had been absent for a long time. It was like a colossal golden diadem with the crown jewel missing.

The queen, who has been everyone's champion, trudges forward with bravery. But for King Nebuchadnezzar, six feet and six inches tall with his massive broad shoulders and bold as a lion, coming home was majestic. The city needed its father's son back on the throne. Human government cannot exist and maintain its momentum without a towering leader. Few men or women have that capacity. King Nebuchadnezzar was a rarity.

The religious leaders however are extremely competitive. Each temple of over fifty in the capital city is certain of its right way in believing. The king's epic has given the ring of assurance to Belteshazzar's God. From the time Belteshazzar had entered Babylon as a captive, His God had left His lasting mark. The temple of the Scrolls is almost as large and well attended as those of Marduk and Ishtar. The king's epic could only increase the interest in the Scrolls—at least temporarily. No temple in the empire could suffer decline without fury.

The king's favor with the multitudes drove all of their unhappiness under the surface. King Nebuchadnezzar and Queen Amytis are still young and years of prosperity await the sprawling borders of their world. After days of celebration, life returns to an increased level of pure splendor. The king begins an empire-wide effort to address pockets of poverty and to repay a multitude of captives for their forced labor. It takes an incredible amount of the empire's wealth to accomplish his goal.

Crown Prince Amel-Marduk is given the responsibility to supervise. The king ceases to require his family or intimate masters and lords to always use royal terms in conversation. As he speaks to his crown prince, he simply talks as father would to his son. He says, "Son, this great task is laid on my heart by the Voice of God in my dream. It is one of the things that brought me to darkness. Our empire has built the most beautiful walls surrounding our cities and structures of massive size—beautiful and elaborate. But we have built them with the pain and even massive deaths on the backs of captive peoples from places we have left in ruins.

"A multitude of Assyrians, Egyptians, Haranians, and the people of the Scrolls were made to toil untold hours with bare necessities. Everyone we can identify must be paid for his or her labor. It's a massive task, my son, that will empty some of our treasure houses, but it is the enormous command of right and honesty. This will warm the hearts of a multitude toward you for the day that you become king of Babylon. My preparation for the empire was on the battlefield. Your preparation can be in the administration of justice."

The celebrated Zion Choir now sings regularly every sacred day in the temple of the Scrolls. The king and queen are regular attendees and absolutely love the great choir and its musicians. The seer Ezekiel is the shepherd over the thousands of people from Zion and teaches the Scrolls regularly. The temple itself is a lovely House of Prayer and a testimony to the faithfulness of Governor Belteshazzar's God.

Amel-Marduk, the crown prince, regularly attends both the temples of Marduk and Ishtar. This helps placate the High Priest Barshlama and keeps a lid on the strong jealousy against the Temple of Zion. Most Babylonians respect the Zion Temple and its God, but still prefer the gods of their heritage. On the surface, there is a religious freedom felt by the majority, but there is strong resentment among the sorcerers, magicians, Chaldeans, and soothsayers. They consider their way of life is in jeopardy, and they are concerned.

The king decides it is time for an extended visit to all the empire. A strong contingent of the brave warriors is near the City of Tyre to hush an uprising. There is another contingent in Upper Egypt suppressing a strong showing among those that are anti-Babylon. The king wants to begin with a trip to see the new bridge the queen dedicated and then travel throughout Palestine to show unity.

The entire empire has become a one-world economy, and prosperity explodes. To talk with his governor, princes, nobles, and kings of the many far-flung provinces in their own palaces or mansions was extremely important. His epic was being read and discussed and he wanted to have his say to everyone possible.

Traveling in his golden carriage with Queen Amytis is like a joyful dream. They are going to move slowly and try to take in every picturesque scene and new building project and to move among their subjects with great compassion. The king is a new man living in faith and showing the brokenness of a transformed person. The two of them have never enjoyed each other so deeply. Every country scene is a joy to absorb. The farms are so different in Chaldea from the farms they would see in Palestine.

As they near Carchemish, the king sees the mileage sign to "Queen Hanna's Bridge." "Mother is so weak and worn," he says. "My sorrows must have taken years from her life. As we finish this tour we are going to spend a few days enjoying her and father's estate. I want to walk back into the marshes and try to remember every possible event of my seven years."

As he finishes these words, he sees the massive bridge towering before him. "My darling, look, that bridge is breathtaking! Almost as spectacular as the Euphrates Bridge in Babylon! I am so honored that you named it after mother. While she was giving her life to reach me you were remembering her. That's perfect."

Amytis speaks of the mighty Euphrates River flowing under the bridge. She says, "This River is life to at least half of all our fruitful estates and plantations. The abundance of waters certainly feeds our rivers that flow all over the western half of Chaldea. The massive date groves we have driven through all day would be desert except for this abundant water supply."

"Remember, Amytis, the marshes where I roamed are fed by this river and the Tigris also. The Pison flows from the west and helps to fill the marshes and produce the millions of pounds of rice and the abundance of fresh water buffaloes. My father's riches came because of these rivers." He reminds Amytis that his mineral exportation commission has found the gold in the Arabian Desert at the head of the Pison.

"We are mining over ten thousand pounds of gold each year from that mine. Our empire is rich just with that one source. Belteshazzar told our team of this fact from the Scrolls of the seer Moses, and was responsible for this accomplishment. These are the most wonderful writings in the world, and full of many words of learning. Living by them makes anyone wealthy."

They have purposefully made this tour of the empire unannounced. Constantly, as the golden carriage comes in view the people become ecstatic. Before the carriage could pass, in most cases, there would be large crowds.

The warriors would move closely and King Nebuchadnezzar and Queen Amytis would step down from the beautiful carriage and both greet the people and even move out among them to shake hands. The queen was always a hugger, and tears would flow from both directions. It is indeed a new day for the king.

Crossing the Queen Hanna Bridge and moving into Syria and on across the northern tip toward the Mediterranean Sea is joyous. The mountain slopes on the Mediterranean are dotted with vineyards of grape, muscadine, and scuppernongs. It was the beginning of harvest and the king and queen were greeted to the taste of the vineyard dresser's best.

The entire company of warriors and support staff, plus the king and queen, learns that traveling without the fanfare of planned celebration was ideal. The excitement of the people is natural and genuine. Even those that had held hard feelings for the king are swayed by the royal atmosphere such a visit inspired. As they approach Tyre, the king decides to visit with the governor that he had just appointed. The previous governor has been part of the uprising and was removed and returned to private life, with a clear warning.

Governor Shafira has just moved into the Governor's Palace, but quickly opens the city under tight security to the king and queen. As the golden carriage rolls down the street toward the palace, encircled by literally hundreds of warriors dressed in their royal style, the people quickly recognize that the king of Babylon is present. All the fear and even anger over the quick victory the warriors of Babylon has affected vanished. If the king of Babylon is not afraid to be in their city, everything must be settled.

King Nebuchadnezzar has never ridden on the causeway from the shores of Tyre out to the center of the island city. It is a pleasant sight, even though some damage was still visible. His own seaport had become the primary import and export location. Tyre was still a grand port of ships and activity. It is a healing visit. The governor needs this support for his daunting task of returning peace to the people.

Traveling to Southern Palestine is nothing less than the previous countries. The farming areas of the poor people are still full of life, peaceful to view, and enjoyable. These simple people were ecstatic to just witness the king and queen riding in the carriage surrounded by the warriors. The appearance of these warriors and their chariots is enough to melt the hearts of enemies that might appear along the way.

King Nebuchadnezzar had inquired from Governor Belteshazzar of the estate of Jeremiah the seer and had directed his carriage driver to visit him. The old seer was broken in humility when he saw the impressive golden carriage of the king. Quickly charging his servants to prepare the best meal available, they leave to perform the task. Jeremiah welcomes the King Nebuchadnezzar and Queen Amytis into his nice but humble home. The king and queen sit in Jeremiah's family room where the Scrolls' are neatly available and talk of Zion, the temple, and the talented choir now living in Babylon.

The king said, "I honor you, Jeremiah, for your faith and your Scroll that I love to read. I must tell you that I wept as I watched your Zion in flames. The grief I felt continues to disturb me because I now know the sacredness of that temple. I saw the walls fall and remembered the words of my father, King Nebopolasser. Your revelations promise it will be built again, and I believe it."

Queen Amytis shares her faith and love in hearing Ezekiel reading and teaching the Scrolls. She says, "Ezekiel is such a faithful lover of your Scrolls and his writings are full of promises. I can almost see the temple he describes that will be built someday. I worship your God," she said to Jeremiah.

The servant kills a young calf and hurriedly roasts the best of the kill. The barley bread is baked and all the trimmings of a feast are ready. As the king and queen ate, they would never forget this meal in a simple seer's home. They left with joy and a sense that they had been in the presence of a Divine visitation.

It is the king's choice not to go near the ruins of the City of Zion. He knows the countryside in that vicinity was mainly a wasteland. Back toward the north and again crossing the Euphrates River at Carchemish, they proceed to visit cities all over the

Mesopotamian Valley. The unannounced visits are exciting. The picture of fruitful estates and plantations on normal working days is an impressive experience. Shaking hands with working farmers was a joy to experience.

Passing through Northern Mesopotamia, they visited several communities of Assyrian people. The king chose to stop as often as possible and renew friendship with them. It is a remarkable surprise when he met former warriors that served under his father. He recognizes several older gentlemen that remembered him romping among the warriors at Uruk. He carefully buries the old antagonism between Assyrians and Chaldeans. Some had read his recent epic and were ready to forgive and forget. They knew the Assyrian Empire would never exist again until the last one World Government.

Several weeks later, after spending time in Uruk, they reach the seaport on the gulf. The city buzzes with the traders, ships, carts and their donkeys, and the busy markets. For the first time in years, the king and queen decide to walk through the market to see the traders in action. Within minutes it became a pandemonium. After hours of enjoying sights, seeing enormous seagoing vessels docked or moving in or out of the port, the king and queen felt like Babylonians instead of just royalty. The city would never forget.

It was time to visit his mother, Queen Hanna. She did not know they were coming until the golden carriage entered the drive. For several months, laborers had been building a road with several simple bridges for the king to visit without having to leave his carriage. The queen is frail, but overjoyed. They sit and talk of all the experiences that had made this trip so wonderful. The queen enjoys every detail.

The king says, "Mother, tomorrow, Amytis and I are going to spend the day in the marshes. This time we will have our warriors for protection and we will even pack a meal to share at my old campsite where I hid. Our lives are so different, and being a king is so enjoyable when you know you are just like everybody else."

His mother replies, "Son, I would love to go with you, but I'm not able. Will you make for your mother a last but precious heart from a bush at that site? I am so grateful that all is well again and this will be my gift from you to remember. I love you and Amytis, my son."

Exhausted, she goes to bed early. When the king and queen returned late the next day from the wild, they discover that Queen Hanna died during the night. Her servants found her during mid morning, but chose not to disturb the king and queen spending time where the king played as a boy and retreated in his sickness.

The queen is buried with the heart that her son made for her at the site he had hidden for those seven years. This was the same place where he had played and used as his hideout when he was an active young lad.

30

The Seer Living in Babylon

565 BC

The gods are in a furious battle over the soul and remains of Queen Hanna. She and King Nebopolasser served Marduk all the days of his kingship, and had dedicated Nabu, their son, to him. This truth and its conflict raged right down to the end of her life, but she had settled her mind. The God of Belteshazzar, the God of Zion, had saved her son out of his insanity, and she surrendered her faith to Him. This clear decision had been firmly stated to her son, King Nebuchadnezzar, and he will, with joy, direct her funeral according to her faith.

Customs of Chaldea required that bodies of the deceased be cremated and placed in a mausoleum or spread over their estates, but Queen Hanna wanted to be buried as the Scrolls determine. She will be honored at the memorial provided for king Nebopolasser in Babylon, but her burial will be private in her garden paradise. Seer Ezekiel came from the capital to officiate. The family is present to grieve together and united in love for one another. But more than for one another, they are here for a respected mother of New Babylon. A small representation of the great choir is present to sing the songs of joy so loved by Queen Hanna.

While the Golden Empire continues to expand and grow richer, the quiet movement of spiritual life is expanding also. The seer Ezekiel, an exceedingly strong voice for the Scrolls, is living a short distance south of Babylon. Right on the Euphrates River, he is writing the Scrolls as directed by the unseen Spirit while shepherding the people removed from Zion. The Royal College, destroyed with the destruction of Zion, has reopened in Babylon. It is a center of learning for Scroll lovers and will be for centuries to come.

Governor Belteshazzar is responsible for directing funds to build and operate this center for learning and copying the Scrolls. The king is supportive and a frequent visitor. The governor and his three vice-governors are regular guest lecturers, and are helping to make this college a strong institution of higher learning. The Doctorate of the Scrolls is only one of many degrees offered. Leaders in and learners of economics, architecture, medicine, languages, engineering, and many other disciplines are given the highest levels of expertise on this campus. It has quickly become one of the finest learning centers in the empire, respected by many, except those strongly prejudiced against the scholars from Zion.

The campus is a lovely sight right on the bank of the Euphrates River. Governor Belteshazzar builds himself a home for the future right beside the grounds. Lecture facilities are spacious, and the dorms are sufficient for several thousand students. The tens of thousands of Babylonian lords, news reporters, businessmen, architectural craftsmen, and every field of learning to direct a worldwide empire must be trained. This learning center immediately becomes one of the best available.

Students from every province of Babylon are enrolling at this star-studded institution. With Governor Belteshazzar helping appoint officers for every position in the empire, this place of learning holds the high ground. No slothfulness is allowed on this campus, and the results are staggering.

Governor Belteshazzar has brought a special and learned scholar from Medea as President of the Royal College. He is the son of Kumrama, the gentleman lord whose estate had welcomed King Cyaxares and the five-year-old Princess Amytis on her first adventure into those mountains. President Benyamin brings a wealth of learning and accomplishments. Giving up estate life and a lordship appointment by his king is not easy, but his opportunity to educate thousands is well worth the price. He is an immediate success. President Benyamin is a third generation captive from the city of Megiddo. His love of the Scrolls is unquestioned, but quiet.

Back in the province of Zion, Jeremiah lives a heartbroken but hopeful life. There is no joy in the fulfillment of his sad declarations made to King Zedekiah. The land around the province of Zion for many miles is waste and destruction. While there is peace and plenty at his estate, most of those left in Zion are poor and undisciplined and can barely survive. Every prediction of his and Ezekiel's Scrolls has come to pass. Other cities of the Zion people are mostly poor and without walls for protection.

Tyre, a neighboring city in upper Palestine, is presently prosperous but full of rebellious talk. Seer Jeremiah knows that it will yet be destroyed. Of all the provinces in the Golden Empire, only the province of Zion is hurting financially, and only Zion and Tyre are still rebellious. Those who should know the most and have been warned by the faithful seers are fairing the worst. Knowledge begets responsibility, and rejected responsibility begets woes and sorrow. It is the code of life that never varies.

Governor Belteshazzar receives a personal letter from Jeremiah. The letter reads:

> To my personal friend, Daniel who brought so much joy to my life many years ago in Zion,
>
>   I often think of the hours we discussed the Scrolls of Moses, King David, and others. The joy of reading that which came from God is never boring. I knew then that you were being prepared to preserve our way of life during the seventy years of captivity. I cannot help but grieve to think

of the even greater suffering we would have endured if you and Azariah, Mishael, and Hananiah had not been ready to be carried as captives to Babylon.

I watched our God preparing you, and saw your tenacity for right, regardless of the cost. You never trembled when the professors threatened to throw you out of the class. You were such gentlemen, and entrusted the whole matter to God over and over again. I'm glad your families are there with you for a life that is certainly far beyond your homes of long ago.

The city of Zion is too sad to view. It is all waste, with wild animals roaming freely in the debris. Owls and other birds of prey still sift through the dirt and dust for morsels of decaying flesh. After nearly fifteen years, the stench is still unbearable.

Poor people are everywhere in the surrounding provinces, trying to eke out a living without the favor of God. I and other Scroll lovers meet regularly for prayer and study, and fill our hearts with the future hopes. What is often depressing is the knowledge that none of us will see better days in this life.

Those appointed to govern us are constantly at war with each other. I expect to be taken by force into Egypt. They have warned me several times about my writings, but I cannot speak, except as God speaks.

Reports from Babylon are spectacular. The king visited me, and what a surprise! He and Queen Amytis truly believe the Scrolls, and that is a miracle. I read his epic, and all I could do was weep with gratefulness that we are friends and fellow travelers after the same faith.

I'm hearing wonderful news of the new Royal College. Several young men among the poor are heading for Babylon as I write. They have letters of recommendation from me, and we need them educated that they may know the marvelous truths. Please consider them as students. They have no funds, but I believe God has directed them to Babylon and to the college.

One of them is named Ezra, one Nehemiah, and the other, Zerubbabel. They are young men in their teens, and the time is ripe for them to be made ready for when the seventy years are finished. Please take special interest and help prepare them to rebuild the city of Zion that we love. Teach them to think and act like you do.

I'm so excited and just plain full of hope. It would be wonderful if I could be young again, and see those walls of Zion gleaming in the sunlight. They will gleam again, and that is what really matters.

Signed, Jeremiah

The young men arrive in Babylon a few days after the "News Chariot" delivers Jeremiah's letter. They wait patiently in the foyer of the president's office for an appointment. President Benyamin steps into the foyer to see three very poor, young teenagers, waiting with smiles of certainty on their faces. He asks them, "Young men, your very smiles capture my attention. Please tell me who you are."

Ezra speaks for them all when he says, "President Benyamin, we are young men from the small farms of Zion. We do not come with riches. In fact, the beauty of this campus and the city of Babylon is overwhelming to us. We come because there is no college in Zion. We are young, our minds are fertile, and we want a full education from an institution where the Scrolls are loved. Are we at the right place?"

"You better believe you are! You are Ezra, and you are Nehemiah." He waits to see if he has the first two names right. They smile and say, "Yes." He continues, "And you are Zerubbabel. Governor Belteshazzar told me of your coming. I have the letter the eminent seer, Jeremiah, wrote introducing you. Welcome to the Royal College in Babylon. You are already enrolled, and rooms in our dorm are prepared. We will put you to learning right away.

"But first, may I tell you that my great grandfather was from Megiddo, and was brought in chains to the Medean Mountains. I am one of you. I am to let the governor know that you are here, and he will come to visit. He is planning an invitation to the Golden Palace for all three of you. Make sure that you are at our temple of Zion on Saturday. You will be introduced as special friends of Seer Jeremiah. Again, welcome."

Shortly, a kind lady comes to show them the campus and their rooms, and to prepare their schedules of classes. They are happy young men—bright with the hope of the Scrolls.

The Royal College allows each religious group to conduct a fellowship for those who hold their ideas and beliefs. The lovers of the Scrolls are, indeed, a large body and their fellowship is lively. Each group is provided a place to meet and fellowship together. Ezra, Nehemiah, and Zerubbabel are overwhelmed at meeting so many followers as themselves. Endless discussions occur around the writings of the different Scrolls.

Frequently, they discuss their concerns about captivity, deportations, and destruction of the city of Zion. A famous question often discussed is when did the prophesied seventy years of captivity begin; at the first deportation, the second or at the destruction of their capital city. When the debate is over, most of them are just happy to be studying the excellent writings they love, and to be educated in their chosen professions.

Ezekiel is the spiritual heart of the Royal College and the temple of Zion. He is building a new home too, adjacent to the governor's home, beside the college grounds. While a popular and frequent speaker at the college, he is careful how he is perceived. He has no interest in social events, but rather to live in constant communion with his God. The temple in Zion is a house of prayer, and Ezekiel protects that with total dedication.

It is beautiful to see the careful devotion of the Scroll lovers. The happiness they manifest is not of the world, or earthly pleasure, nor possessions, but of the inward marvel of a relationship. They may be in a different environment, but the life of Zion still floods their hearts, and they are extremely satisfied.

Seer Ezekiel and the governor are often together to inspire each other and to pray. Shadrach, Meshach, and Abednego would spend part of every day with Ezekiel if they could. His words are always the same, "Yes, yes, come to the temple and we will pray together." They are ever conscious of the wars of the gods. They know that their God directs the prayers of His followers for His purposes to triumph.

Nehemiah has just left class in the Royal College of Babylon and sees Ezra crossing under the elaborate, covered walk. The campus is a garden with nature's best flourishing everywhere. They can see the walls of Babylon, and at night the enormous torches create a glow that seems unreal in its beauty. The Hanging Garden is frequently visited and everyone loves the free time when they can walk in the golden city and shop in the bazaars that are almost everywhere.

"Ezra," he calls in a voice only loud enough for him to hear, "Stop a minute. I must tell you about my class. My teacher for theology is Professor Hammurabi, named after the great Babylonian king of centuries ago. He is a believer of many years from Erech. His father, who still worships Inanna, has a large date plantation, and was general of the warriors of Babylon under King Nebopolasser. What a teacher of our scrolls! He believes they are literal.

"Today, he led us in discussing the seventy years of captivity of the people of Zion, and believes it began with the first captives. That means the captivity began forty-two years ago, and leaves only twenty-eight more years. That makes perfect sense to me."

"If you remember, those are the same dates that Jeremiah has always believed," answers Ezra. "He encouraged me to expect our coming to Babylon to be preparation for us to be a part of the exiles returning to Zion. He used to pause when he said those things. I know he was secretly sad that his life expectancy will not allow him to see that return."

Nehemiah responds, "Being the man of faith and perfectly confident of God's exact actions, based on His revelations, he was excited just in believing. I remember him shouting out his hope, and he would say, 'It's almost as good and wonderful to know it is going to happen as to actually see it happen.' He would then say, 'I'm a happy believer.' Those wonderful statements by Jeremiah still bless me with added assurance."

Zerubbabel comes across the knoll among the flowering trees near the classroom buildings. "What are you two talking about without me?" Together they walk down to the river edge where weeping willows line the sidewalks and sitting areas. "Tell me what you are so happy and excited about. I have brought enough lunch for all of us. Let's just sit here."

Across the Euphrates is a date plantation, and the beautiful trees are hanging with fruit. Workers are busy cleaning away any competitive growth from shrubs and brambles. Others are carefully using special lifts to gather the ripe dates. Their mouths water just watching the action.

After telling Zerubbabel their conversation, they talk at length of the hope that fills the Zion community. Zerubbabel says, "For the most part, the older generation is settled to finish life in Babylon. But we are determined to create a longing for Zion in the younger captives."

The temple is constructed so that the worshippers are facing toward their homes of long ago. The pious will not pray until they are facing west, and not only west, but at the perfect angle toward the ruins of Zion.

31

The Head of Gold Is Dead

562 BC

King Nebuchadnezzar and Queen Amytis have spent the day together reminiscing of the past and considering their approaching forty-third anniversary as king and queen of Babylon. Deep down they know there will never be a city as magnificent and rich as the golden city. The towering fifty-six miles of walls—three hundred feet in height with numerous gates all covered in pure gold—is too beautiful to describe. They had called for their golden carriage and guards and spend the afternoon and evening circling the city. As the torches were lit at dusk they lingered some distance just to admire the beauty.

Returning back to the palace, they decide to walk the Processional for a short distance and chat with ordinary Babylonians. It was a memorial occasion to families and couples enjoying the sights and relaxing when they found themselves with the king and queen. The king is sixty-eight years old and his queen is sixty-seven. They feel healthy and are planning for many years to come.

They meet Governor Belteshazzar and invite him to their family room just to continue to reminisce. The conversation returns to the Divine dream that Belteshazzar had interpreted forty-one years earlier.

The king says, "Governor Belteshazzar, your interpretation of my dream envisioned this golden city and Golden Empire and it was stated that I was the king over all of this. Your God that is now my God also appointed me as the King of Gold. I am grateful that He humbled me so that I can actually enjoy my call and the city instead of being consumed by them. I can remember when I was possessed by it all. Now I know that all is His and He rules in the kingdom of men. When my time is finished I can go in peace.

"I have miserably failed my son and crown prince. In spite of my best efforts since I returned to the throne his demeanor has become impossible. If I should pass suddenly yours and Amytis' strength may help but if he refuses it will be disaster. I fear for the empire with him on the throne. If he replaces the wise but aged lords with his young friends the results will be what you remember in your city of Zion. Arrogant men like I became cannot rule others with success. Even the best of kings must be surrounded by noble men and women.

"Tomorrow, after the business matters are finished, Amytis and I are going to spend time enjoying her beautiful garden. People from the whole world are coming to Babylon just to visit 'The Hanging Garden' and I have spent so little time and it is right beside me. Governor I want you to invite Shadrach, Meshach, and Abednego to come with you and us for this time together. I will order a special meal prepared for the evening after time in the garden."

Matters of the vast empire always break in on happy occasions. They include the problem in the seaport city of Tyre. The king is convinced that there is no option any longer but the complete destruction of the city. His general is given permission to take the necessary force and the huge casting machines of flaming tar balls to settle the matter. The city has been under siege for three years with no success. This large island city, so very proud of its many victories over its enemies, would soon be rubble in the sea.

King Nebuchadnezzar, the skillful warrior himself, has little desire for these kinds of decisions any longer, but his general and the two million warriors demand action. The king decides not to

go but to send his crown prince in his stead. Maybe, General Nebuzaradan could be a great influence on his son and strengthen him
toward maturity in matters of the empire. The king would secretly
speak to the general. The warriors would be ready to leave in seven
days.

"Amytis," the king said, "our friends are here, let's enjoy the afternoon with them."

Climbing about the Hanging Gardens was both strenuous and
invigorating. The sun was especially bright but the cool waters flowing through the garden made it all seem refreshing. Part of the first
level was full of pistachio trees hanging with their fruit, but not
yet ripe for gathering. Walking among these stately specimens was
enjoyable. What an opening picture before they begin the climb.

Behind these trees were areas for the larger animals. The area
for the lions was heavily fortified. Nearby the lions, the tigers, and
cougars were equally secured. All the carnivores were fed from the
wild to help maintain their natural viciousness. Several of these large
creatures were nursing their young and did not relish visitors close
to them. Queen Amytis was especially happy to visit these beautiful
animals with the king beside her. They had been transported from
Medea. She came often but the king had only been here a few times
and that for inspection of the care for the zoo and gardens.

As they ascended among the small trees and flowering shrubs,
the king became talkative.

"I'm amazed at the beauty of these grand gardens. Look," he
said, "at these roses." The rose garden was at the third level and was
a picture of many colors and shapes. The king pauses and begins to
gather a large number. When he had an arm filled he asked a servant
of the queen who was present to care for them for Queen Amytis.

"Take these, he said, and make the biggest basket ever made and
put it on her favorite table in our family room." She laughs with
sheer joy at her Nabu's thoughtfulness.

Slowly they ascended among the world's most beautiful trees, flowers, and animals. Every animal lived in a well-kept area that was created to match their natural habitat. To see rabbits dashing into their open holes in the earthen floor or squirrels hiding in the trees is very interesting.

Parrots chatter among exotic trees from the jungles of Africa while herons stand in what looks like the marshes of the king's place of birth. Again, the king remarks, "Being a king has made my life so complex that I have missed these natural sights. These animals are living so naturally and the beauty of it all makes me feel refreshed and happy. I must come here every week for the rest of my life."

"Nabu," Amytis looks with joy as she speaks, "I have often told you the joy you have given me in this man-made mountain. It is really more beautiful than the real mountains because it brings it all into one huge place. I would need to travel for weeks in Mede to see what we have seen today."

They ascend until they stand among the torches at the top.

"What a sight," the king says. "I have never been up here before. My view of this was from the ground below or at best riding on the walls in our carriage. Surely we can see for many miles."

As the king surveys the countryside, he begins to recognize different locations. "I see Lord Neshrin's date plantation where we have often visited for a quiet afternoon."

He turns to the governor and says, "Look at the Royal College. It is a beautiful campus. No wonder that the youth of the world are enrolled in our excellent learning institution!"

Then the king notices the crowded bazaars at different sites.

"Amytis, tomorrow afternoon we are going shopping our-selves. Remember telling me about riding incognito to the seaport and shopping at a roadside farmers market? After the visit to the bazaars, next we are going to the seaport and we are going to stop at that same market. Can you remember where it is?"

"Nabu, I will never forget where it is. Remember I was on my way to find my love. Everything about those days is etched in my heart forever."

The governor and vice governors have been making conversation together and listening to the king and queen. Just to be with the royal couple is a delight to them. Now the governor sees the value of this time together and speaks.

"King Nebuchadnezzar, we four men were just a little younger than you two when we marched across the desert to Babylon. Having been chosen from the Royal College there in Zion we were afforded some liberties but many of our friends were in chains. I have never told you but we watched several men and women die en route and simply left for birds of prey," says the governor.

"All of that is behind us but it makes us happy to see what changes have occurred in your lives. You two were never like the many kings we had read about. Neither were you like the kings we had lived under. One of our kings, Josiah, was a good man, but very weak before the noble men of Zion. The rest that we have known of our own kings in Zion were no different from other kings of the nations.

"I want to thank you for allowing us to serve. This is without doubt the 'Golden Empire' and there will never be another as rich or as celebrated in so many ways. You have given us good liberty in helping build this empire. You have many talented leaders, numbers of them from Zion or Samarian provinces of long ago removed and some since we were brought to Babylon ourselves. There are also many remarkable leaders from every country that is part of this empire."

Shadrach adds, "We are honored, O, King and Queen, for the life of riches and plenty that we have and enjoy. More than that, we are honored that we can care for the thousands that have been brought from our province of Zion. Caring for them as you have allowed us is well worth our lives here in your world. Our own families are blessed and live in our faith in this province of Babylon."

Carefully they proceed down the many steps into the garden area surrounding the elevated areas. The evening meal is ready in the private quarters of the king and the conversation of animals, different species of flowers and trees fill the evening time as they enjoy the king's cuisine. This meal was prepared to represent the diet restriction of these men from Zion.

When matters of government are completed the next day, the king quickly returns to his beloved Amytis. "Amytis, this is our day to visit the bazaars of our Babylon. Our guards demand that they accompany us. There have been some reports of sabotage and even an effort to attack us but they have secured it all. There is nothing to fear. We are protected by the bravest. As I have learned of the security net that was cast around the estate of my Hanna when I was lost I have ceased to fear anything," he explains.

"Recently, Arioch our captain of the guards told me of twice intercepting enemies that sought to penetrate the net to destroy me. One of these groups was from the Assyrian area and one from the city of Tyre. Both were well planned and well armed but they failed because our guards were so thorough."

As they begin to walk throughout the bazaar, the crowds are ecstatic to see the king and queen up close. They simply chatted and shook hands while Amytis hugs people and the king enjoys the presence of children. One heckler was removed during the evening but the crowd drowned out any annoying words with shouts of love.

Amytis buys a beautiful vase for a special place in her family room while the king acquires a new covering to give his governor. The king also purchases his princess a cape to wear with a new dress that the queen had ordered to be made.

Suddenly the king said to Arioch, "Please go get my princess." When he returned with Princess Kima, she adds total new joy to the large crowds that were everywhere. She immediately became the center of attention. Now sixteen, she is another Amytis, as beautiful and as joyful.

For hours, they moved from bazaar to bazaar and visited thousands. The king asks his captain to get everyone's attention.

"Please quiet a moment, our king wants to speak to you," he says. Being six feet and six inches, the king could easily address the crowd.

"My friends and fellow Babylonians, thank you for allowing my queen and me just to be one of you. The time in these markets has brought me back to my young days. As a boy our Babylonian empire was young and small and father, your king, allowed me to shop and roam the city. Always a guard was close by as we have today, but I loved to buy for myself. Amytis and I just tasted one of the coconut drinks you are all enjoying. It is delicious and I have ordered it for the palace. Also I ate a date bar that I will never forget. Again, thank you for the sheer joy of being your king," the king says.

Roars of thanks and praise filled the air until the king and queen had slowly returned to the palace. The city would hear one person after another as they told their experience of this day.

As soon as the plan could be completed the king and queen are off to the seaport. The warriors are near the city of Tyre and the king gets a daily report but always several days late for travel time. The efficient news chariots bring it quickly to the king.

Traveling to the seaport with all the family except the crown prince is a happy family time. There are grandchildren in the family and Belshazzar is one of them. He is the son of their daughter Nitocris.

The little market where the queen stopped years ago is visited. The same beautiful couple is right there in charge and the queen tells them her story. The wife is quick to remember spotting the queen and saying to her husband, "She looks so much like our queen, she must be her sister." They laugh together as they think of how it all ended with the king back on his throne.

King Nebopolasser's estate is as beautiful as ever and became home to Nebuchadnezzar, Amytis, and the family for a few days.

It was a long deserved vacation for the family. With the place was under tight security all of them are free to roam and play without the restriction of the capital.

After several days at the seaport, now a metropolitan city, the family is back in Babylon. The king receives the report that the island city of Tyre is no more. After years of siege, the warriors were determined to destroy the city and leave nothing behind. They were marching home as wealthy warriors with an abundance of booty for the empire.

The king is happier than he has ever been. Amytis is full of joy. In just a few days they will celebrate forty-three years of their reign as king and queen. Twenty years earlier Cyaxares had died and Amytis had grieved near despair. After returning from Babylon following the king's illness and disappearance, he had suddenly collapsed. The two men of Amytis' life were her father and Nabu. She had endured the time of her Nebuchadnezzar's despair with grace and dignity.

The next morning she awakens and slips quietly to her place of devotion. The king calls her and she is immediately at his side. He says "Amytis, I love you," and he was dead.

Forty-three years as a king, building mammoth walls, massive centers of religion or government structures, and shaping the world empire had taken a toll. Seven years lived in the marshes was a draining experience. His heart was full but tired. With no apparent sickness, it simply stopped. The Head of Gold was dead. Amytis would survive because she had to.

The Babylonian Empire Is Finished

537 BC

From the farthest flung corners of the Babylonian Empire, thousands of people are stunned by the sudden death of their champion. King Nebuchadnezzar was indeed the "Head of Gold" and the men chosen to rule under him are the best. The order of this empire is without parallel and probably impossible to duplicate. The soundness of each decision and appointment keeps the empire humming and quiet. His warriors are indeed "his warriors" and have served the king, not the empire. That made for efficiency as he ruled but will leave the empire vulnerable in his death.

All of the king's governors, judges, lords, and wise men are quick to reach Babylon so as not to miss the funeral of the king. He lies in state after being embalmed by Egypt's best and his burial casket is filled with Babylon's aromas. The enormous arena where he loved to be is the scene of the memorial. The loved Zion Choir is preparing to sing and Seer Ezekiel will officiate. Portions of his epic will be read to show that God had become important in his life.

Almost no one is untouched by the wealth of the Golden Empire. The riches that flow in every direction leave few people with reasons to dislike their king. The one source of distaste is that he had trusted and depended on Belteshazzar and others among the captives of Zion. Belteshazzar's faith in the God of Zion and the miracle of deliverance for the three vice-governors of Babylon created the foundation of his belief in that God. His seven years of insanity and then a return to reason after his humility had made him a new man. He never resorted to haughtiness and pride again. His firm faith had ended the war of the gods over his future.

Babylon is a city of temples and gods and everyone can choose. Those priests, sorcerers, and Chaldeans that had complained about the king's faith had found scarce sympathy.

The tens of thousands of captives from many provinces are now outstanding citizens and will never forget the payment for their labor after his return to the throne. He became a champion for the poor as his epic had reported from the God of Zion. He and Amytis became fellow Babylonians with the people and are loved as never before.

The empire is in deep mourning and extremely fearful of the future without King Nebuchadnezzar.

The crown prince, Amel-Marduk has begun to run with a motley lot and is a coward before the haughty priests of Marduk and Ishtar. The general over the king's warriors had found the crown prince impossible as they conducted the assault on Tyre. He had said, "He certainly is no warrior and has no concept of proper military techniques." The general and his commanders will be trouble for him as he ascends the throne of Babylon. There is already talk about who can replace him when the time comes.

Amel-Marduk wants to ascend the throne before his father's funeral but Queen Amytis absolutely refuses. She and the chief lords, along with the governor of Babylon, will remain in charge. The crown prince is furious but helpless at the moment. The queen is devastated by her loss but pulls herself together for the sake of the empire. The king had prepared the proper documentation to give her the control to effect a wise transition of the throne. She meets with her lords to plan the funeral and to keep everything secure. She is a capable chairwoman of the session. She announces, "To our lords, to the governor of Babylon, and to the crown prince, I begin with deep sorrow but resolve. Our champion, my love, is dead. The final end of his reign must be equal to the successes he has accomplished. He has truly been the 'Head of Gold' and his last years were memorable years. This empire sits on top of the world and we must not fail in his death. The crown prince will ascend the throne at the right time.

"Our Babylonian lords have requested that I continue as queen for an indefinite time and I have consented to do so. You must know that there is great tension between the crown prince, my son, and I, but the signed documents of our deceased king leave me this option. General Nebuzaradan is totally supportive and will be my general and the warriors will be my warriors until I relinquish the throne. This is the best route to take to guarantee a smooth future for the Golden Empire."

At this announcement Crown Prince Amel-Marduk leaves the meeting infuriated. In the few hours since the king's death was announced he has tried to conduct empire business but has been rebuffed by the lords and administrators. Governor Belteshazzar makes a great effort to reconcile the queen and her son but to no avail. He continues to gather his own lords and supporters and prepare for the moment that he can ascend to the throne. He is causing trouble, but the king's guards are in firm control of the palace and all of the royal buildings and royal courtyards. The general and the queen's warriors are firmly in control of the empire.

The queen continues, "The funeral of the king will be equal to his forty-three years as the 'Head of Gold.' I've appointed our faithful lords to take complete control and to direct the celebration of his life and death. The Zion Choir will sing and the Seer of Zion, Ezekiel, will officiate. A special place in the huge arena will be provided for the priest and all the wise men to be seated. No Babylonian will be shunned and no temple will be excluded. King Nebuchadnezzar was everyone's king in life and shall be in death."

News chariots rush the news to all the empire and every route to Babylon is crowded. The "Golden City" and countryside estates for miles are filled. When no home has a spare bed tents are erected. The Babylonian province is alive with mourners. The warriors are everywhere and nothing to denigrate the memory of the king is tolerated. A continuous file of mourners passes down the Processional and into the golden palace. Just to walk past the golden pillars of the colonnade and to enter the beautiful doors of the palace is like a dream. The king's body is in the atrium dressed in royal attire and lies in a golden casket within a wash of flowers.

Passing down the Processional each mourner must pass workers busy preparing a beautiful burial chamber. It is beside the memorial of King Nebopolasser and beautiful Queen Hanna. The guards of the royal grounds are dressed in the special attire reserved for royal functions or when guarding the king in travel. The palace and all of the royal grounds serve as a stronghold of the guards and the warriors. Beautiful chariots of the warriors sit at every strategic location. The warriors are in their chariots with their drivers and all are standing at stark attention with drawn swords. It is a royal death.

The celebration in the arena is massive. After the seats are filled, every inch of standing room is filled. The Zion Choir sings the songs of joy and celebration until the heart of everyone is refreshed. His lords make great orations about his excellent kingship and the beautiful Queen Amytis tells of his commitment to be hers alone.

"Until the end my king assured me that no other women had ever been his in marital love except me. I can assure you that he was my love and I never desired another. The rest of my life I pledge to all this empire, that your interest will be my life. I love my Nabu, your King Nebuchadnezzar and I love you. We must celebrate his life and not his death."

Governor Belteshazzar stands to read from the king's epic that he wrote after his return from the marshes. With notable emotion for King Nebuchadnezzar he gives the king's own confession of faith in God and his assurance that God is sovereign over all the affairs of men.

"Your king, after his expression of faith, obeyed the instruction to turn from evil and to care for the poor in the Babylonian Empire. He directed over one hundred thousand talents of gold to repay the captives that built our beautiful walls, large bridges, and royal buildings. He directed over fifty thousand talents of gold to pay those required to build the Hanging Garden and the Palace of Gold and another fifty thousand to relieve the poor left behind. He gladly did all that he was commanded to do."

Seer Ezekiel gives a hopeful presentation of the future when the entire world will live in peace and chariots of war will be obsolete. He speaks of spears that will prune the date groves and swords that will become the tools of harvest. He tells of temples where all will worship together and children that will play in the midst of lions. He says that all will worship one King and that King will never die.

Queen Amytis stands with her face to the sky as the king's body is slowly moved to his tomb. The tomb of gold is quickly sealed and guards stand in silence. They will change guards every hour until the Babylonian Empire is no more.

Months of peace reign as the queen gives direction to the Golden Empire. The tension in the palace is strong but the noble lords of King Nebuchadnezzar hold the high ground. Governor Belteshazzar and his vice governors fine-tune every administrative function. General Nebuzaradan is ready to serve Queen Amytis for as long as she sits on the throne.

Under great pressure from the crown prince, she sets the date of his ascension to the throne. Nothing changes until he is crowned. Immediately Governor Belteshazzar is dismissed and every lord replaced. A new general takes the office of General Nebuzaradan and the warriors are given new commanders. King Amel-Marduk gives exalted preference to his chosen gods and requires great reverence before himself by everyone. The city of Babylon becomes an armed camp overnight.

Queen Amytis moves quietly among the new lords and wise men seeking to create a tone of cooperation and smoothness. With her guards she is daily among the simple people of the city and acts as an ambassador for the king. She has no fear of any of the temples and seeks good will of all the priests. Every sacred day she is at the temple of Zion and prays earnestly for her son to be wise and to mature into a kingly man. If he fails she knows that she has done her best.

She becomes a regular guest and lectures at the "Royal University." The name had been changed from Royal College to Royal University after meeting the necessary academic standards. Today she is speaking at the assembly of the entire body of approximately ten thousand. Her assigned subject is "Life with a King."

She says, "To President Benyamin, to the governing body, to Chairman Belteshazzar, to the faculty, and to all the student body, it is my joy to stand in your arena before all of you. First I must tell you I have perfect peace after the loss of our king and my love. Our last years were so happy and I live in the joy of their overflow.

"This university is one of my husband's greatest accomplishments. He was a wise king in so many ways." She pauses and then says, "Human government is never easy and trained leaders always make the difference. When my king sent Master Ashpenaz to the Royal College in Zion to bring back the best and brightest young men to train for his administration it was one of his greatest acts. All four of those men are here today—they made the difference in the Babylonian Empire. I honor them before all of you."

She then tells of her life from the mountains of Mede to the present. Her experiences as a princess are explained in such simple terms that the myth connected to the goddess idea simply disappears. She talks of love for her Nabu, seeking to instill a sense of marital faithfulness in the listeners. Telling of her trials and faith during Nebuchadnezzar's darkness makes her a big hit with the students. It will be a long remembered presentation at this learning institution. The applause is deafening.

For almost two years King Amel-Marduk pursues an unrestrained and calculated approach toward changing everything of the laws and policies his father had instituted. Taxes are increased and tariffs on goods flowing throughout the empire are raised drastically. He speaks to his lords and governor with a haughty and brazen air. He opens a harem of concubines and chooses young maidens at will.

Queen Amytis steps into the throne room bypassing all royal protocol and proceeds to ask everyone to leave. She then speaks unceremoniously to Amel, as she calls him.

She says angrily, "My son, you are playing the fool with the Golden Empire built by your father and myself with excellent and noble lords, governors, and administrators. You have freed a wicked man, King Jehoiakim, and placed him on the royal payroll. Your kidnapping of beautiful maidens from their parents to use to satisfy your lust is abominable to the memory of my love, King Nebuchadnezzar. The poor have been forsaken and the captives of many nations that have earned their citizenship you are returning to slavery. The noble people of Babylon will rise up and slay you. Your mother will applaud their action!" She leaves him aghast sitting on the throne.

That night, his guards slip into his bedroom and end his life. A brother-in-law that had honorably served King Nebuchadnezzar and is of like disposition with the late ruler ascends the throne. He is the husband of Nitocris, the third child of Nebuchadnezzar and Amytis. Queen Amytis had aided the now King Neriglissar in this action to save the Babylonian Empire.

Order is restored throughout the city. Governor Belteshazzar and his vice governors are returned to their offices. The noble lords are welcomed back to lead the empire and the general is again placed in charge of the king's warriors. Within a few days the Babylonian Empire is humming with efficiency. The king's harem is closed and the beautiful maidens are returned to their families and in some case their espoused husbands.

Four years later, King Neriglissar dies suddenly of natural causes. His son rules for three months before he is murdered in retaliation for the death of Amel-Marduk.

The husband of King Nebuchadnezzar and Queen Amytis' first daughter ascends the throne. He is the son of the governor of Haran whose mother is a priestess of the moon god Sin. His interest is not the governing of the empire but the building of temples. The great Babylonian Empire begins a slow decline that will never reverse itself.

The king's son, Belshazzar, becomes his co-regent and rules the empire while his father pursues archeological excavations, especially of ancient temples that he then proceeds to rebuild. Again, Governor Belteshazzar is replaced, along with his vice governors. The new lords of the empire are men of like nature with the king and pursue the life of carelessness and debauchery.

King Belshazzar, the grandson of the King of Gold, lives in splendor. Countless parties are his interest and the stately Palace of Gold has become a mockery to the God that has revealed Himself to this city and the empire that flourishes by His order. The war of the gods rages on and sometimes no one can name the winner.

The Persians Are Coming

539 BC

The Babylonian Empire is in disarray from neglect and misdirection. King Nobonidus has little interest in the unlimited challenges of the empire. The warriors have become his personal servants, pursuing with him the dreams of ancient history. The king's son and co-regent is partying instead of reigning. It all seems so mindless with their having full knowledge of the greatness the Babylonian Empire was under King Nebuchadnezzar. The Head of Gold should have had sons and family members of noble character. Life had been too easy in the golden palace.

Province after province is slipping out of the empire with barely a note. Capable governors and princes are acting independently. The large caravans of traders are bypassing Babylon to save the expenditures of high, unreasonable tariffs. The markets of the golden city had been the international center of trade and barter. Now, the cities of Susa and Damascus and even Thebes are exploding in world trade while Babylon is slipping from its prior greatness.

Babylon is still the jewel of beauty and magnificence. The walls shine each night under the glow of its huge torches. The Hanging Garden is one of the world's seven wonders and draws more visitors than all of the other grand sites together. To stand before the golden tomb of the famous King Nebuchadnezzar is a worldwide dream. On the right the palace gleams in the sunshine. On the left is the entrance of Marduk with its golden gates. Watching a chariot race from the Babylonian arena is still a world-class event.

Queen Amytis is ninety years old and as spry as a much younger lady. Anyone that visits Babylon will spend at least one day near the palace or visiting the Hanging Garden just for the pleasure of spotting, Queen Amytis, the crown jewel of the world. She seems to be immortal and often visits the Zion Temple where she prays and weeps over the future of the Babylonian Empire.

Royal University is now the hub of the Babylonian Province. King Nebuchadnezzar had established an endowment of large treasure for this premier institution. It had been created in an untouchable fashion to assure that future kings could not rob it. After being dismissed as governor, Belteshazzar gives his full attention to the university. It is clearly the one world-class higher learning campus. Well-endowed, no person with a record of academic pursuit is rejected. The wisdom that had made the Babylonian Empire the Golden Empire is still alive behind the immense walls that enclose this university that sits right on the Euphrates River.

Nothing really seems different in the Babylonian province or in the golden city but the empire is adrift. The absence of the towering king that had inspired awe and even fear is taking its toll. The two million plus warriors were constantly marching and visible in different parts of the empire while King Nebuchadnezzar was alive. Now, they are only visible occasionally to meet some petty need of King Nobonidus or his co-regent King Belshazzar. The news chariots are almost a fact of the past and missed greatly by the people. It had been inspiring just to watch them race around the empire. They were seen as good news chariots that seemed to spell that all was well.

King Nobonidus is rebuilding the ancient temple of E-Khulkhul in Haran where his mother had been a goddess. It is a temple to the god Sin, worshipped also in Ur, south of Babylon. Belshazzar has sent for the lords from throughout the empire to come to a great feast and celebration in the golden city. Seeing the drift of the empire he is planning to turn the tide by wining and dining all of them into submission.

His invitation is extended. "I, Belshazzar, sitting on the golden throne of King Nebuchadnezzar, am planning for you the greatest feast of Babylonian history. The golden palace, the jewel of the city, is being prepared to receive you in the highest fashion. An abundance of delicacies and fantastic cuisine will satisfy your desires. My harem has been greatly enlarged and there will be no shortage of beautiful maidens to court your favors.

"A terrific race will entertain you on day one. The most determined of our drivers will race for you and I promise that almost every one of them is willing to die to win. There were laws against drivers acting in ways that might endanger another driver but those restrictions have been removed. This will be the race of your life. The prize for the winner is a thousand talents of gold.

"For your pleasure on day two there will be lion and tiger fights. These are exciting events. The animals will be fed raw meat from slain animals for weeks but then allowed to go hungry for several days. Once they are turned loose in the arena enclosure the fights will be to the death. This, too, is a sport from our past that we have recently restored to our city. Many of our citizens are resisting it, but with horrendous pressure I have overruled their rejection. It is indeed a new day in Babylon and we require the presence of every governor, prince, lord, or noble.

"The banquet to be held on the third day will be my big gift to you. No shortage of wine will occur. We will drink to our satisfaction, while my maidens dance and perform. You will find the performances to be the most daring and entertaining acts possible. We will drink to every god that is worshipped in our empire. We will mix our worship of our gods with the acts of our maidens.

"Some anger has been directed toward me because I have not renounced the worship of the God of Zion that my grandfather,

King Nebuchadnezzar, worshipped. At this banquet I will bring the famous vessels taken from Solomon's Temple in Zion and we will drink wine from them while we worship all the gods of your cultures. This will be a liberating event and every god of Babylon will be declared equal."

Babylon is filled to capacity. Excitement for King Belshazzar reign suddenly soars, bought with the promise of unrestrained pleasures. Provinces showing rebellion return to the fold. The great traders start toward the golden city to fill it with their goods and to reopen the international market places. Where King Belshazzar has failed in diplomacy seems to be made up in the promises of unfettered delights and sexual fantasies.

The mood in Babylon is suddenly so different that it is frightening to almost everyone. The temples are alive with sacrifices and the terrible chants of their priests fill the air. Every temple is filled with worshippers and many move from one temple to another. If one god fails another god may save the day.

Sharma is a tall and striking young driver. He weighs a bit over two hundred pounds and has a massive, muscular build. He has been named as the first choice to win. Many recognize him as he walks thru the city.

"Sharma! Sharma!" the crowd begins to shout and he revels in the attention. "Can you win over Meltho and Fesho?" they scream. These two drivers have been declared as the second and third choices, respectively, to win. He takes the opportunity to speak. Standing on a ledge he motions for attention. "I will win!" he shouts, "or I will die in the struggle! This is my greatest opportunity of life. My horse has never lost a race and I cannot return home if I lose. Watch me!" he screams.

The race is dangerous and vicious from the start. The drivers have been pushed to their limit to go for the gold. Nothing is to stop them, life or death. The race lasts for hours. The horses are pushed beyond their limits and some die on the walls and the inclines and declines. Sharma is seen as he and his chariot literally push Fesho's chariot off the wall and he plunges three hundred feet to his death. The crowd roars its approval since Fesho is a dark man from Assyrian territory. Several men die vicious deaths but the chosen champion, Sharma, wins the gold.

The animal fights fill the arena with blood. This had happened often during an earlier period in this same arena, but the mood of the Babylonian Empire had changed just as King Nebuchadnezzar and Queen Amytis had changed. The return to this kind of event seems to fill the city with a darkness that even the supporters find scary.

It is banquet time in the Palace of Gold built to give vision to the golden empire. The king is excited and filled with pleasure over his celebration. The promise of returning the Babylonian Empire to its former greatness inspires him to the brim.

He does not consider that the news of this fantastic celebration and the clear announcement that it will be a party of drunkenness has gone to his enemies also. The Persians are busy planning a new world empire and have set their sights on Babylon. It is the perfect time to take the city.

The party begins and the palace is full of the king's lords, governors, wise men, princes, and nobles. Maidens from the king's harem are dressed in their most provocative attire. Wine is offered like water; tasty and satisfying and totally inebriating. It is not long before the king is in a stupor.

For all to hear, he says, "Servants, I said servants, go quickly to the treasure house. There is a room marked, 'Not to be touched' and signed King Nebuchadnezzar. Beneath that sign it says, 'The vessels from Solomon's Temple—preserved for the future temple.' Bring them! Bring all of them! Place them here before me. Do it quickly before I cannot remember what to say."

In a few minutes, because the king's temper is at a feverous pitch, the servants rush into the palace with vessel after vessel. There are hundreds and they gleam in golden splendor. Still faintly visible are the words, "Holy unto the Lord, Holy unto the Lord."

"Forget those words!" screams the king, "Come quickly and get you a vessel! Fill it with my excellent wine! Maybe we can make God drunk and He will come down to play with us!" For hours they pass the vessels among themselves and drink the wine of the king. As they drink they praise every god whose name they can remember.

Suddenly a scream splits the air. The revelry of the whole palace is quickly silenced, and gloom like thick darkness fills the house. "Look! Look!" one after the other cries. A hand without a body is moving across the wall over the king's head. Words are being written but no one knows the language. The atmosphere is still except for quiet wailing and weeping. The king breaks out in a deathly shake. His joints are loose and his knees are clattering so loud that those near him can hear the strange sounds.

"Where are my wise men, my soothsayers, my Chaldeans, and my astrologers?" he cries. "Tell me what those words are saying! Where did that hand come from? Is this a trick?"

The Chaldeans and all his leading religious men gather as many as are not so drunk they cannot stand. They speak together, they shake their heads, and they fumble for words, and finally just blurt out, "We do not know. We have never seen that language." They tremble because the king is full of fear and rage and never is he more dangerous.

Someone goes quickly to the Royal College and finds Queen Amytis. She had left the palace before the celebration to began prayer at the Zion Temple. She comes quickly because of fear for her grandson. It is the day she has been expecting because he has departed so far from right.

"Belshazzar, my grandson, the news will not be good and only Belteshazzar, the man for whom you were named, can give you the interpretation. He is the man in this kingdom in who is the Spirit of the Holy God. He will tell you what the hand has said."

Belteshazzar comes quickly. The king is now completely sober and says, "Belteshazzar, I know you and I have been told that you can make interpretations, and dissolve doubts: now if you can read the writing, and make known to me the interpretation thereof, you shall be clothed with scarlet, and have a chain of gold about your neck, and shall be the third ruler in the kingdom."

Belteshazzar answers him wisely, "Let thy gifts be to thyself, and give thy rewards to another; yet I will read the writing unto the king, and make known to him the interpretation. O, King, the Most High God gave your father Nebuchadnezzar sovereignty and greatness and glory and splendor.

"But when his heart was lifted up, and his mind hardened in pride, he was deposed from his kingly throne, and they took his glory from him:

"And he was driven from the sons of men; and his heart was made like the beasts, and his dwelling was with the wild asses: they fed him with grass like oxen, and his body was wet with the dew of heaven; till he knew that the most high God ruled in the kingdom of men, and that he appointeth over it whomsoever he will.

"And thou his son, O, Belshazzar, hast not humbled thine heart, though thou knewest all this. But hast lifted up thyself against the Lord of heaven; and they have brought the vessels of his house before thee, and thou, and thy lords, thy wives, and thy concubines, have drunk wine in them; and thou hast praised the gods of silver, and gold, of brass, iron, wood, and stone, which see not, nor hear, nor know: and the God in whose hand thy breath is, and whose are all thy ways, hast thou not glorified:

"And this is the writing that was written, MENE, MENE, TEKEL, and UPHARSIN.

"This is the interpretation of the thing: MENE; God hath numbered thy kingdom, and finished it.

"TEKEL; Thou art weighed in the balances, and art found wanting.

"PERES; Thy kingdom is divided, and given to the Medes and Persians."

While the king is listening to the interpretation, the waters of the massive Euphrates stop. Somewhere north of Babylon, the Persian Army has damned the river. As the waters drain to a halt under the city walls, the Persian warriors march toward the city. Hundreds of them enter by the riverbed. Quickly, while the city leaders are in a drunken stupor, the Persian warriors open every magnificent gate and take the Golden City of Babylon. The Golden Empire dies hard, but it dies.

King Belshazzar is slain with the thousands of his lords and mighty men; but drunken men. The Babylonian Empire is no more. The city immediately comes under Persian rule. The Royal University does not miss a day of classes and Queen Amytis moves to a lovely home near the university campus where she will live out her life among the captives of Zion.

About the Author

Joseph Chambers began writing while pastoring his second church in Rockwell, NC, (1958–64). Juanita, his well-educated wife, helped him as he learned to read and begin writing weekly articles for their church newsletter. After many years of writing these articles, he wrote his first book, *Miracles, My Father's Delight* (Pathway Publishing House).

After coming to Charlotte to pastor, he began a monthly prophecy publication that has been a blessing in many countries. He also wrote his next book, *A Palace for the Antichrist* (New Leaf Publishing Company) with foreword by Tim LaHaye, co-writer of the highly successful *Left Behind* series. He wrote two books that were self-published by he and his wife's ministry. The fifth book was released December 2006 entitled *The Masterpiece: A Powerful Look at the Book of Revelation* (21st Century Press). He has written over six hundred articles that have been distributed in many countries.

The Bethany Theological Seminary awarded him a doctorate in sacred literature in 1999 because of excellence in sacred literature. Rev. Chambers has led two great seminars at that institution. He had previously received a doctorate from the Indiana Christian University for a statewide movement he organized and led in North Carolina. This effort was to protect children from the effect of pornographic literature. There had been a large number of articles written and published in connection with this task, plus a tremendous amount of press.

Nebuchadnezzar: The Head of Gold is the first novel in a series entitled The Battle of the Gods. There will be seven books in the complete series covering history from 630 BC to the future eternal kingdom. The Book of Daniel is the foundation of this endeavor.

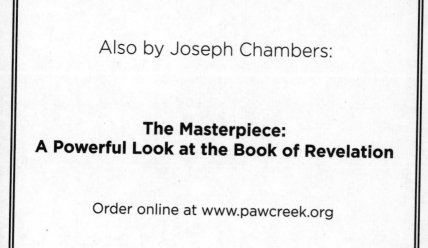

Also by Joseph Chambers:

**The Masterpiece:
A Powerful Look at the Book of Revelation**

Order online at www.pawcreek.org